ADVANCE PRAISE FOR
THE ELECTION HEIST

"A political thriller that will keep you at the edge of your seat, unable to put it down."

—LADY BRIGITTE GABRIEL, bestselling author, founder and chairman, ACT for America

"Americans will be shocked to learn that even their paper ballots are not secure if the software that counts them can be compromised. In addition to being top rate entertainment, *The Election Heist* was a real eye opener."

—REP. JOHN RUTHERFORD, FL-4

"In 2020, governments still do not take the threat of a major election security breach seriously. Ken Timmerman gets it! His scenario in this book is all too plausible, which means the realities are chilling... A good and timely read."

—TOM MALATESTA, nationally recognized cyber security expert

"If you don't think election security is important, think again. Ken Timmerman's new book shows why all of us should be worried about the 2020 election."

—STEPHEN MOORE, economic advisor to President Trump and Heritage Foundation senior fellow

"Ken Timmerman has written another page-turner, with all the suspense of election drama, voter recounts, and political high-stakes poker the way the game is played in today's super-charged political reality. If you enjoy the scheming of talented but devious political operatives, media personalities angling to make their careers on a 'gotcha' moment, and the winner-take-all gambles today's candidates for political office must take, this is a book you can't afford to miss."

—Jerome R. Corsi, Ph.D., bestselling author of *The Obama Nation, Unfit For Command*, and other books

"Every American voter who cares about the integrity of our election processes, regardless of political affiliation, should read *The Election Heist*. Only someone who has been in the political warfare trenches like Ken Timmerman could write such a timely, political thriller 'work of fiction' like this."

—Hon. Joseph E. Schmitz, former Inspector General of the Department of Defense and author, *The Inspector General Handbook: Fraud, Waste, Abuse, and Other Constitutional "Enemies, Foreign and Domestic"*

"Thank God voting machines in America are secure for now, otherwise *The Election Heist* provides a fictional account of a horrible disaster very different from the nightmare we already face of corrupted voter rolls, absentee ballot fraud, and administrative incompetence in election offices across the country."

—J. Christian Adams, member of President Donald Trump's advisory commission on election integrity, President of the Public Interest Legal Foundation, Department of Justice voting veteran and *New York Times* bestselling author of *Injustice*

ALSO BY KENNETH R. TIMMERMAN

FICTION

ISIS Begins

Honor Killing

The Wren Hunt

NONFICTION

Deception: The Making of the YouTube Video Hillary and Obama Blamed for Benghazi

Dark Forces: The Truth About What Happened in Benghazi

Shadow Warriors: The Untold Story of Traitors, Saboteurs, and the Party of Surrender

Countdown to Crisis: The Coming Nuclear Showdown with Iran

The French Betrayal of America

Preachers of Hate: Islam and the War on America

Shakedown: Exposing the Real Jesse Jackson

The Death Lobby: How the West Armed Iraq

La Grande Fauche: La Fuite des Technologies vers l'Est (Gorbachev's Technology War)

Fanning the Flames: Guns, Greed, and Geopolitics in the Gulf War

www.kentimmerman.com

THE ELECTION HEIST

BY KENNETH R. TIMMERMAN

Post Hill PRESS

A POST HILL PRESS BOOK
ISBN: 978-1-64293-573-8
ISBN (eBook): 978-1-64293-574-5

The Election Heist

Cover art by KC Jones

This is a work of fiction. While a number of public persons, places, and institutions make appearances in this book, they are used fictitiously. With one exception, as noted in Chapter 12, their character and dialogue are solely the product of the author's imagination and are not intended to portray real persons, places, or organizations. Please do not call the FBI with the secret location of the hackers who plot to steal the 2020 election. It does not exist.

Post Hill Press
New York • Nashville
posthillpress.com

Published in the United States of America

CAST OF CHARACTERS

Nelson Aguilar, Republican congressional candidate
    Brady Aguilar, his fourteen-year old son and campaign IT director
    Ken Adams, aka "the Crocodile," campaign consultant
    Annie "AB" Bryant, campaign manager
    Camilla Broadstreet, volunteer coordinator

Rep. Hugh McKenzie, incumbent Democrat congressman
    Williston ("Willie") Adams, his wife
    Morton Nash, campaign consultant
    Jennifer Lindh, campaign manager
    Nader Homayounfar, IT director
    Stan Harris, director of opposition research

Gov. Cheryl Tomlinson ("Mrs. T"), Democratic presidential nominee
Sen. Vincent Bellinger ("Uncle Vinnie"), her running mate
T. Claudius Granger ("Granger"), campaign fixer and talking head
Navid Chaudry, Granger's IT director, in charge of the "secret switch"

Gordon Utz, Maryland state IT manager, Annie Bryant's boyfriend
Lisa Rasmussen, Maryland state supervisor of elections
Jim Clairborne, FBI deputy supervisory agent in charge of Cyber Division
Tyrone Masterson ("Rone"), his partner
Gail Copeland, volunteer attorney helping the Aguilar campaign
Harvey Simon, DNC lawyer assigned to McKenzie campaign

Kirk Norton, governor of Florida
Shelley Hughes-Jackson, Florida secretary of state
Lula Rowe, Florida director of elections
Catherine Herrera, supervisor of elections, Nassau County, FL
Milford Gaines, supervisor of elections, Okaloosa County, FL

Ricky Brewer, host of *The Razor's Edge*, MSNBC
Benjamin Bryant, host of *Fox News Sunday*
Galen Beaty, Kristina Brower, co-hosts of Fox News election coverage
Matt Hall, Aaron Duffy, on-air personalities, Fox News
Keith Cobb, host of CNN election night coverage
Rick Hoglan, CNN numbers man

To all true patriots of whatever party, who recognize that our representative democracy depends on free, fair, and verifiable elections. No one should be afraid to identify themselves at the polls, or fear that their votes will not be counted as they were cast.

And to the campaign volunteers who give of themselves for what they believe: Thank you for all you have taught me and know that you do not labor in vain.

"…I do not know whom to believe. If we win, our methods are subject to impeachment for possible fraud. If the enemy wins, it is the same thing exactly—doubt, suspicion, irritation go with the consequence, whatever it may be."

–GEN. LEW WALLACE, writing to his wife, Susan, while serving as a partisan observer during the 1876 presidential election recount.

TABLE OF CONTENTS

PART I

THE CAMPAIGN

Rep. Hugh McKenzie, a four-term incumbent from a liberal Maryland district in the Washington, DC, suburbs, was not looking forward to this meeting. He had cruised through every election he had ever contested, thanks to political savvy, connections, and lots of special interest cash. But now, for the first time in his political career, he was in trouble.

He had been redistricted. And the new district threw in more than a hundred thousand hard-core Republican voters from rural and upper class areas. It was a disaster.

The party leadership didn't so much as hiccup when the court handed down its decision. Even as he cooled his heels on the ornate tile of the majority leader's anteroom, with its magnificent view over the National Mall, Hugh McKenzie was simmering. *Gus did this to me for a reason,* he thought. He could feel himself going red at the gills. *Control. Deep breaths. Focus on the ask.*

By the time Majority Leader Clarence ("Gus") Antly welcomed him into his enormous office, McKenzie was all business.

"Why isn't the party contesting this court order?" he said. "We're going to lose one seat, for sure. Maybe two."

"You'll be fine, Hugh-boy," Antly said. "You've got $2 million in the bank, a shot at leadership, and you keep telling me how much the Jews love you."

If there was one thing McKenzie hated more than the Jews in his own district, it was being reminded of his bullying father, who had called him Hugh-boy all of his life. He felt the heat returning to his cheeks.

"Besides," the South Carolinian went on, putting on a drawl, "if we contest Maryland then the Republicans are going to contest Iowa and Pennsylvania, where we win big."

McKenzie pulled out a color-coded map of the new district from his leather document folder and laid it on the table. "Those yahoos up there hate us. They hate *me*!" he said forcefully, slapping at the large rural areas on the map.

"What do you care," Antly said. "You call it fly-over country when you mock the president."

McKenzie persisted, pointing elsewhere on the map. "Down here, along the Potomac, the median income is over two hundred thousand dollars a year. And they hate me there, too."

"Stop your whinin'," Antly said. "I've seen the numbers. You've got fifty-point-two percent registered Democrats. That's a lock."

"Yeah, but many of them don't vote. Hispanics never vote. I've got thirty-five percent Hispanic, ten percent Asian, and only five percent African American."

"So make 'em vote," the Majority Leader said.

"What do you mean?"

Antly stood up and walked over to the floor-to-ceiling window framed in light walnut, stained and smoothed from generations of politicians massaging the wood as they schemed.

"Just go out and do your job, Hugh-boy," he said. "You'll figure it out."

2

McKenzie's predicament deepened four months later when the Republicans nominated a strong, well-funded candidate to oppose him in the November election. It was the first time he had ever faced real opposition in his entire political career, at the state level or in Congress, and an uncomfortable ache started to gnaw at his stomach.

He was going to have to fight. Walk the parades instead of drive. Marshal real volunteers instead of paid campaign workers. Actually debate. Maybe even go door-to-door. And all of this while he was trying to do the People's business in the House.

"Look, we'll just lean on our friends," Willie said. "You won't have to do house parties except with big donors. And don't even think of door-to-door. *Citizens United* is the gift that keeps on giving."

Williston ("Willie") Adams, his wife of twenty-one years, came from a patrician family near Baltimore but did everything she could to hide that fact. She worked as the legislative coordinator for the biggest federal workers union in Maryland: AFGE. They had discussed the Supreme Court decision in

Citizens United on and off for years. Early on, McKenzie had campaigned against it and had joined a dozen Democrats and a Republican in sponsoring legislation ("*Bipartisan* legislation!" he always insisted) that would walk back *Citizens United* and ban "dark money" from politics. But they always knew there was a perverse flip side to the decision, since it allowed McKenzie and fellow Democrats to raise unlimited money from labor unions and trial lawyers as long as those donors didn't give the appearance of "coordinating" their expenses with the campaign.

"So you want me to benefit from the very thing I've been fighting against for so many years?"

"Of course," she said. "Why wouldn't we?"

"Because Aguilar is no dummy. He'll figure that out in a heartbeat and roast me for acting contrary to my own principles."

"Since when have politicians *not* been hypocrites?" Willie asked.

"Seriously?" He was hurt she could suggest such a thing so readily.

"You'll be fine. But this race is going to be expensive, maybe the most expensive in the nation."

"And even if I win, I've got to do it all over again in two years," he said glumly.

"That's the nature of the beast. But you're up for leadership. As long as we keep the majority, that means power. And money."

"A big if," he said, letting his mind wander. "But then, maybe we'll finally be able to afford sending Katie and Jack to Harvard and Stanford, instead of College Park."

That had always been their dream. Years ago, they bought a wildly over-priced bungalow on a leafy street—a ten-minute walk from downtown Bethesda—because it put their children in a tony public school district. Over the years, as they paid off the mortgage, they'd been able to expand it, though never to the

McMansion size of many of his neighbors. *Way too ostentatious*, Willie had argued.

But Harvard and Stanford? Nobody had to know. That could be their secret. And their gift to their kids, payback for all those soccer games and PTA meetings he'd never attended when they were small. No University of Maryland for them.

Maybe there is an upside to this fight, he thought. Maybe it would be worth spending a sweaty summer campaigning.

3

y Labor Day, McKenzie's internal polls were showing him below 50 percent, a deadly sign for an incumbent politician just two months from the election.

Probably the worst moment had been the Wheaton street fair in mid-August. McKenzie had set up in a corner of the large tent for dignitaries at the back end of the central square. Wheaton was the heart of the heart of the *barrio,* a melting pot of Hispanic communities that regularly voted Democrat at 70 percent or more. Surrounded on three sides by gaily painted two- and three-story buildings, and on the far side by a street closed off with Jersey barriers, the square was filled with smoky food stalls and face-painters and souvenir sellers. Kids were running around with giant water pistols, spraying each other and their overheated parents. Two different mariachi bands competed with each other from opposite sides of the square. It was loud. No, it was *raucous,* McKenzie thought. Sweaty and raucous and very foreign.

Willie had taken their two children to her family's compound on the beach in Rehoboth for the month, so McKenzie was alone with his campaign manager, Jennifer Lindh, behind the long campaign table. About twenty paid volunteers were milling around, wearing dark blue t-shirts stamped with McKenzie's handsome face and his auburn curls. (He liked to think of it as his JFK Jr. face, fresh and just slightly sun-burned.) The campaign workers made forays into the crowd, bringing in unsuspecting voters to meet the Congressman. *Voters, really?* McKenzie thought. Half of them didn't speak English and were probably illegals. Sorry. Undocumented immigrants.

He went along with the charade, shaking hands, patting the heads of the children, pretending to smile when some youngster turned a water pistol on him, leaving a long wet streak down his sweaty white shirt and dribbling down his khakis like flecks of pee. Then his campaign workers would give the voter—*really?*—a campaign t-shirt and off they would go, little water pistol monsters and all.

After two hours of this, McKenzie was ready to call it quits.

"How many t-shirts have we given away?" he asked Jenn.

She looked up from foraging in the boxes behind the table. "At least four boxes of them. Say, maybe a hundred?"

"Do you see a hundred people out there wearing our t-shirt? I mean, besides our own volunteers?"

Jenn shook a finger at him. "You gotta stop this," she said. "Sometimes I think you like making yourself depressed. You're just overheated, that's all. Drink some water."

"No, you're right. I'm depressed," he said.

Behind him, on a dais beneath the tent, municipal employees were testing the sound system as the dignitaries started to gather. As the area's United States Representative, he was expected to give a brief speech. Nothing political, of course, just congratulations on this wonderful event, how as Americans we celebrate our diversity, ya-di-ya-di-yadda.

And when the chairman of the town council introduced him, that's exactly what he did. He took the sweaty microphone and resisted the urge to find something to wipe it down and introduced himself. "For the past eight years, I have had the honor and the privilege to be your representative in the People's House, the greatest House in the world, the Congress of the United States of America," he said.

Before he could start on his diversity speech, one of the mariachi bands started to play, only this time it sounded like they were inside the tent. It was so loud there was no way anyone would be able to hear him, but he pressed on anyway, holding the microphone closer to his lips. *We'll make this short*, he thought. *That's all they want anyway, just to see me. Look, little monster, there's our congressman.*

McKenzie waved to the crowd, preparing to hand back the microphone, when he finally saw the mariachi players in their sombreros snaking through the crowd at the far end of the tent, swaying and calling out, rattling marimbas, trumpets, and smaller brass instruments playing a staccato dance. He turned to the chairman of the town council with an annoyed frown but was met with a complacent shrug as if to say, *that's how it is here in Wheaton, amigo.*

Dumbstruck, McKenzie just stood there, gaping, as the mariachi line made its way through the crowd toward the dais. And then it struck him that they were all dressed in red, and as he looked more carefully he gave an inward groan because they were wearing t-shirts of his opponent, Nelson Aguilar. And the whole tent was now full of them. An undulating raucous red sea.

At the back of the line came Aguilar himself, smiling broadly, waving, shaking outstretched hands, kissing women on the cheeks, hefting babies and posing for selfies with the moms. *He's a natural,* McKenzie thought. *And that beautiful suit. Hard to believe he doesn't even break a sweat.*

McKenzie turned to Jenn. "This is a disaster," he said. "Let's get out of here before it becomes an embarrassment."

4

Nelson Aguilar was everything the Democrats feared most. He was handsome, Hispanic, rich, and conservative. The son of immigrants, he had made a successful career as a broadcast journalist, first on local radio and later as a financial reporter on a popular cable TV network. After many years in New York, he returned to the *barrio* in suburban Wheaton, Maryland, bought the local Hispanic radio station, and turned it into a modest media empire. At forty-six years old, he was at the peak of his powers.

Through his daily broadcasts, Nelson Aguilar owned the Hispanic day workers, the Salvadorian maids, the Guatemalteco, and the Mexican landscapers. He seduced the building cleaners, the hotel workers, the middle-aged couples who ran the nail salon. With his media savvy, he won the young geeks who sold cell phones in the malls.

But most importantly, for financing his first-ever political campaign, Aguilar had used his radio empire to work his way into the Maryland business establishment, with its millionaire Rotary clubs, its power lawyers, its discreet golf courses tucked away behind walls of trees, its mega-buck developers, its Potomac and Severn River yachts, its Eastern Shore duck camps and St. Michael's estates. Nelson Aguilar knew who was up, who was down. And especially, who was fed up bearing the yoke of taxes and regulations coming from Washington, DC, and secretly welcomed the relief provided to them by President Trump.

And he knew how to reach them personally to reassure them. He had the Crocodile to thank for that. Give them plausible deniability, the Crocodile liked to say, but always show them your power. And that power came from his voice.

"You came here the hard way," he exhorted his supporters at the end of his daily broadcast commentary. "You came here for the dream—that great, beautiful, American dream, that great blessing that came from God on high. And yet, there are some who want to take that dream away from you. I call them the central planners, but you know who they are. They want to steal your American dream. They want to tax you back to poverty. They want to regulate your small businesses out of business for their Green New Deal. And chief among them right here in Wheaton is Hugh McKenzie!"

By the time he swept through the primary, decimating his rivals (a small businessman who awkwardly tried to appeal to core Trump supporters, a lunatic libertarian, and a pro-choice lawyer from Montgomery County), he had raised his first million. That got the attention of the national party bigwigs and the media. By the time of the Wheaton fair, he had cleared $2.5 million and was locked in a dead heat in the polls with his Democrat rival—44 percent to 44 percent—despite the heavy pro-Democrat demographic.

"This one is yours to lose," the Crocodile said that evening, after what they were now calling the Mariachi coup, when they sent Hugh McKenzie scurrying off the dais like a cockroach. "Even the Cook Report is now saying this District is in play."

Officially the Crocodile, as he liked to call him, was his campaign consultant. But to Aguilar, Ken Adams was a miracle worker. He had brought him from nowhere to win a smashing victory in a primary normally dominated by the Party's most conservative activists, for whom Hispanic meant sponger and border jumper and MS-13 gang-banger, or so at least the media claimed. Now the Crocodile was setting out a roadmap to victory in November. Woo the big donors. Focus on the message. Just be yourself, because it's you they love, boss. Nelson Aguilar, the son of immigrants, was going to the United States Congress. And it didn't turn his head in the least.

5

arly the following afternoon, the Crocodile was explaining how this next meeting was to go down as they cruised northward along a rural stretch of Georgia Avenue in a black Suburban leased by the campaign.

"Marguerite Parker—she'll ask you to call her 'Midge'—is one of three siblings. The two brothers, David and Peter, run the stud farms. The biggest stud farms in Maryland. Probably in the States, if you ask me. We'll be driving by one of them soon here in Woodbine, on the other side of Route 70." He gestured at the rolling fields and pastureland of Howard County, and Aguilar thought, *if he weren't the Crocodile, with his bald pate and rough, deeply-tanned skin, he could be an oracle, a prophet, a soothsayer. Whatever.*

"Midge is also a rider. It's a passion of hers. Dressage. You're going to see a couple of very expensive saddles hanging around her office, thrown over banisters, casual-like. Just say something innocuous. You know, like nice saddle, or something."

"Graciela used to ride."

"You can say that."

"I always watched. She never let me ride."

"Even better. She'll maybe ask you about that. Feel comfortable talking about her?"

Aguilar closed his eyes for a moment and the image of Graciela hit him full force as she sat erect with the reins, sweating and happy, on her eight-year-old tawny thoroughbred stallion. What's his name? *Bogart.* How could I forget?

"She died of breast cancer when Brady was nine. That was five years ago. I've been doing my best to give him a Christian upbringing as a single dad ever since."

"That's good."

"It also happens to be true." Aguilar laughed.

"That's what I like about you, *amigo*," the Crocodile said easily. "Always deep and true."

The Crocodile let that sink in for a moment, but Aguilar wasn't embarrassed. He genuinely liked the man. "Like you, too, *cocodrilo*," he said.

"So," the Crocodile said, pulling a file folder from the bag beneath his seat and set it on the center armrest for Aguilar. "This is where we are going, the Westminster School for Disadvantaged Girls. It's Midge's other passion. They cater to young women who get in trouble, mostly from minority communities. Gang members. Drugs. Teenage pregnancy. Whatever. But especially she takes in those girls who get pregnant and offers them a home."

"What about the babies?"

"They team up with a specialized adoption agency to place the babies in loving Christian families."

"This is God's work," Aguilar said solemnly. He was impressed. The Left always accused pro-lifers like himself of having no heart for young girls who felt that having an "unwanted" baby would ruin their lives forever. What a ridiculous term. *That* was heartless. God *always* wants the babies. "So she is giving these girls a second chance. And saving their babies at the same time."

"That's right. I knew the two of you would be a perfect fit."

Adams slowed the car as they approached Westminster and the junction with Route 140.

"By the way," he said. "Midge didn't get her money from the stud farms. That's hardly ever a money-making proposition. It's like buying a boat. There are only two moments of happiness: the day you buy it, and the day you get rid of it."

"So what's her secret?" Aguilar asked.

"She was a partner in the original venture capital firm that launched Facebook. She came away with one-quarter of one percent of the stock. Do the math."

"Good call," Aguilar said.

"I'll make the ask. I guarantee you, she won't flinch."

The brick-columned mansion housing the school sat up on a hill, overlooking centuries-old oak and walnut trees. As they pulled into the circular drive, Aguilar noted the white picket fence in the side yard. *It's a horse fence*, he thought. Had to be. But where was the tape or the wires?

A tallish older woman opened the main door, obviously waiting for them. She was bean-pole thin, stern, and wore a plain white dress with faint blue roses. Aguilar shot Ken Adams a questioning glance.

"Nurse Ratched, not Midge."

"Glad you warned me!"

"Ms. Parker has set out tea in her office upstairs. If you would follow me," she said.

Midge Parker was sifting through papers at an enormous desk, back to the window, and rose as soon as her assistant knocked and opened the door. In front of her, the low table was set with tea plates, cups and saucers, knives and forks, and a rectangular platter of cucumber sandwiches without crusts. Aguilar deployed his charm, leading the conversation gently as the Crocodile had instructed. He complimented her on the saddle in the hallway, they talked a bit about horses, he mentioned Graciela and being a single dad. But instead of talking more about himself, he asked her about the school and what they were doing for the girls.

Ten minutes later, she put down her tea cup briskly and gave them a mischievous grin. "Here I am, going on about myself all this time, when that's not at all what you came here to talk about," she said.

"Bless you, Ms. Parker, for what you are doing," Aguilar said.

"It's Midge," she said. "Please, call me Midge."

"Midge."

"Well, Midge. You know why we are here," the Crocodile picked up.

"I know why, but I don't know how much," she said.

Aguilar laughed. "More than you can possibly imagine."

She laughed as well. "I think if anybody else said that to me, sir, I might be offended."

"It's whatever God puts in your heart."

The rest of the meeting went like a charm. Midge Parker made out a check on the spot for $500,000 in the name of the non-profit organization Adams jotted down on a Post-It note. That non-profit, in turn, would wire the money to Americans for the Dream, the super PAC Adams had set up to support the Aguilar campaign. In this way, Ms. Parker's name would never appear in public disclosures. That was exactly the way she wanted it—just as many other donors the Crocodile had contacted on Aguilar's behalf.

As they drove back down Georgia Avenue to Aguilar's office in Wheaton, Aguilar reflected on this special arrangement. Why did they have to go to such lengths to disguise the names of their donors, he wondered. Because the Left would go after them in a heartbeat. They would destroy their businesses. They would destroy their families. They would destroy them personally. Why? Because that's what they did.

That's also why the Crocodile insisted on driving to such meetings, even though they had plenty of drivers available. No one else needed to know. Loose lips sink ships, as he had told Aguilar many times already. Keep it close and personal.

It also gave the Crocodile face-time with the candidate. After another long silence, Aguilar could hear it coming. Another baring of souls. Mine.

"You *have* put Annie behind you, right?" the Crocodile asked after a while.

"What do you mean?"

"You know what I mean. We can't have any of that, not on this campaign."

"I am a widower."

"Doesn't matter."

"Do you think I should fire her?"

"For Pete's sake, no! That would be horrible."

"Ken, I can assure you that I am quite capable of having a professional relationship with a beautiful female who, in another life, would undoubtedly exert a powerful attraction on me."

"Oh, I don't know about the other life," the Crocodile came back. "Everyone can see the sparks."

Aguilar chuckled. "I guess you're right. It must be obvious. But I assure you, we've already had that conversation."

"You and Annie?"

"*Cabron*, who else?"

"Tell me, boss. I need to know."

"Okay."

So Aguilar told him. Haltingly. The whole story—or most of it, anyway. He didn't need to explain to the Crocodile how attractive his female campaign manager was. Any red-blooded male could see that. Luckily for Aguilar, Annie Bryant—"AB" for short—was as gracious as she was beautiful and smart.

"I know her pedigree. Don't forget, I was the one who brought her on to the campaign," the Crocodile said.

A graduate of a well-respected Christian undergraduate college, Annie Bryant had earned a law degree from Pepperdine University in California. From there, she interned on Capitol Hill where Ken Adams spotted her and hired her as a minority staff counsel to the Judiciary committee. From there, he brought her on the Aguilar campaign.

One afternoon in mid-summer, after everyone else had left the campaign headquarters down the street from his office, Aguilar lingered. Annie was in her cubicle, running the numbers on the latest poll.

"I asked her out to dinner. No more, no less."

"Oh no," the Crocodile leered. "There's more."

"She said no. That was it."

The Crocodile took his foot off the accelerator, his eyes from the road, and turned to stare him full in the face.

"What did you say when she said no? Your exact words, please. Indulge me, boss."

Nelson Aguilar was not one to blush. He had the easy manners of someone who was fully at home with himself, who had nothing to hide. He liked to think that he spoke to others as he spoke to God. Now was not the moment to do otherwise.

"Okay, I said. I understand."

"Is that all?"

"No. She said she was in a relationship, and I said, lucky guy."

"And?"

"And I said that her steadfastness or whatever it was only increased my deep admiration for her. With your permission, we won't mention this again and I will only inquire as to your general well-being, I think is how I put it."

"Will she back you up on that? Don't get me wrong, boss. But this is in your best interest."

"I get it. We're going to be under increasing scrutiny. So ask her yourself. Ask her when I'm not around. I think she's solid. And, I really do envy that other guy, whoever he is."

6

The Thursday after Labor Day, the two candidates were to meet for their first face-to-face debate at the Leisure World retirement center in northern Silver Spring. It was the largest polling place in all of Montgomery County, if not all of Maryland, and was a coveted spot for politicians of both parties to trawl for votes. The debate was organized by the Association of Retired Federal Employees (ARFE), and for Democrat Hugh McKenzie, that sponsorship allayed whatever fears he might have had about meeting Aguilar face to face. Not only did his wife, Willie Adams, work for the ARFE parent organization, but Jennifer Lindh, his campaign manager, used to work for ARFE itself.

"You've discussed all the ground rules with the organizers, correct?" he asked Jennifer as their driver took them round the Beltway from Bethesda to the Connecticut Avenue exit.

"Down to the color of the coffee mugs," she said. "Royal blue, if you're asking."

"No sand-bagging this time. No mariachi bands. Right?"

"No surprises, that's right," she confirmed.

And of course, she was wrong. Nelson Aguilar had out-smarted them—again. But it wasn't apparent at first.

They had built into the schedule a fifteen-minute meet and greet before the debate, and to Hugh McKenzie everything seemed on track. The clubhouse was packed with his support-ers, many of them wearing his JFK Jr. t-shirt, and all of them wanted to shake hands, remind him how they'd met, or how much they hated Donald Trump. Everyone wanted to know why the Democrats had let up on impeachment after the bi-partisan vote to remove Trump from office in Senate. Not going there, he said. That's the trap they have laid for us. Let's impeach him in November, dontcha think?

He was feeling pretty upbeat until he spied the Crocodile. (Even Hugh McKenzie referred to him by his nickname, which had become infamous from all the years Ken Adams had prowled Capitol Hill.)

"How ya doin', Congressman?" Adams said, all smiles.

"Just great until I saw you."

"Hey, it's just a friendly hello. No barbs. I don't bite. Really!"

"I didn't appreciate that stunt in Wheaton," McKenzie said quietly. He didn't think anyone else could hear him given the hubbub of voices all around them.

"It wasn't a stunt, Congressman. That was real."

"I bet."

"But don't take it personal. It's all politics. You know that. One day we do our best to drag each other into the mud. The next, we work side by side on legislation. I look forward to that again."

"You mean, after your guy loses?"

"Ha! No, after you do," the Crocodile said.

And then he vanished, melting beneath the surface of the crowd.

Damn it, Jenn, where are you! McKenzie fumed. All of a sudden he felt terribly alone. Where was she when he needed her?

7

The format was simple. The ARFE moderator, Richard August, sat between the two candidates at a bare cafeteria-style table. He had a list of topics he had prepared for that afternoon's debate. Each candidate had two minutes for an opening statement, two minutes per question, and one minute to rebut. At the end, they would have another two minutes each to close. The timer, who was seated directly below them in the front row, would hold up a yellow card when they had fifteen seconds remaining and a red card when their time had expired.

McKenzie won the coin toss and elected to close, letting Aguilar go first.

For the first couple of minutes or so, there were no surprises. Aguilar launched into his life story: Mexican immigrant, TV reporter, small businessman, etc. McKenzie had become so familiar with his opponent's background he could recite it himself, so he spent the time surveying the audience. There were only a handful of Hispanic faces, he noted. Most of them were in their twenties—students, possibly. But there was one gentleman in a suit in the back. Small business owner, perhaps? Keep an eye on that one. The rest of them seemed to be friendlies, retired government employees. *My people*, he thought. Jenn was in the far corner in the back and gave him a confident nod. *Good work, Jenn!*

When it was his turn, he graciously praised his opponent. "I am pleased to see that our Republican friends have finally had the wisdom to nominate someone who doesn't look like most of them," he said. "Diversity is our strength. That is why I have always supported comprehensive immigration reform. We absolutely must resolve this humanitarian crisis at our borders and keep ICE from breaking up families and putting children in cages."

Something was wrong. He didn't feel the warm ripples of agreement flowing from the audience. There was even a hint of hostility he was unaccustomed to. *What was it?*

When he began talking about his opposition to the Trump tax cuts for millionaires and billionaires, he began to see what it was. There were four middle-aged white women sitting in the third row, directly in front of him. At first, he had thought they were ARFE workers, placed there strategically by Jenn. But now he could see they were scowling at him. Scowling! Unbelievable. He made a note to find a more sympathetic face and engage that person directly in the next round.

"Our first topic this afternoon revolves around health care. Congressman, you have said publicly that you support Medicare-For-All. Mr. Aguilar, you are opposed. Why?"

Aguilar leaned into the microphone, thanked the moderator for the question, and then he did the unthinkable: He actually stood up.

"Let me tell you a story," he said, walking up to the front of the stage, where he could almost touch the audience. "My late wife originally came from Venezuela. My parents were Mexican. Came here legally, by the way."

The scowlers broke into good-hearted laughter. So they *were* plants, McKenzie thought.

"Look at Venezuela today," he went on. "The country is imploding. They say that over the past year, the average citizen in Venezuela has lost over forty pounds—and that's not because dieting has suddenly become a thing."

The scowlers laughed again. *Damn!*

"Like Cuba and many other socialist countries, Venezuela has free health care. Free health care for all! Just think of it! Medicare-For-All is a hallmark of socialist countries. Today in Venezuela, nobody can find a doctor because all the doctors have fled. In Canada, where some doctors remain, people have to wait weeks to see someone. Is that what we want for this county? Socialized medicine? Long waits to see a doctor? Rationed health care services? Government bureaucrats determining who gets a heart transplant, and who dies? I believe we need to return to a free market system, with patient choice and market pricing and the doctor-patient relationship at its core."

The moderator turned to him. McKenzie took his micro phone from the stand and turned to address him instead of the audience.

"Before getting to health care, I'd like to ask our moderator if it's okay for me to stand to address the audience, or would he rather have us sit behind the table, as we had agreed?"

He caught Jenn's eye at the back of the room. She was nodding her head ever so slightly in approval. That's right. Take back control.

Richard August pulled on his wispy beard and nodded. "You're right, Congressman. If you and Mr. Aguilar would remain seated, that would be best."

"Now, as to Medicare-For-All," he began.

McKenzie explained how our health system was failing. People were having to pay more and more for insurance, while the drug companies were making billions and billions of profits by gouging consumers.

"*But you voted for Obamacare!*" one of the scowlers called out.

"Madame," said the moderator. "Please don't interrupt the Congressman."

He couldn't believe they had actually heckled him. Not just scowled, but heckled! This was supposed to be his home turf.

"Actually, I never voted for Obamacare," he said icily. "I was first elected after it became law. But I am proud to admit that I support it—with some necessary changes. That's what Medicare-For-All is about."

The next question was about McKenzie's plan to set a national minimum wage of fifteen dollars an hour, so he got two minutes to make the case. He carefully avoided looking at the scowlers but found a good ARFE member just to their left to engage. He must have been seventy-five if he was a day and had a lachrymose tick in one eye, causing him to dab at it with a handkerchief. McKenzie smiled and never took his eyes off the man.

"*Twenty-dollar Big Macs,*" one of the scowlers heckled.

"Madame, that's the last time I'm going to warn you," the moderator said. "Please reserve your comments until after the debate."

How can they get away with it, McKenzie wondered? *If I tried something like that—what? What would Aguilar do? Would he whine and complain? No, he would turn it to his advantage! Of course!*

"Would a fifteen-dollar national minimum wage raise the price of some consumer goods? Yes, of course it would," McKenzie said, looking directly at the hecklers. "But the prices that would go up are already so ridiculously low that I doubt it would affect you, Madame, or anyone in this room. But the fifteen-dollar wage would dramatically affect those at the lowest rungs of society, who are just barely making ends meet as it is. We are talking about fundamental fairness here, not Keynesian economics or having to pay a little more for a hamburger."

That was better, he thought. As he set the microphone back in its stand he snuck a glance at Jenn. She nodded her approval.

It went on like that for the rest of the hour. Aguilar was in the zone. He appealed directly to the ARFE members, telling personal stories, moving his body and gesturing almost rhythmically. The charisma just oozed off of him, even seated. Nevertheless, McKenzie felt he was holding his own. He was asking the audience to cut through the marshmallows and consider hard facts. And always, remember who the real enemy was: President Trump.

"Donald Trump has demeaned the presidency," he said. "He says things on a daily basis that no president would have ever dreamed of saying before. America has become a laughingstock around the world." Turning to his opponent, he gave a wry smile: "And do you think Mexico is going to pay for that wall?"

He paused dramatically, daring Aguilar to speak, but his opponent merely gave a friendly shrug, as if he didn't know the answer. "Not a chance," McKenzie told the audience.

Now it was time for their closing statements. Hugh McKenzie tuned out his opponent as he methodically ticked down the mental list of what he was going to say. Fix the immigration mess Trump has created. Medicare-For-All, not Trump's health care for none. Minimum wage. Election reform. And of course, the Green New Deal, because in twelve years the planet faced a deadly ultimatum. If we don't act by then to reverse the course we are in, science tells us we will never be able to dial back the deadly spiral of catastrophic global warming. Whole nations will go underwater as the icecaps melt. Forests will burn. Crops will be scorched so bad it'll make the Dust Bowl look like springtime in Florida. We can't afford to take these risks, which my opponent shrugs off. I am asking for your support to send me back to Congress for another two years to work on your behalf.

He saw the yellow card flash below and sat up straight. *It's time to put this one away*, McKenzie thought.

But Aguilar just blew through his time, without even a pause. The timer held up the red card, but he appeared not to notice. She waved it several times without getting his attention. Finally, the moderator jumped in.

"Mr. Aguilar, I'm afraid your time has expired."

Aguilar was in the middle of a story. He was talking about his career as a war correspondent, and everyone in the room was rapt with his every word.

"I do apologize, Mr. August. But I wonder if the audience would indulge me for another two minutes? They of course should give the Congressman an extra two minutes, as well. What do you think, folks? May I finish my story?"

The scowlers howled their approval, thumping their feet and clapping. To McKenzie's dismay, people started clapping in the back of the auditorium. And then in the middle. Soon enough, they were calling out, "Yes! Yes! Yes!" from all over. Aguilar turned to the moderator sheepishly.

"What do you say, Mr. August?"

The moderator threw up his hands in acquiescence. "Reset the two-minute clock," he said to the timer.

What was so important for him to blow through his time, McKenzie wondered? He started to tune in, but he couldn't figure out why Aguilar thought telling war stories would advance his cause. *These are my people. They're hard-core Democrats. Most of them are against war. All wars. The Iraq war was a disaster. And now we have a president just itching to go to war with Iran. Why should they sympathize with that?*

"And so, in early January 2009, they sent me to a small town in Israel way down in the Negev desert on the border with Gaza. It was called Sderot. The producers back in New York insisted we all wear these huge bullet-proof vests. I'm sure you've seen them. It makes you feel a bit ridiculous, but you know what? They said if we didn't, it would void both our health coverage and our life insurance! My wife would have killed me if I had done that!"

Everyone laughed. Even McKenzie found himself giving a small huff. *Where was this going?*

"You may remember, these were the final days of the George W. Bush administration. It was called Operation Cast Lead. The Israelis knew they had one last chance before Obama took office to do serious damage to Hamas.

"Why was that so important? Because Hamas was launching thousands of rockets—more than four thousand, if I remember correctly—into Israeli towns and villages. That's why they sent me to Sderot. It was getting pounded day after day.

"Sometimes we did our live feed from the air raid shelters. One time we were down there with local residents for an entire day, babies and moms, old men and women. Most of the young men had been called up to military service.

"But if you listened to just about any other news channel, all you heard about was Israeli aggression, the Israeli invasion, indiscriminate bombing. Already people were accusing Israel of war crimes."

Aguilar paused dramatically and turned to McKenzie. *You've got to be kidding*, he thought.

"One of them is sitting right next to me here at this table. Congressman Hugh McKenzie."

The timer held up the yellow card. Aguilar pressed on.

"Perhaps in your time, Congressman, you can explain to folks here why you accused Israel of committing war crimes when in fact all she was doing was defending herself? You were still in the state Senate, down in Annapolis. That makes it all the more extraordinary. How can you call yourself a supporter of Israel when you make common cause with Israel's enemies?"

A prolonged hissing came from the audience, and it wasn't just coming from the scowlers but seemingly everywhere. This was not how he was intending to conclude. But McKenzie knew better than to respond immediately to such a hot button accusation. That was a beginner's mistake, and he was anything but a beginner.

"I have four minutes, right?" he asked the moderator.

"That's right, Congressman." Robert August turned to the timer. "Four minutes."

McKenzie picked up the microphone, his lips pressed together, red in the face. For a good fifteen seconds, he said nothing, just shaking his head. *It's good at times to show your anger*, he thought. Let them feel how unjust this is.

"I'm going to get to that scurrilous accusation in just a minute. But first, let me conclude by sketching out my plans for making sure American prosperity benefits all Americans, not just millionaires and billionaires."

And so he gave his closing speech pretty much as he had been intending, except that he drew it out a bit longer. When three minutes had gone by, one of the scowlers piped up.

"What about Israel?" she called out.

"I'm getting to Israel," he said flatly.

"Answer the question!" another one said.

"Mr. Aguilar is referring to a letter that was being circulated by the Council on American Islamic Relations, a widely respected civil rights organization, that was signed by more than sixty members of the Maryland Senate and House of Delegates, including quite a few from his own party."

"Did you sign it?" an older man called out. It was the man with the lachrymose twitch whom McKenzie had thought was on his side.

"Sir, this was a letter being circulated by a well-respected civil rights group, and the stories we were hearing out of Gaza were horrific. Of course I signed it. It called on Israel to respect the Geneva Conventions and to refrain from targeting civilians. It did not accuse them of war crimes."

The timer held up the yellow card. McKenzie could feel the sweat run down the back of his shirt.

"I hope this incident has been instructive of the kind of misrepresentations and outright lies my opponent has been using in this campaign. I would ask that you look at my record, and vote your values. Who do you want representing you in Washington, a man who will say anything to get elected? Or someone with a proven track record of helping those who have been left behind by the Trump economy?"

The moderator banged down his gavel, and the room erupted in applause, but McKenzie wasn't fool enough to think it was directed at him.

8

From then on, it only got worse.

A few days later, McKenzie was heading into the Capitol with his driver, skimming the *Washington Post* and the *New York Times* with the local traffic station playing in the background. Both papers enthusiastically reported on plans by the Democrat nominee for president, Governor Cheryl Tomlinson of Illinois, and her running mate, Senator Vincent Bellinger of New York, to roll out their Medicare-For-All proposal that evening at a Town Hall meeting near Scranton, Pennsylvania. *Sounds like they're channeling good old Joe Biden*, McKenzie thought. Too bad about what happened to him after winning the primaries.

But Tomlinson was a great choice—undoubtedly the Democrat who had the best chance of beating Donald Trump. She had grown up on the south side of Chicago and spent much of her youth as a gang member, running crack for the Black P Stone Rangers. Weren't they somehow tied to Jesse Jackson? A vague memory of some right-wing hit job on the revered civil rights icon stirred in the back of his mind. That's right, *Shakedown:*

Exposing the Real Jesse Jackson. And that photograph of Rev. Jackson sitting at the feet of Jeff Fort, the notorious gang leader who was sent to jail for life on terrorism charges. The Reverend pretty much disappeared from politics for years after that! Tomlinson paid her dues, did time in jail, where she came to Jesus and found her husband, who went on to become a charismatic preacher once they were released. She ran the business side of his ministry, building it into a mini-empire, with books, speaking tours, and a mega-church just down the street from the Rev. Louis Farrakhan's Mosque Maryam. Known locally as "Mrs. T," she was elected governor six years ago in her first-ever run for elected office.

He made a note to watch the Town Hall meeting that evening, most likely from his office in the Rayburn building.

Then he heard his name.

"Joachim, turn up the radio, please!" he called to the driver.

"...But you know the truth: It's health care for none. Nelson Aguilar knows you deserve to keep more of your hard-earned pay. Let's send Congressman McKenzie home to his family. Vote for Nelson Aguilar on November 3rd. Paid for by Americans for the Dream."

Paid for by who? he thought. Must be a Super PAC. So that's in addition to the $2.5 million he's already raised. Nice.

He picked up his iPhone and called Jenn.

"Did you hear the attack ad on WTOP just now?"

She had not.

"Well, turn it on and keep listening. Get someone to make a transcript. And get Stan Harris to do a run on the Super PAC. It's called Americans for the Dream. I want to know how much they've raised, how much they've spent, who their donors are, the works. See if there are any cross-overs between the campaign and the Super PAC. That could be illegal. And see if any of our media buyers know any of theirs. We need all committee chairs for an hour this afternoon at the DNC. Coordinate with Lisa in my office to find the best hour for me."

Next he dialed Derek Greenwald, his finance chairman. His secretary said he was just heading into a meeting. "Tell him it's Congressman McKenzie and he needs to get back to me within the next half hour," he said.

After that, he dialed Mark Margolis, his pollster. It rang three times. Four. *Mark wouldn't dare not pick up the phone*, he thought, *not with the amount I'm paying him.*

"Mark, I need you to do a quick tracking poll this morning. No, nothing on specific issues. Just the quick and dirty. Approval rating. Name recognition. Who you're voting for in November. Maybe a presidential preference. Keep the universe manageable, but I want you to pay special attention to demographics. Hispanic. Jewish. Soccer moms. We need it for this afternoon's staff meeting. Ask Jenn for the time. And I'll want you to run some comparisons as well to see the trend lines."

For a moment he let himself marvel at the contrast between his mind, racing along at 150 mph, and the leisurely pace of the black SUV as they followed the meanders and gentle rapids of Rock Creek on Beach Drive. They were just thirty minutes from the seat of power of the most powerful nation on earth, and here they were immersed in a leafy forest, with giant rocks left behind by the glaciers strewn on the hillsides like prehistoric monuments. *There's not another place like this on earth*, he thought. And he had no intention of giving it up.

He knew what he had to do. After all, he was a pro.

9

They met at 4:30 PM, after the House adjourned for the day, in a large conference room on the third floor of the Democratic National Committee headquarters. It was common practice for Members to use the DNC building for election purposes, since it was actually illegal for them to conduct campaign activities—even just simple phone calls—while they were on the grounds of the Capitol. The Republicans had a similar arrangement with the RNC on 1st Street SE, right across from the Metro, with the advantage that they could repair to the Capitol Hill Club for drinks once their business was done. No such luck at the DNC, whose rinky-dink café couldn't compare. McKenzie had walked through the Rayburn House Office Building basement to Longworth, then surfaced on New Jersey Avenue and continued down toward D Street, SE, Joachim guarding his flank. It was only two blocks, but with the Washington, DC, humidity he was drenched by the time he arrived. He stopped in the men's room and tried to mop himself dry with paper towels.

Good Lord, he thought when he entered the cramped conference room. *Am I really paying all these people?* They were as numerous as his congressional staff. And most of them were getting paid much more.

"Alright, people," Jenn started out. "This thing is tightening, so we've all got to be on our toes."

She'd been a good catch, McKenzie thought. Willie's colleague from the union. If she hadn't gone into politics, what would she be doing today? He realized for an instant he was stumped. He didn't know anything else besides politics.

"Let me bring you all up to speed. This morning, a Super PAC supporting our opponent's campaign began airing attack ads on WTOP, WMAL, and other DC-area radio, and tonight they are booked to go up on cable television as well. Here is the first one that aired this morning."

She swiped her phone, turned on the speaker, and set it on the conference table so they could all hear.

> *"Twenty-five percent. That's the amount Congressman Hugh McKenzie wants to grab from your paycheck. He plans to take it every week. Every two weeks. Every month.*
>
> *Just think of that: twenty-five percent less in your pocket from every paycheck. And that's in addition to all the other taxes they are taking.*
>
> *He calls it Medicare-For-All. But you know the truth: It's health care for none.*
>
> *Nelson Aguilar knows you deserve to keep more of your hard-earned pay. Let's send Congressman McKenzie home to his family. Vote for Nelson Aguilar on November 3rd. Paid for by Americans for the Dream."*

For a moment, they all sat in stunned silence as the emotional impact of the attack ad sank in. *That was a low swipe,*

McKenzie thought. This guy was determined to play gutter politics. Or was it just politics? Whatever. He could play, too.

"Stan, I'd like you to fill us in on what you've found out about this Super PAC that's running the ads," Jenn said.

Stan Harris had been an investigative reporter for *Newsweek*, and then the Daily Beast, and was one of the best around. He worked as a consultant to this and to several other campaigns— Democrats, only—renting out the services of the investigative firm he and another former journalist had set up five years ago. Their job was to dig dirt on Republicans and cover up the holes.

"All we could do this morning was a public records search," he said. "They incorporated just two weeks ago, offices with a Republican law firm on L Street. Straw man as Treasurer. But they've already filed their first forty-eight-hour notice. And it's a biggy."

"How big?" McKenzie asked.

"$1.2 million, Congressman. Apparently from just two donors."

"Do we know their names?"

"One of them, yes. At least, we have a pretty good feel for it. You know the Facebook billionaire up in Westminster, Midge Parker? She donated 500 grand to a 501c4 called People's Choice about ten days ago. People's Choice turned around and made a $500,000 donation to Americans for the Dream the next day."

"What about the rest of the money," McKenzie said. "The other 700 grand?"

"It came from a 501c4 called the National Republican Trust. They've been fundraising and donating to races all across the country, so it's harder to see a direct tie-in…. We also have identified their media buyer," he added.

Jenn stepped back in. "Kwanda?" she said. "Have you checked with our guys? Do they know them?"

Kwanda Armstrong was among the younger members of his team. *Don't let the afro fool you,* McKenzie thought. She'd been a journalism major at Morgan State University, one of the historic African-American colleges in Maryland. Good school, actually. None of this new age nonsense, gender studies, phony history. She went on to earn a Master's in communications from Georgetown. As communications director, she was one of the best.

"Oh yes," she said. "CapitolNet, Inc. is big. They've been in the business for over two decades. They only do Republicans. And they've got leverage."

"How so?" McKenzie asked.

"Here's the bad news, Congressman," Kwanda said. "They've bought up every available political spot in the DC market for the next ten days."

"What? How can they do that?"

"Well the how isn't all that difficult. Remember, they've got $1.2 million in cash. Right?"

"You mean, we've been shut out for the next ten days? Silenced? Sidelined?"

"That's about it," Kwanda said.

"You could always file a complaint with the FEC," Jenn said.

"Right," McKenzie said. "And by the time they got around to considering it, we'll all be looking for jobs."

This was a disaster, and it sent him reeling into a funk.

"Before you get all depressed," Jenn said, trying to put on a light touch. "You need to listen to what Mark and Morton have got to say."

"That tracking poll you asked me to do this morning?" Mark Margolis began. "Here are the results."

He handed around twenty stapled copies of the poll, so everyone could follow the numbers. It included pages and pages of graphs and pie charts showing the main demographics supporting and opposing each candidate.

"The biggest takeaway, Congressman, is that your support is not eroding in any significant fashion," Margolis said. "Take a look at the tracker on page three."

They all turned to the bar chart and saw that McKenzie's numbers, while they had eroded from a high 54 percent favorable in the spring, they were still close to 48 percent and hadn't fallen in the past two weeks despite all the bad publicity.

"Even more significant," Margolis said, "is the Trump favorable/unfavorable. His unfavorable in the district has gone up from fifty-eight percent to over sixty-two percent, with only twenty-eight percent holding a favorable or very favorable opinion of the president. That is your ticket to re-election, if I might say so, Congressman."

McKenzie wasn't quite so sure. Trump's unfavorables had hovered around 50 percent right up until the night before the election in 2016, and yet look at what happened. He lost the nation-wide popular vote by three million, for sure, but by focusing his efforts on states he could swing with just a few thousand votes, it gave him that big margin of victory in the electoral college by night's end. *Luckily we have no electoral college in congressional races.*

"Let me remind everybody about the basic numbers here."

That was Morton Nash, his campaign consultant. No, his *highly paid* campaign consultant, recommended by the Democratic Congressional Campaign Committee, the DCCC. They were the ones who ultimately controlled the biggest purse strings, and they were all in the pocket of the Majority Leader, Gus Antly.

"Congressman, I know you are worried about demographics," Nash began. "And it's true, according to Mark's data, the

Hispanic vote is starting to soften up a bit. But don't forget the basic voter registration numbers of the new district. Rounding the numbers, you've got fifty percent Dems, thirty percent Republicans, and twenty percent independents, whack-jobs, or no affiliation.

"Now, history shows us that in just about any election, you're going lose ten percent of your own party. So subtract five percent for you, three percent for Aguilar. So he's plus two on that metric.

"In the past six election cycles in this district, independents have broken sixty-forty for us. Let's say it's a bad year, because of redistricting, and they break fifty-fifty—although Mark's numbers don't show that. But for the sake of argument, that gives our opponent forty-two percent at the end of the night. And that's *his best case* scenario. You beat him fifty-eight to forty-two. In any normal race that's called a landslide, Congressman," Nash concluded.

McKenzie knew the numbers. He had heard them many times before. And yet, somehow he didn't find them reassuring.

"What about his impact on the Hispanic vote? They account for fully thirty-five percent of registered voters," he said. "Mark?"

His pollster flipped through the pages of data and asked everyone to look at page sixteen.

"Hispanics register Democrat at a significantly higher rate than the general population," he said. "The current stats show them at sixty-six percent Democrat, six percent Republican, and twenty-eight percent unaffiliated."

"So what if we lost twenty percent of the Hispanic Democrats? What if we lost half of them?" McKenzie asked.

Morton Nash, the campaign consultant, took in a deep breath. "That wouldn't be good," he said finally. "But that's not going to happen. Because you've got a secret weapon you haven't even begun to exploit."

McKenzie gave him a querulous look. *A secret weapon, really? Aguilar's got more money than I do, that's pretty clear. At least for now.*

"Congressman, you've got the frank."

10

cKenzie couldn't believe what he had just heard coming from the lips of a DCCC political consultant. At first, he just wanted to laugh. He was being urged to commit a felony and use his taxpayer-funded privilege of postage-free communications with his constituents to push a partisan advantage.

The frank—or more accurately, the Franking Privilege—was something all members could access. It gave them the ability of communicating at no cost with their constituents through direct mail, as long as what they communicated could legitimately be seen as official business *not* directly related to an election.

The Franking Privilege was first enacted by the Continental Congress in 1775 to allow members to keep constituents informed about matters of government. Instead of placing a stamp on the envelope, members placed their signature. That practice has continued to this day. Every time Congressman McKenzie sent a "newsletter" to his constituents, which was about once every two years, it was "stamped" with his signature and a special congressional commission reimbursed the Post Office for each piece of mail sent.

He rarely used it, and when he did, it was in election years.

But he had never used it so close to an actual election. If he recalled correctly, there was a ban on using the frank for any communication with constituents within ninety days of an election. They were well beyond that now.

"How do you propose getting around the ninety-day ban?" he asked Nash.

"Congressman, that's much less of a problem than you think, especially in your case. I've already looked into this. You've only used the frank a half-dozen times since you were elected to Congress eight years ago. General practice allows you to use it three to four times a year. The last franked letter you sent out was in June—and it's the only one you've sent this year. You can easily argue—and the Commission can't really object—that you have been quite conservative in your use of this congressional privilege. You only need to use it twice in the next two weeks, as I see it. Three times, max. And we will carefully craft those communications to fit within the law, all the while they respond and crush the insidious lies your opponent is spreading through paid media. Then we'll follow up with paid mailers and be back up on radio and TV."

It was tempting, on the surface. But everything he had ever learned in law school was screaming at him to reject the proposal outright.

"The Ethics Committee is split evenly along party lines. They can't possibly allow such a thing."

Nash gave a little bow, pretending to take off his hat. "Thank you, Congressman. You have just made my point. The Ethics Committee is indeed bi-partisan, and it is split three to three. I think I can just about guarantee you that you will not lose a single one of the three Democrats on that committee should it ever come up for a vote."

He didn't like the smell of it. He was a lawyer, after all. Morton Nash was suggesting that the rule of law was contingent on the ability to enforce the law, not the principles of the law or its statutes. That was an invitation to corruption, a banana republic. Buy off the judges and you get off scot free.

"Since you seem skeptical, let me spell it out to you, Congressman. Your opponent releases an attack ad with lies about your record on Medicare-For-All. You respond with a newsletter to your constituents that reproduces portions of the Congressional Record that explicitly rebut what your opponent has said. In other words, you are setting the record straight—but not with your own words or editorializing, but with the words of the Congressional Record. That is explicitly what the franking statutes allow."

McKenzie still didn't like it, but he had to admit, it was tempting.

"Send me a memo from the DCCC general counsel's office. I want to see the actual statutes and their reading of the statutes."

Nash was ready for him. He opened his leather document case and took out a memo, printed on official letterhead of the DCCC, and tossed it across the table to him with a smirk.

"That's why you pay me the big bucks, Congressman. I'm worth every dime."

II

Nelson Aguilar was in his element. The fire marshal capacity of the Iglesia Cristo Está Vivo below the Wheaton mall was 1,200, and it was packed to the rafters. His campaign had rented the space for the rally, so there could be no phony accusation that Pastor Victor Hermosa was endorsing Aguilar from the pulpit, which would be a violation of the Johnson amendment and could lead to his church losing its non-profit status. The pastor was indeed on hand that night but as a member of the audience, not up on the stage with Aguilar. He made no public statement or endorsement. He didn't have to.

The Crocodile had pulled off another coup and convinced the outgoing Comptroller of Maryland, a lifelong Democrat, to introduce Aguilar. Ken Adams knew all about the contempt the Comptroller felt for Congressman McKenzie, which dated from the days when the two men had served together in the Maryland state senate from neighboring districts. They hadn't liked each other then, and they absolutely despised each other now. But until tonight both men had kept their feelings behind closed doors. Comptroller Sastry Karna had already announced he was retiring after two terms, and rumors abounded that he was amassing a war chest to run for the U.S. Senate as soon as a seat opened up. The Crocodile bet that Karna would be unable to pass up an opportunity to inflict a mortal wound on a potential competitor for that Senate seat, and he had been right.

"He's laying it on pretty thick." The Crocodile grinned.

"You knew he would," Aguilar said.

They were waiting in the pastor's dressing room behind the altar, which had been stripped of all religious ornaments for tonight's rally except for the giant cross suspended from the ceiling. The Crocodile knew that Aguilar would be walking around on stage, interacting with the audience, so he had instructed the lighting crew to steer him back to center stage periodically and discreetly light up the cross over his head. Nothing too ostentatious. No crown of thorns. No halo. Just a subtle blessing from on high.

"My friends, these reckless policies Congressman McKenzie is proposing amount to nothing less than socialism," Karna was saying. "I am a Democrat. You all know that. But I am not a socialist and I never will be," he shouted out.

The crowd responded with an uproar, and then they began chanting, "Aguilar! Aguilar!"

Karna turned toward the dressing room, and the Crocodile gave a nod. It was time.

As he joined the Comptroller on the stage, Aguilar looked out over the audience, drinking in their wild applause. He found familiar faces and gave them the thumbs up. Annie Bryant was near the fire exit about midway up the hall. He gave her a special wave, and for an instant, locked his eyes on hers.

"My friends," he began. "Just look at you. You are the faces of today's America. You are not Democrats. You are not Republicans. You are Americans!" he said, and the crowd cheered.

"You are not Latino, you are not black, or Asian, or this hyphen or that. You are Americans! And we *all* rejoice in the American dream! You are living testimony that the dream lives on and will continue to live for as long as we prevent the socialists from destroying it, because God wants America to be free."

Ken Adams drank in Aguilar's words. He let them flow over him, surround him, despite every professional instinct to listen with a critical ear. He had never met a politician who had such a remarkable empathy for his audience. Aguilar sensed their mood. He could feel their enthusiasm and channel it to his purpose; and when it seemed he might lose control, he pulled in on the mast and rode them into shore. There was nothing he would change. There was no advice he could give. It was disconcerting! This was as close to perfect pitch as he had ever seen. If Aguilar couldn't beat McKenzie, nobody could.

"You may have heard that my opponent recently went down to the Mexican border. Do you know what he was doing there? He didn't go visit with the brave men and women of our border patrol. He didn't even go to the detention centers he criticizes so much. No. He actually went *across* the border to a migrant camp inside Mexico, and brought Spanish-speaking lawyers with him to coach illegals on how to break our law. As if we didn't have enough MS 13 members here already. Can you believe it?"

The crowd began chanting, *"No paseran! No paseran! No paseran!"*

"Friends, I know many of you in this room. Some of you have been so kind as to invite me into your homes and into your churches. Let me ask you a few questions—and let's make sure the Fake News can hear your answers."

Oh my God, the Crocodile thought. *He's doing a Trump. And he's getting away with it.* The news media were all in the well down in front. They would have to turn their cameras around to face the crowd if they were to capture the responses Aguilar was eliciting. And you knew they would never do it. That's why he'd positioned two volunteers with small video cams down in the well. One was to stay focused on the candidate, but the other was to capture the audience reaction, which they were live-casting on Facebook.

"So we 'know' from our friends here in the media"—the audience hissed—"that the president is cruel. He is racist. He has unleashed ICE to carry out raids all across the country. They are splitting up families. Tearing mothers away from their children. Taking Grandma away in handcuffs."

A deadly silence came over the room. Had Aguilar crossed a line? Even with his "own" people that he knew so well? The Crocodile watched the so-called journalists down in the well. They all had pens poised to their notebooks, blood dripping from their lips.

"How many of you here in this room have had ICE come to your house?"

No one raised their hand.

"Don't be shy. If they really have come, they know who you are."

People laughed. Two hands went up, but that was it.

"And how many of you saw Mom get deported? None? Well, what about Grandma? Anyone see Grandma get dragged away in handcuffs by ICE?"

The Crocodile knew where he was going. It was a risk, but a well-calculated risk. He was going to face the attackers head on and cut them off at the knees.

"Of course not. But the Fake News won't report that. Will you, guys? No, you won't be reporting that. You won't report that this president is finally deporting the criminals and the gangsters who are tearing our communities apart. They broke our laws coming here and continued to break them ever since. I say good riddance to them!"

The audience cheered, but not a single news camera turned to face them.

"Congressman McKenzie cares more about people coming illegally into our beautiful, wonderful, God-blessed country than he does about you: American citizens. He wants to give them 'free' health care. That's right. He wants to take twenty-five percent out of your paychecks and give it to people who jump the line and break our laws to come here illegally."

He was right on the edge, the Crocodile thought. *The media could play this very badly, but would they dare?*

"You know what it's like in El Salvador, in Honduras, in Guatemala," Aguilar said. "You know what happens when the police are taking bribes from the gangs and the drug lords. When the politicians drop to their knees, begging for big payoffs from the cartels. My opponent wants America to be like the countries most of us have fled. He wants to erode our rule of law.

"So let me ask you a simple question: Do you want to live in a lawless nation, where drug kingpins and gang lords set the rules?"

The church erupted in a single voice. Their cheering went on for nearly a minute, so Aguilar let the microphone drop to his side and exchanged greetings with people he spotted all over the room.

"We can change the laws," he went on once the chanting died down. "And if you elect me to Congress, I will. But we cannot—cannot—allow this country to become a lawless nation, like the banana republics we fled. If we lose America, where else can we go? This is the last safe haven on earth for a free people. God blessed this country and will continue to bless this country—if we are smart enough and brave enough to defend it and defend our freedom and the rule of law."

That was his cue. The Crocodile turned to the stage manager behind him, who punched a few buttons, filling the church with the mariachi band theme song of the campaign. Everyone in the pews came onto their feet and began forming lines, swaying to the music, hands on the hips of the person in front of them.

Aguilar stood on the stage, waving to the raucous cheers for several minutes, then joined the Crocodile backstage.

"Well, boss. You did it. You did well."

"You think it went down okay? Not too risky?"

"No, you hit it just right," the Crocodile said. "Because, see, you've got something that no other candidate has got, and everyone in that church knows it. You're one of them. You're not a phony like McKenzie, born with a silver spoon. You have risen despite the obstacles. And so you give them hope that they can rise, too. You have *earned* the right to speak the truth to them. You have earned it from them. And that's why you're going to win, boss. That's why you're going to win."

12

ongressman Hugh McKenzie pretended indifference as the NBC make-up artist began to powder his face for *The Razor's Edge,* but secretly he was grateful for the solid tan she had selected. While he knew Ricky Brewer was going to be asking him about his debate with Aguilar, he wasn't sure how he would react if he actually played a video. It had been the worst performance of his political career, and he was still kicking himself for getting sucker punched into playing defense. Politics 101: Never make excuses, never explain, but attack, attack, attack. *And he flunked.*

"How 'bout your hair, Congressman? Just a spray or two to keep it in place?"

"I leave it to you," he said affably. "I am in your hands."

Former CIA Director Pat Counihan was on screen with Brewer, but he couldn't hear what they were saying. He ought to get a medal, though. A profile in courage. Standing up to Trump, even as he faced increasing scrutiny and even legal jeopardy for his actions during the final months of the Obama presidency. Warning about Russian interference in our elections. And the

Republicans continued to wave it off as if it happened all the time. Maybe it did, actually. People forget the Cold War. That's what Dad says. The Russians have been all over us for one hundred years. But that would be a Republican talking point.

Jenn and his bodyman, Joachim, were waiting for him in the cramped green room. Counihan was still on screen.

"Turn it up," he said. "I ought to hear what he's saying in case I need to respond."

They were discussing Senate Majority Leader Mitch McConnell, and his refusal to allow legislation to come to the floor that would change election laws across the country. *Moscow Mitch*, they were calling him. Ouch! Of course, they were Democrat-sponsored bills—one of them his.

> **Ricky Brewer:** *Yesterday, FBI director Christopher Wray raised the prospect of foreign actors manipulating voter data but said his bureau was working relentlessly to prevent it.*
>
> **FBI Director Wray:** *We have yet to see attacks manipulating or deleting election- and voter-related data, or attacks that actually take election management systems off-line. But we know that our adversaries are relentless. So are we.*
>
> **Brewer (to Counihan):** *So what do you think the worst case would be that would possibly screw up our notion of who actually won the election?*
>
> **Counihan:** *I think if the Russians or someone else did something to disrupt the electoral systems, going in and maybe taking down some of the registration rolls, preventing individuals from getting to the voting booths, or manipulating some of the tabulations that*

might be sent from one precinct to headquarters. It really raises questions about the integrity of the election. And my concern is, would Donald Trump at that stage claim that the election was fraudulent because of interference from individuals in some basement somewhere, that they manipulated it?[1]

He turned to Jenn. "Can they actually do that? Interfere in the reported vote?"

"You mean in the precinct by precinct totals that are sent to the counties, and then to the states? That's way above my pay grade, Congressman. But it's an interesting notion, isn't it?"

"That's not what the Russians did in 2016."

"No," she said. "I've never heard anybody claim that the Russians actually penetrated the electoral systems. What they did was bad enough."

"Sure. But it could have been worse."

He made a mental note to speak to his IT guy about the mechanics of how the electronic voting machines worked, how they counted the votes, and how those votes were tabulated precinct by precinct. Were there technical tweaks he could offer as legislation that might shield voting machines from being hacked?

The producer ducked her head into the green room. "You're on, Congressman. Please follow me."

Counihan was back in the makeup chair, getting his face daubed with wipes, when McKenzie went by. "Good job, Mr. Director. Wish you were still there."

Counihan's Irish-red skin was re-emerging from beneath the makeup. "Oh, thank you Congressman," he said. "And good luck with your race. I hear you're going to need it!"

---

1   John Brennan: "Our Election Systems Need to be Strengthened," interview with Chris Matthews on *Hardball,* July 26, 2019.

Well, good day to you, too, he thought. *That was a helluva thing to say to someone as they were about to go on live television. I thought he was supposed to be on our side.*

Brewer was drinking coffee and surveying a computer screen embedded beneath the round plastic table of *The Razor's Edge* set. He didn't look up until the producer had seated McKenzie across the table and brought him a clean mug of water.

"Okay," Brewer said, reaching out to shake his hand. "This is how it's going to go. I'm going to do a brief recap of what Director Counihan just said, then I'm going to introduce you as a principal co-sponsor of one of the election reform bills. You heard what he said, right?"

"Most of it," McKenzie said.

"The gist is, without your bill, our electoral systems are still vulnerable to hacking. So you can riff off that all you like for the first two minutes or so."

"Sure," McKenzie said. Brewer was scrolling down his computer screen. *If you didn't know how the set looked to television viewers, you would never guess it by sitting here*, he thought. Instead of that magnificent view of the Washington monument—Gus Antly's view, from the Majority Leader's office in the Capitol Building—all you saw was a blurry cityscape of lights. The deep walnut paneling was real, or sort of, but there wasn't much of it. It seemed so informal you could almost be lulled into thinking you were at some kind of high school drama rehearsal. Brewer wore sandals and jeans beneath the table.

"After that, I'm going to put you on the razor's edge."

"Okay," he said hesitantly.

"I'm not going to mess with you, Congressman. But everyone's seen the video of that debate of yours now that the president tweeted it out. It's gotten something like three million views. So I'm going to ask you the same questions. Are you anti-Israel?

Are you really suggesting an additional twenty-five percent withholding tax to pay for Medicare-for-All? What do you say to the 85 million people, maybe more, who stand to lose their private health insurance? Do you really think that's a winning platform for Democrats against this president? You get my drift."

"I do," he said.

"Okay. Here we go."

Brewer sat up straight, growing a good six inches right in front of his eyes, and launched into his famous introduction, speaking so fast it was hard to untangle his words.

The first segment went well. Just as he had promised, Brewer teed it up and let him present his election reform legislation, interrupting only with prompts, so he would keep moving at the rapid pace of the show.

"So is there any chance of Moscow Mitch bringing this bill to the Senate floor before the election?" he said.

"In all honesty, probably not, Ricky," McKenzie said.

Without transition, Brewer went on. "You and your Republican opponent squared off last week in a debate that sent fur flying. Not your usual style, if I might say so, Congressman."

"No, it wasn't. And my opponent is not the usual opponent. He's used every low trick and—"

"Let's have a look."

Before he could finish his sentence, there he was on screen, red-faced, flustered, as a voice heckled him from the audience.

"What about Israel?"

"I'm getting to Israel."

"Answer the question," the heckler shouted.

"So, Congressman. What about Israel?" Brewer said. "And what was that all about?"

"Ricky, first of all, let me just say that I'm a bit surprised that you would give airtime to hecklers who in all probability were paid for by my opponent's campaign. This is a phony issue, dredged up by a bunch of bottom-feeding muckrakers who couldn't care less about Israel let alone my own beliefs."

"So what are those beliefs, Congressman? Is it true you signed a letter condemning Israel that was being circulated by the Council on American-Islamic Relations, CAIR? Not exactly a neutral group. They were unindicted co-conspirators in the biggest terror-funding prosecution ever."

"Before I was elected to Congress, I joined a group of bi-partisan lawmakers in the Maryland state legislature that sent a letter to the UN Secretary General, raising concerns about human rights abuses during the Israeli invasion of Gaza during which it was reported thousands of civilians died."

"But thousands of civilians didn't die, Congressman. There was an investigation—"

"—which that letter helped prompt—"

"—found that at least a quarter of the casualties on the Palestinian side were in fact known armed militants, and another half were suspected to have taken part in the fighting. One thousand three hundred and forty-one Palestinian casualties in all."

"We didn't know that then. What we knew was the horrible footage we were seeing on television of UN schools being bombed, children in the streets."

"And it turned out that a lot of those children were in fact being used as human shields. Take a look."

Brewer rolled tape from Al-Aqsa TV of Hamas leaders calling on children to form a human shield at Hamas positions in Gaza to prevent Israeli air strikes. It then cut away to children standing in front of a sand-bagged checkpoint, flashing the

V for Victory sign, while Hamas fighters loaded mortars just meters away.

"I can tell you, Ricky. We didn't see any of that footage at the time. And I would say now that Israel—"

"This is when the Israelis began a tactic known as 'roof-knocking,'" Brewer broke in. "Pretty smart, if you think of it. First they launch a warning shot on the roof of a building they know is being used as a firing position by Hamas. Then a couple of minutes later, they take it down. Have a look."

> *"The first shot means 'get out,'" a female narrator with a British accent said indignantly as a small explosion lifted dust off the roof of an apartment block. "And the second one means business. It's called roof-knocking. It's supposed to minimize civilian deaths."*

"As I was saying," McKenzie cut back in, "since then we've seen Israel take some pretty extraordinary measures to avoid civilian casualties, even putting their own soldiers in danger."

"You call yourself a big supporter of Israel."

"I am, Ricky. And my constituents know that. I have been a strong proponent of funding for the Arrow anti-missile program and for maintaining Israel's qualitative military edge. I've voted for David's Sling. I've voted for the F-35. I've voted for Iron Dome. For my opponent to suggest anything different is just a lie. But I'm not surprised."

"Yeah, well that seems to be the Republican playbook, doesn't it. So let's turn to Medicare-For-All and that twenty-five percent tax."

"Another lie," McKenzie said.

"Watch this," Brewer said, pointing to the screen dramatically. Nelson Aguilar came on screen, and he was exhorting a crowd of young Hispanics.

"Twenty-five percent. That's the amount Congressman McKenzie wants to grab from your paycheck every week. Every week. Just think of it. Twenty-five percent less in your pocket every week. He calls it Medicare-For-All. But you know the truth: it's just plain socialism."

"Is Medicare-For-All socialism, Congressman?"

"Of course not, Ricky. It's just a new and improved version—much needed, I will admit—of Obamacare. My constituents have been begging me for years not to let the Republicans take away Obamacare, which guarantees their access to affordable health care."

"And so, under your plan, would 85 million people lose their private health insurance?"

"Look. Under our Medicare-For-All proposal—"

"Would they lose their insurance? True, or not true?"

"That depends."

"But they might?"

"So, we spend more on health care than any nation on earth. Our mixed public/private system has built-in fraud waste and abuse that is mind-boggling. We as a nation have to move toward a single payer system. And that's what Medicare-For-All does. It moves us closer to single payer."

"In plain speak, that means no private insurance. Your opponent calls it socialism."

"He can call it whatever he likes. But his solution only benefits millionaires and billionaires. It would pour billions of dollars into the coffers of Big Pharma and the insurance companies while denying access to health care to millions of hard-working middle class Americans."

"Just Americans, Congressman? We've got fifteen seconds. Would you deny health care to undocumented immigrants and asylum seekers?"

"Ricky, that's a topic worthy of a discussion that will take much more than fifteen seconds. But in a word, no, I wouldn't deny anyone coverage who was working within our system."

Brewer turned away to face the main camera. "Thank you, Congressman Hugh McKenzie. You've been on *The Razor's Edge*."

The red light above the camera went off, and the producer shouted, "Clear." McKenzie took a deep breath and exhaled gratefully.

"You did pretty well, Congressman," Brewer said. "Hope to see you back. And good luck to you, sir."

"Thanks. Everybody's telling me how much I'm going to need it."

"You'll be fine," Brewer said. "That's what I'm hearing. Don't let 'em get to you."

13

The polls began to stabilize by late September, showing him down by four points (forty-two to forty-six) with 12 percent undecided. Morton Nash, his campaign consultant, remained upbeat because the steady erosion of his favorables they'd been monitoring over the past few months had bottomed out and forty-six was still beatable. He had crafted a series of negative mailers about Aguilar that were about to drop, and now they were up on TV and radio as well. The campaign had underestimated Aguilar at the beginning, and brought Nash on board in a panic to right the ship. They should have hit hard on Aguilar's negatives much earlier. Nash argued that Aguilar's central campaign message, about the rule of law, was about to backfire—with a little help. "It's all about the messaging," he said at the daily staff meeting. "From here to Election Day, we've got two goals. Win over the undecideds, and peel back his support among female Hispanic voters, who will vote with their heart, not their head. We do that, and we win."

"Aguilar wants to deport Grandma?" McKenzie said.

"That's right, Congressman. But don't worry: you don't have to say that."

McKenzie knew Nash was right, but he still didn't like it.

"What about winning fair and square?" he said.

"There is no fair and square, Congressman. This is politics. Either you win, or you lose. Do you want to win?"

McKenzie was planning to air his misgivings to the Democrats' vice-presidential nominee, Senator Vince Bellinger, once they had wrapped up the first debate prep session. They had served together in the House when McKenzie was a freshman, before Bellinger went on to win the vacant U.S. Senate seat from New York. Bellinger had urged the campaign to select McKenzie to play Vice President Mike Pence because he had never seen anyone who so perfectly captured the vice president's sanctimoniousness. "He's a natural," Bellinger had argued. "I need to practice ignoring it."

The mock debate had gone well. McKenzie thought he had scored some points using Aguilar's attacks on Medicare-For-All, which Bellinger initially fumbled. "How can you possibly go before the American people and tell them that eighty-five million of them—eighty-five million!—are going to lose their insurance because of a cockamamie scheme that puts the government in charge of your health care?"

"With all due respect, Mr. Vice President, that's not what will happen," Bellinger said.

Bellinger's handler from the campaign, former DNC chairman Nathan Bullock, jumped up and started screaming at the cameramen and the two debaters to stop. "Horse pucky, Senator. Grow a pair. Don't let Pence wrap you up in his phony compassion shtick."

Bellinger looked down at his notes. "How about this?" he said. Turning to face the cameras directly, he shook his head in sorrow. "It is so disappointing, Mr. Vice President, to hear you lie and lie and lie again. You know that's not going to happen. And everybody in America knows. We're going to transition into Medicare-For-All while leaving private insurance in place for those that want to keep it."

"Better. Throw it back at him," Bullock said.

And so it went for another two hours, back and forth. McKenzie found himself almost believing the Republican talking points he had practiced for the mock debates. Many of them dovetailed what Aguilar was using against him. *Maybe that is the answer*, he thought. Don't focus on his uniqueness. Paint him as just another Republican taking orders from the party in Washington. We've been here before, people. Don't let yourselves be fooled by the fancy tricks, the mariachi bands and celebrities. Nelson Aguilar is just part of the machine.

On second thought, maybe not.

"You did well, buddy. Maybe a bit too well," Bellinger said once they have finished. "Sounds like you've let your guy get into your head. That was pretty damn convincing!"

"Isn't that what the campaign wanted?"

He tried to turn it into a joke, but Bellinger saw through it.

"I hear you're in trouble."

"It's true. I'm behind in the tracking polls."

"In that district? That's got to be one of the safest Democrat seats in the nation."

"Not after re-districting," he said.

"If my memory is correct, it's still over fifty percent Democrat."

"Fifty point two."

"So what happened? You get caught harassing a female staffer? Suggest soccer moms should quit their jobs and stay home to take care of the kids?"

"No. My opponent has got a ton of money. He's Hispanic. He's a businessman. And, well, everybody treats him like a rock star. Even the media!"

Bellinger wrapped an arm around his shoulder and drew him off to the side where the staffers couldn't hear them. "Sounds to me like you need some insurance," he said.

"I was hoping for another one million dollars from the Party."

"Your Uncle Vinnie's got better than that. I have somebody you need to meet."

He wrote a familiar name on a yellow Post-It note, along with a cell phone number, then put his finger to his lips.

"Don't talk on the phone," Bellinger said. "Just tell him Uncle Vinnie asked you to meet. See if he can't join us at the next debate prep. Then it's all yours, Hugh-boy."

Hugh-boy! When was it going to stop?

14

The first week of October went by in a whirl. Congress was out of session and everyone was in full campaign mode. Aguilar was doing rallies almost every night, or so it seemed, bringing hundreds of people into churches and schools. Stan Harris, McKenzie's opposition research guy, was all over them. He had guerilla campaign workers filming every minute of them, filming the crowds, and especially, filming the candidate when he thought he was speaking privately to big donors.

"We've got great stuff, Congressman," he said at the next campaign meeting at DNC headquarters. "We've got amazing footage. Look at this."

Harris played tape of Aguilar in his suit, top two buttons of his dress shirt unbuttoned, showing a giant gold cross on his chest, with a hand up to his face to hide what he was saying to a person so enormous that "porcine" would be an understatement. The other person was holding out a check.

"Fat cats give dark money to Republican candidate," Harris said. "My guy got his camera on the other side of that hand. See the zeros on the check? We'll put in subtitles when we do the ad. What he's saying through all the background noise is, 'I've got your back, boss.' That's your opponent, Congressman. Don't believe what he says about representing the little people. He's in the pocket of the special interests. He's with the millionaires and the billionaires. That's the punch line."

McKenzie let it sink in for a minute. It sure looked bad for Aguilar, that's for sure.

"Any way we can get the Super PAC to do that so I don't have to say I approve of this message?"

Morton Nash, who had written those lines and discussed them earlier with Harris, twirled a finger in the air in exasperation. "Of course, Congressman. That's the plan."

He did a couple of house parties that week, meeting with his own versions of the Republican pig, who turned out to represent the restaurant and food chain lobby—*a fitting irony*, McKenzie thought. He had Jenn walk his donors through the numbers, making sure they all understood that he was in trouble—just enough trouble to get them to open their wallets, but not enough trouble to despair of victory. Then he gave his stump speech: Medicare-For-All; fifteen-dollar minimum wage; Green New Deal; and, for the one event with Jewish donors in Potomac, Israel's qualitative military edge.

But through all of it, Hugh McKenzie was distracted. It was as if he was watching himself perform down on a stage while he sat on a cloud, dreaming of other things. The actor down there knew his lines and recited them perfectly. But up here on the cloud was the candidate, anticipating the meeting with T. Claudius Granger after the next vice-presidential debate prep.

To his relief, Granger was waiting for him. His was a well-known face from the Sunday talk shows, but nobody pretended to notice he was there. He sat in the back row of the conference room at Myers, Ogilvy, Pantazis, and Pugh, the Democrat law firm on Vermont Avenue that was hosting the secret debate prep sessions, well-shielded from the media. Granger came to the campaign from Governor Tomlinson's black mafia. In his early sixties, he was distinguished, well-dressed, and soft-spoken, and on television defended Mrs. T. and her campaign better than the official spokesperson. But behind the scenes he was the campaign hatchet man, their fixer. Once everyone else had left after the debate prep, he motioned for McKenzie to join him. Jenn naturally stood up with him and approached. Granger gave her a gracious bow and took her hand.

"The Congressman and I are about to have a discussion, Miss—what was your name again?"

"Lindh. Jennifer Lindh."

"Miss Lindh," he said, letting go of her hand. "I understand that you and the bodyman were about to go sit with the receptionist until the congressman and I have finished our little chat."

Jenn gave McKenzie a querulous look, but he just shook his head. "Yes, I guess we were," she said finally. "By the way, do you have a first name, Mr. Granger?"

"Just Granger," he said. He wasn't going to tell her, or anybody for that matter, that he never wanted to be called Thomas. He was an avenging angel, not an Uncle Tom.

Once they had left, Granger motioned for McKenzie to sit down.

"I hear you have a problem," he said before McKenzie could say anything. "I have solutions. That's why Mrs. T. pays me all this money. I fix things so well that nobody realizes they were broken."

McKenzie knew vaguely about the Democrat presidential nominee's background as a Chicago gang member and raised an eyebrow.

"Oh, I can see what you're thinking," Granger said. "Shame on you, cracker."

"No, I wasn't—"

"Oh yes you was." Granger gave a great belly laugh, making fun of them both. "Yeah, that's right. I came out of the Black P Stone Rangers, just like her. And I did time for it, too. But that was years ago. Went to law school while I was in the slammer. Me and Mrs. T go back a long ways…. Now please explain to me why this wetback boy is giving you such a run for *our* money."

So, McKenzie laid it all out. Aguilar had money, he had charisma, and he had the Hispanic vote. Since that was usually a solid demographic for Democrats, and close to 35 percent of the registered Democrats in the district were Hispanic, he was in trouble.

"So I hear," Granger said.

He drummed his fingertips against the wooden arm of the leather swivel chair, as if pondering what he was about to say.

"We have a special program," he said finally. "It's very close hold. Normally, we wouldn't give access to anyone outside the campaign. But since you've become a favorite of Uncle Vinnie, he convinced me to make an exception. We certainly wouldn't want to lose your vote in Congress. This will give you a guarantee."

He wrote a name and a phone number on a Post-It note and smoothed it onto the arm of McKenzie's chair.

"Have your IT guy give Navid a call. Tell him Granger told you we're all in. They are to set up a meeting. Just the two of them. No one else can know about this. Not even your wife."

Not my wife? McKenzie wondered. She hated the Republican yahoos in the new district more than he did.

"If one word of this ever gets out, we are all dead men. Understand?" Granger gave him a look that chilled him to the bone. Apparently, he wasn't just talking about losing an election. Nor was he talking metaphorically.

"Speaking of IT," McKenzie said, trying to make light of the implied threat. "I was on *The Razor's Edge* last week just after Director Counihan was talking about how the Russians or somebody in a basement might hack our electoral systems during this election."

"Yeah, we weren't very happy about that," Granger said. "Sometimes Director Counihan would do better to keep his mouth shut. You did pretty well, by the way."

Granger got up. That was it. He was dismissed.

15

"**N**elson Aguilar: paid for by millionaires and billionaires. Hugh McKenzie: the people's representative. Brought to you by Progress Maryland, not affiliated with any political campaign."

The Crocodile was fuming. He was pacing Aguilar's office at the radio station, tapping stacks of paper, thumping bookshelves. He was red in the face. If the cause of his concern hadn't been so serious, Aguilar would have laughed at seeing him so out of sorts. The Crocodile never lost his cool, let alone his temper. But this latest attack ad from the McKenzie campaign was all over cable television, and they had just finished watching it together. For the third time. It was scurrilous. And it was untrue—or mostly so.

"You know what happens right after that sequence they aired with the guy from the National Restaurant Association? You remember what I said?"

Aguilar chuckled. "Of course I do."

"That was *me* speaking, not you. I am the one who's saying—to *you*—'I've got your back, boss.' Because that's what I do. Everybody knows that's what I do."

"That's right."

"It wasn't *you* making a promise to a donor. It was *me* protecting *you*!"

"It's true," said Annie. For all the Crocodile's sustained proximity to her candidate, she was happy to back him up.

"And then I grabbed the check from that idiot before he could give it to you. You are never *ever* supposed to touch money."

"And I don't. I didn't."

"No, but it sure looks like it the way they filmed it. They made it look like that fat idiot was giving money to you personally. Or buying favors. Or whatever. Bad, bad, bad!"

The Crocodile had no hair on his head to tear out, but his arms were flapping, his fists shaking at Heaven.

"We've got to hit back immediately. AB," he said, turning to Annie, who had been listening to his tirade sympathetically, "we've got airtime booked on all the networks, right?"

"We're maxed out. That's right."

"Can we shift the spot we had planned for tomorrow evening and rotate in a counter-attack?"

"What did you have in mind?"

The Crocodile stopped pacing, suddenly taken aback. "I don't know, actually. So much to choose from."

Aguilar couldn't help but feel a hint of amusement as he watched the Crocodile fret. As a TV reporter working in war zones, Aguilar had been shot at. He'd been bombed. He'd been spat upon by angry crowds at political rallies. He'd been physically assaulted by Antifa thugs. Through all of it, he always kept his cameras rolling, and if he was doing a live feed, he kept on talking. *That's what we have to do now*, he thought. *Just keep on talking and let the bombs fall where they may. God will do the rest.*

"*Relajas!* Chill out, my friend. Don't let them get under your skin."

"What are you thinking?" the Crocodile said.

"You all have done amazing work. We're hitting him every day. Annie, remind us of what's coming up."

She had the media buy sheet on her clipboard and read out the titles of their upcoming ads.

"'Secure the border,' 'Medi-scare,' 'American dream,' 'Fair weather friend.' That one's about Israel," she said.

The Crocodile picked up the thread. "So fifty-fifty, attack and support," he said. "Remind me what's in the border piece."

Annie pulled up the script. They had actual footage of Congressman McKenzie crossing the border into Mexico and meeting with groups of asylum-seekers, including a close-up of a flyer he was handing out. It was mostly in Spanish with the English words highlighted. "He's telling them what they are supposed to say when they get stopped by the border patrol."

"So he's actually coaching them on how to break the law."

"That's the punch line. 'Hugh McKenzie: law breaker, not lawmaker.'"

"That's it!" the Crocodile said. "Let's rotate that in starting tomorrow."

"I'm ahead of you," Annie said. "Already done."

Annie had a glow to her that was hard to miss, Aguilar thought. Perhaps she was pregnant? He remembered how Graciela had glowed. It filled her eyes with a kind of dreamy haze and gave a special smoothness to her skin. It started early on, too. It wasn't just with Brady, who was turning fifteen, but with the one they had lost early to a miscarriage. *Precious lives,* he thought. *Precious, precious lives.*

"Just thinking out loud," he said. "Annie, do you have any idea how many babies have been lost in Maryland because of late-term abortions? Specifically, to procedures that the Congressman has supported?"

"Not off hand, but we can find out."

"The Rockville street fair's coming up this weekend. McKenzie is sure to have a booth. What about calling on volunteers to picket him, holding up tiny coffins of the babies he helped to abort?"

"Rockville's got a big Asian population," the Crocodile said. "They're mostly pro-life. But that's pretty in-your-face."

"Isn't that what you said we needed to do?"

"It might be illegal."

"We've got plenty of Republican lawyers on call. Find out exactly *how* to do it legally and let's get on it."

Aguilar was running a lean campaign, even with all the money he had brought in. He used consultants, not paid staff members, to handle high-end donors, direct mail, polling, data management, accounting, and media buys. For all the rest, he relied on volunteers—including for legal advice and his FEC filings.

"You've been pretty silent. What do you think, Camilla?"

Camilla Broadstreet was the best volunteer coordinator who had ever worked in Maryland. Or anywhere, for that matter. And because of that, she was one of the few paid staff. She brought the volunteers together once a week for a light dinner and drinks so they could schmooze with the candidate. It was part of her technique. She knew the value of star power as a motivator, and Aguilar knew how to turn it on. His volunteers would walk through hoops of fire to get him elected—and in campaign terms, that meant waving signs on highways in the rain, checking in donors at house parties, stuffing envelopes, working social media—and marching and singing in ninety-five-degree heat at parades and street festivals. When she wasn't employed on a political campaign, Camilla toured the country as a motivational speaker, giving high-priced speeches about growing up bicultural and making it in a color-blind society. She, like Annie, had been hired by the Crocodile.

"I'm Roman Catholic. What do you think I think?" she said.

"How about the Latina girls?"

"Oh, this goes beyond the Latinas," Camilla said. "We've got all kinds of people who get up at six in the morning to hold silent vigils in front of Dr. Carhart's abortion mill. They've been doing it for over a year. Anglo housewives. Retirees. Even middle-aged gay men."

"If the lawyers will sign off on it, it sounds like a plan," the Crocodile said. "But we're going to need to hire security from now on for our own events, to keep their oppo research guys from getting those close shots."

16

There was a reason Annie Bryant had a "glow" about her. It wasn't because she was pregnant: She was in love. As she watched Aguilar handle this mini-crisis, she couldn't help but recall the afternoon when he had hit on her. It was so innocent, actually. He was charming, polite. Old worldly, even. Gallant was probably the word. At any rate, she wasn't one of the Me-Too lynch mob and never had been tempted to join them. She liked men. She enjoyed their company. Indeed, she preferred them to most of the women she knew, especially those who thrived in the Washington, DC, swamp. And she had no problem enjoying Aguilar's company and letting him know without umbrage where she stood. She was in love—with someone else.

She still wondered if the meeting hadn't been a set-up by Gordon's mom, Marcie, whom she had met during an earlier campaign event while working as staff counsel for Andy Harris, the only Republican member of Congress left in Maryland. Marcie was a good Republican, a staunch conservative, and you could count on her to show up at every campaign event. She volunteered to go door-to-door, lick envelopes, whatever. And never asked for anything in exchange. But she also was dead broke. That made no difference as far as Harris was concerned. But it meant that she was always going on about her son "the computer nerd" who worked down in Annapolis but still lived at home, helping her with the rent.

Gordon was a genius, Marcie said. Even at an early age, when husband number two (not Gordon's father) had left her, he had displayed a rare talent that—if wrongly nurtured—could have sent him over to the dark side. In the eighth grade, he was furious when an English teacher gave him an F for a presentation on *Huckleberry Finn* that he had sweated over for hours. It was so unfair, he groused. He was upset for a week. And then, Mom got a call from the school principal asking her to come to his office. Gordon was waiting there when she arrived, his chin all the way down to his shoes. Clearly, the principal had been treating him as a juvenile delinquent and was about to exile him to Outer Slobovia. He was so huffy, trying to get her to share his indignation, but when she learned what her son had done, she laughed out loud.

"You mean he hacked the school's server and changed his grade to an A?" she said. "And you want to suspend him for that? There were no broken windows, no smashed chairs, no broken jaws, not even a little scrape during recess. Nobody got hurt and nothing was damaged. You should be putting him in AP math and science, instead!"

When she told Annie the story the first time—and she told it several times before Annie finally got to meet the former child prodigy—she said that once they got home, she had asked Gordon to explain to her what he had done. He went on about how he had found a "back door" into the school's main server, and then simply logged on as the system administrator, altered the grading database, and left. (The actual term he had used was "SQL injection," but it went so far beyond her she never even attempted to register it). He never tampered with anybody else's grades. He never told anyone else how he had done it. She was still angry with that school principal all these years later.

They corresponded regularly by email, mostly one-way from Marcie, who loved to forward conservative blog posts that poked fun of liberals. (Her favorite was a headline that read, "Singlehandedly," above an attractive photo of Alexandria Ocasio-Cortez. Down below, it read: "Putting an end to dumb blonde jokes.") So when Marcie forwarded her the invitation to the local Republican Club meeting at the Red Horse Tavern in Frederick where Gordon would be making a presentation on the new voting systems the state would be using in the next election, Annie said, what the heck. It was only a fifteen-minute drive up to the Golden Mile from her small townhouse in Urbana, and she had nothing better to do. That was before the campaign, of course.

The minute she saw him, she felt as if she had known him for ages. He was just as Marcie had described him. Tallish and gangly, a bit awkward, even shy. But once he started speaking, he commanded the total attention of everyone in the room. He was low-key, precise, and intense. He didn't just know everything there was about the new voting machines, but he had read all the vulnerabilities that were floating around on the Web and was prepared for all their natural skepticism, given that the Democrats had really pushed hard for these particular machines despite a horrible track record of errors and breakdowns in the paper-ballot scanners. He was handsome enough and would grow better-looking with age, she remembered thinking. But that wasn't what initially caught her attention. It was his intelligence. *Want to know a secret, guys? It's not your looks that attract women. It's not money or flashy cars. It's your brains.* She had a soft spot for intelligent men. Jocks and party-boys had never been her thing.

How to get his attention was something else entirely. She hung around after the Q&A, drinking a glass of mediocre Merlot, while a crowd of club members hovered around Gordon, the guys drinking beer from the bottle. He politely declined the beer but did finally accept a glass of Sauvignon Blanc from the president of the club. She liked that.

Finally she saw an opening and went up to him to say hello. She said that she worked in Congressman Harris's office, and she was sure the Congressman would be very interested to hear what he had been saying. Did he have a written version of his briefing he could email her?

"Sure," he said. "Just give me your card."

And that was that.

She was going to make him chase her.

Or so she thought.

The next time they met, she was *sure* Mom had arranged it. Marcie asked her to "show the flag" for Congressman Harris at the Maryland Wine Festival, which was being held on the sprawling grounds of the Carroll County Farm Museum in Westminster, just at the edge of his district. The Congressman wasn't planning to attend—not good politics to be seen with a wine glass around your neck as you swayed from winery to winery amidst crowds of happy drunks on a beautiful sunny September afternoon—so Annie agreed to hang out at the Republican Party booth. And sure enough, not an hour had gone by when Gordon showed up to say hello to his mom.

"You two *have* met, haven't you," she said with innocence so fake it wouldn't get a crab to bite.

Of course they had, Gordon said. A bit awkwardly, for sure, but that got them to small talk: the voting machine presentation, how did the Congressman like it.... And, low and behold, Mom was suddenly nowhere to be seen.

After a bit, it dawned on him. He saw the glass around her neck, and said, "I see you came prepared. We've got old friends who own Elk Run Vineyard on Liberty Road. They've got a booth just around the corner. Would you like to come taste their rosé?"

Carol Wilson was on duty, along with a male volunteer who helped out at the festivals, while her husband was back at the vineyard fixing the hydraulics on one of their tractors ahead of the harvest. She welcomed Gordon like a son and gave them each solid pours of the Cold Friday rosé.

"Why Cold Friday?" Annie asked.

"Because it was freezing cold the first year we harvested that plot!" Carol laughed.

They went on to sample the new Citrine rosé (a mix of Chardonnay and Pinot noir), the Cabernet Franc, and the Red Door Cabernet blend, and on the third glass decided they liked Red Door the best.

"What are you doing next Friday night?" Gordon asked.

"I thought I was having dinner with you," she said.

And so it began, slowly.

Gordon invited her to the Surf House in Urbana, a recent addition to the bedroom community that attempted to reproduce the atmosphere of a beachside eatery, surfboards on the walls, tiki bar outside, fishing nets suspended from the ceiling, and large screen TVs with videos of surfing competitions on endless loop.

"Do you like Cava?" was his first question.

She said she did, and after two glasses he started to loosen up. She found herself enjoying his sense of humor, his self-deprecating way of telling stories about himself, and his taste for wine. They split an entrée of grilled squid that was surprisingly tender, and by the time their fish came, they had finished the Cava.

"We should have a New Zealand Sauvignon Blanc with the fish," he said.

"Good thing I don't have to drive far," she said. "How about you?"

"I'm still at Mom's house in New Market. But there's a back road from here up to Old National Pike so I don't have to go out on 70."

"Sounds dangerous," she said.

"I've been driving it since I was a kid. In fact, that's where I learned how to drive—before I got my license."

Gordon lived in a completely different world from hers, and it was refreshing to get away from politics. He'd been a gamer all the way through college and told her stories of his exploits on Azeroth in World of Warcraft while at College Park. She let the words flow over her, blending in with the pleasant buzz from the wine, and through it she undressed him in her mind. *He still had a boy's body,* she thought. Little hair on his chest, the tight stomach, the thin waist. But those fine, long fingers. The blond hair that fell carelessly across his forehead like corn silk. And the innocence! He would be a few years younger than she was. *So now I'm a cougar,* she thought. But that's okay. Without doing anything in particular, just being himself, he created an aura around them, a private world that encompassed them both. She felt warm and encompassed, as if he held the two of them in his arms.

Still, Annie was determined not to rush things. There was nothing worse in her book than being a vamp. They were all over the Hill, those young women with the fancy degrees and a lust for power who were determined to sleep their way to the top. The biggest prize was a Congressman. A chief of staff would do, or a majority chief counsel. But when needed, they would settle for junior staffers their own age to stay in practice or just for fun. Annie had graduated from a Christian college that tried—and failed miserably—to teach the virtues of chastity to its students. Then it was law school on the Left Coast where no one pretended virtue, let alone chastity. Because she was smart and endowed with athletic good looks, she had her pick of her fellow students. But since coming to the Hill eight years ago, she had become much more selective. The rumor mill churned non-stop, chewing up the innocent and the guilty and spitting them out in pieces. Mixing sex with office politics was deadly.

She let Gordon court her over a period of several weeks. Dinners here and there, weekend excursions to Baltimore or local vineyards. But still, he made no move. So in the end, she gave him a little push. She invited him to demonstrate the cooking skills he had boasted about—at her place. She made sure there was lots of wine.

And the rest was history.

After their third bout of love-making, he turned on his side and stroked her cheek, dialing her dark hair behind her ears.

"You are so gentle with me. Thank you," he said. "You are so patient. So kind."

"Shh," she said. "I am happy. You don't have to talk."

"I do! For me, it was the first time," he said.

"Really?" she said. That got her to sit up. "You could have fooled me."

"I'm glad I did," he said. "Now I've got to make up for lost time."

The injection of carnality into their relationship removed the tension that had been building for several weeks. Now they found themselves hungry for each other, so much so that they would leave restaurants just barely finishing their main course and a bottle of wine, rushing back to Annie's bed. She was happy. And she noticed that her face took on a new glow. And she didn't mind that others, including Nelson Aguilar, could see it.

17

Nader Homayounfar looked again at the address he had scribbled down: 920 Pennsylvania Avenue, SE. It was a strange place for a tech firm to have its offices, a neighborhood of hundred-year-old brick townhouses on the wrong side of Capitol Hill. But that was unmistakably what Navid had told him. *Yes, Southeast,* he said, when Nader had questioned him. *Behind Capitol Hill. There's a bus but it's a nice walk this time of year.*

It was now less than three weeks before the election, and Nader's boss, Representative Hugh McKenzie, was seriously underwater in the polls. An atmosphere of gloom hung over his congressional office. Staffers were quietly updating their résumés and avoiding each other in the corridor. At campaign meetings at DNC headquarters, Morton Nash was running the numbers precinct by precinct on a huge whiteboard, showing how they could still win and where they should deploy the candidate and their advertising dollars. But everyone knew Nash was grasping at straws. This meeting was supposed to get them back on their feet, McKenzie told Nader quietly. Just you and this guy, Navid. *Granger's guy.*

It's ironic that most of the IT managers on the Hill, at least the Democrats, are Asians, he thought. Mostly Indian or Pakistani Muslims, with a sprinkling of Iranian-Americans on top. The anonymity of sitting behind a computer screen shielded them from social awkwardness. But that still didn't explain the numbers. Was there a math gene or computer gene that they shared? Maybe the Indian and Pakistani computer geeks were Parsees. That would explain it. One big distant family, reconnecting via 4chan and the nets.

Nader did a double-take when he saw the name on the bronze plaque by the door. JT Government Services was familiar to anyone who followed politics, indeed, to anyone who watched cable news for more than an hour a day. Set up by Rick Jourdain, a former journalist, and Roger Turpin, a confidant of Governor Tomlinson and frequent TV commentator, the firm was known to be handling opposition research on Trump for the DNC. Turpin was always showing up on Rachel Maddow's show on MSNBC, teasing out dark ties between Trump and Putin, Trump and neo-Nazis, Trump and the deplorable of the week. It was deep, it was complex, and it was dirty, so the narrative went. But IT wizardry didn't figure in the skill set of Turpin and Jourdain. Nader half-wondered if he had come to the wrong address.

He slipped his business card to the receptionist, whose crescent-shaped glass desk neatly embraced the marble staircase spiraling to the upper floors. "I'm here for Navid," he said. She took the card and nodded, continuing to talk to someone over her headset, and typed out a message. A few minutes later, an Indo-Pak head peered from around the corner and called his name.

"I work with Navid," the young man said.

He escorted Nader to the end of a white corridor to an unmarked door secured with a digital lock and an optical scanner. "The War Room," he said. "Please put your cell phone and any electronics you're carrying in the box." It was a black metal container with a hinged door. The inside had slots with foam protectors that held a dozen phones and a large flat area big enough for a laptop. It was a Faraday box, designed to block all electromagnetic emissions, including cellphone and Wi-Fi signals.

Downstairs, the corridor emptied out into a vast underground vault, where a dozen people sat in elevated rows of desks as in a movie theater, each with two monitors and a giant central display above the pit so they could all watch. For now, only the side screens were lit, showing five different TV channels, with a single word floating across the main display: SECURE. Navid's office was off to the side, walled in milky glass. On his door was a nameplate that read:

Tits or GTFO

It was famous from the hacker Rules of the Internet, and Nader recognized it immediately. Because so few females were ever admitted to the hacker clubs, Rule #31 required a physical display of feminine attributes, either by live video or a screenshot, as a way of weeding out imposters. Below it was a poster of a brightly colored circuit breaker. "We call it the Secret Switch," the young man said. "The Holy Grail of campaign IT."

"So you've found it?" Nader asked, humoring him. "The Secret Switch?"

"Ask Navid."

And so he did.

"This is like totally secret, man," Navid said, drumming his fingers on his glass desktop. "Granger and my guys are the only ones who have any idea what we are doing. Jourdain and Turpin are clueless. Everything's on a need-to-know basis. Hence, the SCIF and the air gap on all our programming machines. So are you need-to-know?"

"That's what Granger says."

"Really? Maybe you don't realize where this is leading. How do I know I can trust you and your guy?"

"Get out your *dak-tagh*."

"My what?"

"Your *dak-tagh*. Let us cut palms together and see who is loyal."

"Man, like, what are you talking about?"

"Klingon! When Martok first arrives on Deep Space Nine at the head of the Klingon invasion of Cardassia, he gets out his warrior knife and slits his palm and gets Captain Sisko and Major Kira to do the same. If they bleed real blood, they are not changelings and aren't out to betray him.

"It was on last night," he added sheepishly.

Navid burst out laughing. "That's good. Hahahahaha…. Here we do a hash," he said, referring to an encrypted version of a plaintext word. He sent a page to the printer and swiveled around to snatch it before it flew onto the floor. He glanced at it, bug-eyed, and handed it to Nader, It read:

11dac30c3ead3482f98ccf70675810c7

It was a rite of passage among the black hats, the hacktivists who graduated from 4chan to Anonymous to jail time or the FBI, or who just kept their heads down and scrubbed their online profiles, scrupulously practicing electronic hygiene. This particular hash was famous, so it wasn't much of a test. Nader glanced at it, then airplaned the sheet back onto Navid's paperless desk.

"Parmy," he said.

Navid grinned wildly, and they bumped fists. "You're in."

He pulled up a PowerPoint and sent it to a monitor embedded in the glass window that gave onto the staff pool, and the surrounding glass darkened. The first slide was familiar: It showed the red/blue breakdown of the 2016 presidential election, county by county, with narrow blue streaks along the East and West Coasts and around a few major cities submerged in a vast red sea.

"It looks like a blow-out for Trump, but actually the election was decided by 77,000 votes in just three states: Pennsylvania, Michigan, and Wisconsin. It's very easy to imagine things having turned out very differently. In 2020, they will."

"You don't know that," Nader objected.

"Oh, but I do," Navid said.

He put up a map that differentiated the states by the type of voting machines they used. Forty-three states would be using voting machines that were no longer manufactured. And while all but ten of them had said they intended to replace the old machines, only a handful actually appropriated the funds to do so. "So, for the most part, we will be dealing with the old machines. But who cares! Old technologies, known vulnerabilities. New machines, new vulnerabilities. Hahahahaha."

Nader could feel his eyes growing wider and his jaw dropping. "You're going to hack the election." It was a statement, not a question.

"No, no, no, no, no," Navid said. "We are going to exploit vulnerabilities. Plural. Call it boutique exploits, custom-tailored for each situation. Not a silver bullet but a hail of silver bullets. A Gatling gun of silver bullets. A nuclear war of silver bullets! Hahahahaha."

The next map color-coded the states and counties in various shades of reds, pinks, purples, and blues.

"Now here's the bad news: Our national election infrastructure is actually a patchwork of several thousand networks, so there really isn't a national election infrastructure you can hack. It's all done at the state and county level. And each one has a different system. Like ten thousand of them. Complicated, right?

"But that's also the good news, for us at least. Some of these systems are relatively strong. Those are in red. Some are pathetically weak, wide open to script kiddies, blue. But red or blue, none of them are safe. Give me enough time and resources, I guarantee you we can flip the secret switch, in and out with no fingerprints. Hahahahaha."

There were so many exploits, so many entry points, the hardest thing was deciding which one to attack. And not all of the vulnerabilities involved the machines. Many were baked into the behavioral pattern of hard-core Democrat voters, poll watchers, and election judges.

"Take Florida, for example. All across the state, even in Republican counties, you've got Democrat snowbirds who will be showing up to vote after they have cast absentee ballots in New York, New Jersey, Connecticut, and Maryland."

"Aren't they afraid of getting caught?" Nader said.

"Are you kidding? We made sure the state legislature never appropriated the funds the governor earmarked to link up to the ERIC system, which would allow the county boards to check their poll books against other states for duplicate votes. Besides, even if they made a positive match, they'd have to convene a grand jury and investigate each case individually. So no one ever gets prosecuted. I mean, like, *never*.

"Plus, you still have counties that use the old Direct Record Electronic or DRE machines. Why? Because they've got to facilitate voting for people with disabilities who can't fill out a paper ballot, so it's back to the old touch screens. The touch screens! Hahahahaha. Don't you love the ADA? Those Edsels are so easy to penetrate that a pair of eleven-year-olds at DEF CON broke into them in about ten minutes. A pro can do it in less than a minute. Then you just upload your time bomb to the PCMCIA card and the on-board tabulator, and away you go. Good old-fashioned black box voting. No paper trail. Nothing. At one minute past eight, your results become the machine's results, and it daisy-chains to the whole precinct. You want fifty-four to forty-six? That's what you get. You want razor thin? Whatever! Once the results are uploaded or the PCMCIA card is taken out, the code erases itself without a trace. You've got DREs in some of our target counties in Florida, Virginia, and Pennsylvania, and a handful of other states as well. I mean, like, we *own* the DREs. We could stop right there and win the election. But why stop when you're having fun! Hahahahaha.

"Some of the DRE machines have been upgraded to generate a paper ballot that theoretically can be audited. When the voter presses the button to cast his finished ballot, our patch kicks in and alters the result, so the paper ballot shows the altered vote, not the original one. When the votes are tallied from the machine onto the removable PCMCIA card and uploaded onto the GEMS server, it's our vote count that shows up. And if anyone ever cares to check, the paper ballots will match.

"Our best friends are the IT guys who work in all these election boards. They are absolutely convinced their systems are secure. Why? Because they designed them! They maintain them! Nobody can hack *them*! They are invincible! Hahahahaha.

"Take optical scanners. All the so-called experts are convinced that optical scanners are secure. Unlike the DREs, you fill in a paper ballot by hand, it gets scanned and tabulated and drops into a sealed box where it's preserved for an eventual recount. So we can't remotely generate the paper ballots or alter them. But for all the counties that have adopted them, only a handful do anything more than token audits to reconcile the paper ballots with the tabulated vote count announced on election night. Most of them just sample one percent of the precincts, running the paper ballots through the tabulators again. Thanks to us, they get the same results.

"When an election is decided within the margin of error, as it was in 2016, either candidate plausibly can win. But if he or she wins by three or four percent—way beyond the legal limit for a recount—who's going to pay to make copies of all those paper ballots and the personnel to count them by hand? And even if they do, it will take days. And by that time, the whole nation will have known who the next president is, and if you tell them they were wrong and it's actually the other guy, you'll have chaos. Riots! Blood in the streets! And I haven't even mentioned SQL injection into the manufacturer's FTP sites to alter the patches they send out to their clients. Or the fact that the tabulators don't actually count the paper ballots, but the image files. Can't you see, our elections are secure! Look at the Iowa caucuses! What can possibly go wrong! Hahahahaha...."

"This is illegal, right?" Nader said.

"Dude, are you kidding? By the time you get home tonight, you will have broken some law. Probably more."

McKenzie's Maryland district habitually went Democrat. The redistricting commission predicted that even with the influx of new Republican voters, it would still elect a Democrat with 60.7 percent of the vote. Forget Aguilar's campaign, his appeal to Hispanics, or his internal polls.

"Polls are notoriously wrong," Navid said. "That's the line to take. You want to program a result close to the original projections, then point to the redistricting commission. No surprise here, big margin, move along. With the way Aguilar's spending money on media buys, he probably won't have enough to pay for a recount. And even if he did, what would he find? We will arrange to lose enough of the paper ballots to cast doubt onto the accuracy of any recount. Chaos, man. Chaos! Hahahahaha!"

18

McKenzie stayed behind after the campaign meeting waiting for Nader. The word from his pollster that afternoon had been bleak. Even Nash, the ever-upbeat campaign consultant, was advising desperate measures, things he had never done to win an election. They needed to fund a massive get-out-the-vote drive, focusing on places like Takoma Park and Bethesda and downtown Rockville—their strongholds. They needed to saturate the airwaves, radio and TV, with attack ads and with their closing argument, back-to-back if possible. McKenzie needed to be at every street festival, even the Great Frederick Fair, the heart of the heart of Yahoo Land. (There are more Democrats in Frederick than you think, Nash said.) They also needed phone banks to call the snowbirds and explain to them that they could request an absentee ballot from the State Board of Elections on the Friday before Election Day, as long as they postmarked it by Election Day. Under Maryland law, they had the right to vote if they were still a resident of the state. No need to put a fine point on it. Let them decide where duty lies, Nash said.

The latest Quinnipiac poll had them down 44–52 with only 4 percent undecided. It was going to be a tough climb, but it was still possible, Nash said. As early voting began in more than a dozen states, Trump's unfavorables, which had been running well over 50 percent for most of the campaign, dipped down below 50 percent for the first time. The race was tightening as voters began to pay attention, some of them for the first time.

Kwanda Armstrong, their comms director, planned to unleash a barrage of targeted Facebook and YouTube ads. She had a team of volunteers and paid IT guys, separate from Nader's operation, putting together truly nasty videos and memes disparaging their opponent and his *barrio* allure. Nash believed they could socially engineer hard-core deplorables who normally would vote Republican to split their ticket or at the very least not vote for Aguilar. Identifying these targets was a piece of cake.

What truly shocked him, though, was the disconnect between the mainstream media, who were screaming at Trump, and the mood on the street, where no one seemed to care. It had become a thing in black neighborhoods for young men to strut around with Keep America Great caps. At the Rockville street fair, when Aguilar supporters swarmed his booth with garish posters of newborn babies torn from the womb, he fully expected his supporters to come to the rescue and push them back. But no one came. Where were the outraged soccer moms? The college kids? The feminists and queers? Had they all gone into hiding? Didn't they care about protecting a woman's right to choose? He had always thought he had his finger on the pulse of his district, but now he was beginning to wonder.

"So what about Granger's guy?" he asked, when Nader finally showed up.

The DCCC director had tucked him into one of the sound-proofed cubicles members used for fundraising calls. Nader closed the door, put a finger to his lips, and spread open the black Faraday pouch Navid had given him. He placed his phone inside and mimed for McKenzie to do the same. The Congressman made his sour face.

"What's the deal?" he said.

"It's necessary, Congressman. No discussions in the open."

When the phones had been locked down, Nader started to explain. "It's a piece of cake for a malicious hacker to inject a Remote Access Trojan into your phone. We call them RATs. You won't notice it, but your phone will become like an FBI wiretap, even when it's turned off. These pouches cut the signal. It's like the SCIF in the Capitol Building where everyone went to read the unredacted Mueller Report."

"Nobody read the Mueller Report," McKenzie said.

"Okay, the impeachment transcripts. Whatever. You get what I mean."

"So does Granger's guy have some kind of golden key?"

"I think he does, Congressman. Perhaps, many of them. Mrs. T is going to win the presidential, and you are going to be re-elected, within one-tenth of a percentage point of the projections in the GRAC."

That was the Governor's Redistricting Advisory Commission, the group that designed the new districts after the court mandate that struck down the gerrymander. Their statisticians looked at historical voting patterns and demographics and came up with precinct by precinct, street by street, even block by block vote tallies, and crunched the numbers to generate projections for the district as a whole.

"That was sixty-one to thirty-nine Democrat, give or take a few tenths. That's pretty much what the polls are now showing—for my opponent."

"Yeah, well. As Navid says, screw the polls. Nobody believes them anyhow. The GRAC projections are solid stuff. Just rely on them, and you'll be good."

McKenzie sat on a corner of the desk and pressed his jaw into his fist. Where was the limit of plausible deniability, he wondered. Were you aware, Congressman, that Granger and his IT team were actively plotting a criminal conspiracy to hijack the elections? No, sir. I saw no indication of that at the time. *Really?* Really. I know of no specific act. Better to keep it that way.

"What do we need to do?" he said finally.

"Didn't sound to me like you have to do anything, sir. Granger has selected you for the program."

"The program?"

"That's what they're calling it. The 'secret switch.'"

"The what?"

"Actually, you don't need to know that, Congressman."

McKenzie looked at him skeptically.

"Unless you want to," he said quickly. "Do you want to know?"

McKenzie let the words hang out there between them like a smoke ring.

"I suppose not," he said finally. "But if they do this, we win?"

"That's right. We win."

19

The last week of the campaign passed in a blur. The national media, of course, was fixated on the presidential race. Fox News carried live coverage of the Trump rallies, sometimes three or four per day, while the rest of the national media tracked Mrs. T. and Senator Bellinger as they drilled down on core Democratic audiences in Pennsylvania, Michigan, Iowa, Florida, and Minnesota. They weren't making the same mistake Hillary Clinton had made in 2016. They were out there, campaigning. Hardball, all the way.

The McKenzie-Aguilar match-up was turning out to be the third most expensive congressional race in the country, with total spending by the campaigns and outside groups topping $15 million. Billionaire Republican donor Sheldon Adelson had jumped on board the Aguilar bandwagon, with a $2.5 million donation to his Super Pac, Americans for the Dream. Silicon Valley Democrat Tom Steyer and financier George Soros matched him, with $1.25 million each to McKenzie's Super Pac, Progress Maryland. The airwaves were awash with attack ads. It was unclear if they were having any impact on actual voters.

McKenzie followed the counsel of Morton Nash, his campaign consultant, and reluctantly put in an appearance at the Great Frederick Fair, where the biggest attractions were funnel cake and the afternoon tractor pull. The gigantic monster trucks were so loud you couldn't even hear yourself think. This is what the yahoos did in their spare time. *Really?* Watch jacked up monster trucks and Mad Max hot rods square off with iron sleds the size of railroad cars, plows dug into the dirt? He hung back in his campaign booth, where unfortunately he could see Aguilar, or catch glimpses of him at least, greeting voters two hundred feet across the walkway.

To get out, he had to pass in front of the Republican booth, so he got Jenn to marshal their volunteers, forming a protective phalanx around him. The last thing he wanted was another public confrontation with Aguilar.

"Congressman, git on in 'ere!" he heard from the last Quonset hut of the permanent fairgrounds.

It turned out to be Tim May, co-host of *Mid Maryland Live* on WFMD, the local news talk station, conservative, of course. May was broadcasting live from the Great Frederick Fair and waved McKenzie over as he shouted into his microphone.

"And lookie here who we just spotted walkin' by. It's Congressman Hugh McKenzie, Democrat from Merrie-land's Eighth Con-gressional Dis-trict! Welcome, Congressman! Come on in 'ere! Don't walk away now, he'ah?"

Jenn threw up her arms and shrugged. It was up to him.

McKenzie detested May's corn-pone Maryland accent. How many real people still talked like that, anyway? Except, of course, on yahoo radio. Tim May was a former sheriff, a respected arson inspector, and sometime pastor of a local countryside church. His co-host, Frank Mitchell, masqueraded as a lieder-hosen, garlic-raising, leftover hippy vegetarian and city-dweller, but

McKenzie was sure that was just a pose. They were the local version of Hannity and Colmes, with Hannity ever dominant and his left-wing man an apparent pushover.

"You're on *Mid-Maryland Live* from the Great Frederick Fair, with Congressman Hugh McKenzie. Boy, have I got some questions for you, Congressman."

"I'm sure you do, Tim. But maybe we should just take calls from your listeners. What do you say?"

May was surprisingly polite to him for the first ten minutes and apologized several times for not having him on sooner. He allowed him to talk uninterrupted about Medicare-For-All and the rest of his legislative agenda.

"I gotta ask you, Congressman, what you think of our president, Donald Trump. Now I don't gotta remin' you, we're on live radio, so keep it clean!"

McKenzie harrumphed, his version of a laugh. "Well, you know, Tim, I'm no fan of the president. But I've got to give our listeners some hope. I am convinced he's going down on November 3rd."

"Whoa now, pardner. What makes you think that? All the polls have been tightening, and if 2016 is any measure, he's gonna come back and win big time, uh-huh, uh-huh. Whaddya say to that, Frank?"

"Let's listen to the Congressman, Tim. He's our guest, not me."

"Oh yea, that's right. Well, Congressman. Take it away!"

"I think history teaches us to be very wary of the polls, Tim. Take my own district. My opponent would appear to be leading in the polls, but my internal polling suggests that is not the case."

Tim May actually winked. "So give us the scoop, Congressman. What do your polls show?"

"They show us winning by a healthy margin. In fact, I'd say they show us winning pretty close to what the historical averages of this district show."

"Folks, you just heard it from the horse's rear—sorry, the horse's mouth," May said, stifling a guffaw. "Sorry about that, Congressman. Old habits die hard. I was just thinkin'a my ole' buddy 'ere, Frank. No offense intended."

"And none taken, Tim."

When they got back into the Suburban, McKenzie kicked the front seat. "Damn, why did I have to say that?" he said.

"He was goading you," Jenn said. "Nobody is going to take that seriously. Besides, nobody really listens to WFMD anyway. It's just barely covers Frederick, Carroll and Washington Counties. And the northern tip of Montgomery, mostly Republicans anyway."

After Frederick, Takoma Park was a relief. This was the beating blue heart of his blue district, where Democrats out-registered Republicans ten to one. Takoma Park was known as the first American community to declare itself a nuclear-free zone. To reduce their carbon footprint, they had banned cars from downtown and sponsored communal truck gardens for residents who didn't have their own yards. Since almost everyone owned lavishly restored Victorian houses or upgraded post-war bungalows, the truck gardens became the communal weed patch.

The street fair was preceded by the LGBTQ pride parade. McKenzie had his volunteers marched in front of the 1968 yellow Mustang convertible loaned by a supporter, carrying campaign banners and tossing out rainbow-colored candies. He waved from the back seat and got sunburned.

Later, at the Democratic Party booth, he spied Aguilar walking through the crowd. *Pretty gutsy for him to wander around here where there's not a Republican in sight,* he thought.

"Say, isn't that what's-his-name, the liberal commentator on Fox News?" he asked Jenn.

"José Gonzales."

"Yeah, him. Look."

Gonzales was talking with Aguilar, arm wrapped around his shoulder, as if they were best buddies.

"We need a fly on the wall for that conversation," McKenzie smirked.

Jenn instructed one of their paid volunteers to doff his campaign t-shirt, join the crowd that had formed around the pair, and bring back cell phone video.

"So what were they saying?" she asked, when he came back a few minutes later.

The volunteer had only caught the end of the conversation but remarked that the two were pretty friendly.

"Yeah, we saw that," McKenzie said.

"So, Gonzales was saying, 'Nobody's ever asked me that before.'"

"Asked him what?"

"Aguilar asked for his vote," the volunteer said.

McKenzie felt the heat rise to his cheeks. Then he shook it off.

"We're all forgetting something," he said. "Those two have been pals for years. Remember all those faux debates on Fox? Gonzales is a closet Republican. Everybody knows that."

The Wednesday before Election Day, McKenzie made a tour of the early voting sites. The plan was to mingle with voters as they waited in line, Jenn by his side, with campaign volunteers handing out palm cards before the voters reached him. Jenn had him ignore the voters who dumped the cards. He spotted many faces he recognized from campaign rallies, union members, CASA de

Maryland volunteers, and an imam from the Georgia Avenue mosque.

"I'm Congressman Hugh McKenzie, and I'm asking for your vote," he said, going up to strangers Jenn pointed out. "I'm here to represent *you*, not the millionaires and the billionaires."

They were at the Silver Spring Civic Building downtown, and the lines—even at mid-day—wound back several hundred feet across Veterans Place. He was astonished not just at the crowds, but their composition. There was hardly an Anglo face anywhere. These voters were Hispanic, Black African, Caribbean, Asian, Middle-Eastern, and who knows what strange mixes of peoples. *This is not the Maryland I grew up in,* he thought. *But these are my people now. My opponent and his president want to send them back to where they came from—as if they had someplace to go.* Most of them shook his hand politely. Some did a double-take, looking at his face, then at his palm card, then back at him, and bursting out, "Oh my gosh, it's you!"

"Some people say it's JFK, Jr. You know, John-John?"

"No, no. It's you!"

"Yeah, I guess we look alike," he joked. "I'm Congressman Hugh McKenzie, and I'm hoping you will remember to vote for me when you get inside."

And then, in the distance, he heard the rattling of marimbas and the trill of Mexican trumpets, and he groaned.

"Here he comes," he said to Jenn.

They tried to back away from the line of voters, but a crowd pressed into them from behind, swaying and stomping and cat-calling to the mariachi band of Nelson Aguilar pouring in from a nearby street. McKenzie and Jenn were at the bottom of the square and could clearly make out his nemesis over the heads of the crowd, shaking hands, blowing kisses, dancing arm in arm with teenagers, followed by a half-dozen television crews. He was a rock star and everyone seemed to know him, and if they didn't, they wanted to. Someone thrust a campaign poster toward him, and he autographed it with a big black marker. A middle-aged woman extended her bare forearm, and he autographed that, too. The crowd began chanting, "Aguilar! Aguilar!"

"Time to make ourselves small," Jenn said.

We already are, McKenzie thought.

20

At midnight, the security shift changed at the Civic Building. A half hour after the new man came on duty, he left the control room with its banks of closed circuit TV monitors and went to the break room to brew a pot of coffee. He did this every night, and after sipping an initial cup, put the coffee in a thermos and brought it back with him for the late-night vigil. It normally took him ten minutes—fifteen, at the most, if he took his time in the rest room or stopped to read the latest Department of Labor or OSHA poster informing him of his rights.

Tonight was no different. The longest hours were those between two and five AM, after the revelers went home and there wasn't a sound in the neighborhood except for the occasional police siren whomping up Georgia Avenue after some speeder. He needed enough coffee to make it through the dead hours, so habitually he brewed a large pot.

At exactly 12:32 AM, a man wearing what appeared to be an official Montgomery County Board of Elections badge emerged from a storeroom, went into the control room, opened a metal panel, and fiddled with some wires from a small device he withdrew from his jacket pocket. At 12:34, he unlocked the door to the media center and walked halfway down the row of voting machines. Each machine was a squat box—a desktop computer, in fact—elevated from the floor on four metal legs. The touch screen voting module was secured person-high on top of the computer, with a curtain that could be pulled around it to give the voter privacy. Standing at the rear of the machine, obscured by the curtain, the man fished a squat metal key from a pocket and inserted it into the rear door of the computer. He gave a quarter turn to the left and the simple swivel lock released, allowing him to fold down the door.

At 12:35, he inserted a USB stick into a slot and turned on the computer. Forty-five seconds later, he shut down the computer, put the USB stick back in his pocket, and relocked the computer door. At 12:36, he closed the door of the media room behind him and started walking toward the service entrance at the rear of the building by the garbage cans. At 12:37, he emerged onto the dark street, looked around him, and gently pulled the door closed behind him. In less than a minute, he made it around the corner to where he had parked his car in a legal parking spot hours earlier.

When the night watchman returned to his post four minutes later, he set his thermos and coffee mug on the desk and noticed the four blank screens in the bank of closed circuit TV monitors. He banged on the metal housing, but they didn't flicker. He tried turning them on and off, but that had no effect, either. Finally, he went to the breaker panel by the door and noticed that two of the breakers had tripped. He flipped them off and then on and the screens behind him lit up. *Musta been a power surge,* he muttered. *And not even a storm!*

21

At fourteen years old, Brady Aguilar had transformed his bedroom into a video arcade. Atop a spare curved desk, he had positioned two 25" G-sync gaming monitors powered by a Ryzen 5 3600 CPU on a Prime B450M-A motherboard, installed by his own anxious hands in a P400S box. The Ryzen chip set had six cores, clocked in at 4.2 gigahertz, and could accommodate up to 64 Gigs of DDR4 memory. It was one of the most powerful gaming systems you could buy—at least, with his limited budget. With the monitors, 500 gigs of SSD flash storage, a GeForce RTX 2060 video card, and a 1 Terabyte hard drive, it had cost him just over $1,050, money squirreled away from lawn chores and snow shoveling.

When he finished his homework early, or during late summer afternoons, he would close the blackout curtains over the windows behind the monitors. But with the days shortening now at the end of October, he could turn from his virtual universe and gaze at the squirrels jumping branches in the giant walnut tree in the backyard to come down to earth. His favorites these days were *Grand Auto Theft V* for the action and *Elder Scrolls V* to enchant his mind.

But Brady wasn't just a gamer. He used the second monitor for more serious pursuits, and that's what he was doing tonight. He was the main IT guy for his dad's congressional campaign, responsible for the campaign website, their social media, and their email accounts. His screen name was *abuelo*. Only AB, his dad, and the Crocodile knew his true identity. He wanted the volunteers to think he was an adult—maybe even a much older adult they could spoof, if such was their intention. He had played enough *Dark Souls 3* to be wary of people pretending to be someone they were not. Infiltrators could be anywhere or everywhere.

He was checking the logs when he noticed that someone had been sending identical emails to a dozen different volunteers. When he opened the source code, he saw that the sender had spoofed a seemingly ordinary dot com address in the U.S., but that the underlying IP address was someplace in Russia. The email had the subject line, "Campaign tracker" and purported to offer a free of charge service that allowed users to track how their campaign was rated on various social media sites. Two campaign volunteers had apparently clicked on the link.

"Dad!" he said later that night when his father returned home to make dinner. "We've been hacked!"

"What do you mean hacked? Who? How?"

"Someone has been sending spear-phishing emails to campaign volunteers to get them to click on a malicious link. That someone stole their credentials to log onto our system and install a Gh0st RAT. That's a form of malware, a Trojan horse that piggy-backs onto normal system processes so you can't detect it. Then it steals your connection and communicates remotely with whoever injected it, all the while you're surfing the internet or whatever."

Aguilar raised his eyebrows. "You got me, *chico*," he said. "What does that mean in normal speak?"

"It means we have a serious security breach of the campaign's computers. Theoretically, the intruder could do any number of things—deface the campaign website, publish fake tweets or Facebook posts in your name. Or even get access to the campaign bank accounts. They basically have access to everything."

The next morning, the Thursday before the election, Aguilar raised the issue with AB and the Crocodile.

"This is bad, boss," the Crocodile said. "You should take it to the FBI. They could do a Hillary on us."

"What do you mean?"

"Steal somebody's emails. Publish them. Embarrass us."

"Have you put embarrassing information in your emails?" Aguilar shook his finger at him. "Naughty, naughty!"

"It's serious, boss. Look at how McKenzie exploited that idiot from the restaurant association and his campaign check. They could take anything and twist it to make it look nefarious. They could steal our media plan."

Annie had a different idea.

"I know an IT guy I can take this to," she said. "If he thinks it's serious, he'll know whom we should approach at the FBI."

The Crocodile cocked an eyebrow at her. "How's that?" he said.

"He works for the State Board of Elections. In fact, he manages the tech side for all of the state's 19,000 electronic voting machines. He works with the manufacturer when they install software updates, and makes sure that all the counties properly train precinct workers. And he handles security."

"Is this just a guy?" the Crocodile said.

Annie's cheeks reddened slightly, but she said nothing.

"So, it's more than just a guy."

"Ken, leave her alone. It doesn't matter who it is," Aguilar said. "I think we should be happy for his help."

22

After Annie's phone call that morning, Gordon Utz decided to run a security check on the voter registration database. As he was going through the access logs, it leapt out at him: Someone was attempting a brute force attack. The same IP address was trying repeatedly to log onto the system, apparently without success. They were probably using Hashcat, Forge, RainbowCrack, or John the Ripper. These were popular brute forcing tools that allowed a would-be intruder to try millions of password combinations using rainbow tables, a kind of password dictionary of pre-computed hashes of plaintext words and character sets. This greatly reduced the access time needed to penetrate the system and could crack passwords up to fourteen characters in length in less than a minute.

Gordon smiled to himself: He was better than the hackers. He had added "salt" to his cryptographic hashing routine, random characters that were not visible to users but frustrated most rainbow table hackers. It was kind of like spelling your name and adding 71B9 (or any similar combination of letters and numbers) at the beginning or end of it in hidden text.

Whoever was attempting to penetrate the database was also spoofing their IP address. It looked like the attack originated from the Washington, DC, area, but as he traced it back, he saw that it resolved to a server located in the Russian Federation.

"Even the Russian address could be a spoof," he told Lisa Rasmussen, the state supervisor of elections. She was an appointed official who had been in office for over twenty years. When she had started working in Annapolis they still used printed voter rolls and punch card voting machines, but she prided herself on keeping up with the technology—if not herself, at least by hiring brilliant geeks like Gordon Utz.

"I've never been a believer in Russian hacker paranoia," she said. "Maybe it's just a bunch of kids in some basement somewhere. Did they get in?"

"Not that I can see," Gordon said.

"What else do we have on that server?"

"There's an FTP folder with the training manuals for the voting machines. We need to make it accessible to all the precinct captains for training."

"Can you give it another layer of protection?"

"You bet. But I still think we should go to the FBI."

Gordon drove up Route 50 from Annapolis against the early rush hour traffic and made it to the FBI's Washington Field Office across from the national architectural museum by 4:00 PM. He had requested to meet with Jim Clairborne, the deputy chief of Cyber Division tasked with election security.

Since the alleged Russian breach of the DNC in 2016, the FBI had beefed up its election security operation to where they now had dozens of agents whose main job was to hold the hands of election officials around the country. They set up public websites to announce cybersecurity training programs and best practices and made it look like they were taking the threat of election hacking seriously. They had a nationwide database called ERIC that allowed election officials to match voter rolls across states to identify voter fraud, but fewer than half the states had signed up. In truth, Election Security was not a happy place to work. Most of the agents assigned there felt they had been sidelined from the real work of the FBI. They should have been out cruising in unmarked Ford Fusions, meeting confidential informants in fancy hotels.

Clairborne greeted Gordon in the lobby and took him through security into an office suite deep inside the building, then took his suit jacket off to expose the snub-nosed Glock 19 handgun he wore like a fashion appendage. He was around six-foot-two and made Gordon feel like some middle school sixty-pound weakling.

"This is my partner, Rone," he said, introducing a bearded man wearing jeans and a button-down blue shirt stretched to the limits of his biceps. It was easy to imagine the pair of them in desert camo gear, carrying M4s.

"So what's this about a potential breach?" he drawled.

Gordon explained what he had discovered that morning.

"Did this come from ALBERT?" Clairborne asked.

ALBERT was a private network monitoring system that the Department of Homeland Security recommended state and local governments join, since it reduced the number of brush fires the FBI had to put out.

"We don't subscribe to ALBERT. We do our own monitoring," Gordon said.

"Well, ALBERT would have provided us with a baseline, since it rejects most known network anomalies amateur netsec guys think are security breaches."

Gordon was used to the government gobbledygook and couldn't help but pick up the underlying disdain dripping from Clairborne's words.

"Did you take this to Lisa Rasmussen?" he went on.

"I have," Gordon said.

"And?"

"She feels as you do, apparently, there's no there there."

"So what else is there to discuss?" Clairborne exchanged a frustrated smirk with Rone, who was doodling on a yellow legal pad.

"Actually, a lot," Gordon said. "There's a lot of there there. First of all, the server they attempted to penetrate contains an FTP folder with all the instruction manuals and maintenance records of our voting machines. Every time Dominant Technologies announces a patch, we keep a record of when it was installed and who installed it."

"Was there any penetration? Any data exfil?"

"Not that I could see."

"Do any damage?"

"Not yet."

"Maybe you've got a concerned citizen worried you guys are not doing your job. Some 300-pound kid in a basement having fun."

"It's not a joke, sir."

"Did you install the latest security patch from the manufacturer? It should have gone out last month."

"I did. I worked on that personally with their rep and redid the hash."

"Then you're chasing ghosts, brother. Come back when you have an actual penetration."

"With all due respect, Mr. Clairborne, I think you should have a look at that Russian IP address."

"Russian, really?"

He cast a cursory glance at the print-out Gordon had placed on his desk. "This looks like a Washington, DC, server, not a Russian one."

"If you ping that server, it resolves to a dot RU domain name," he said.

Rone picked up the printout, showing interest for the first time. "Really?" he said.

"Really," Gordon agreed.

"Alright, we'll have a look," Clairborne said.

When he had escorted Gordon back through security, he stopped at the front office to speak with his administrator.

"Did my guy from the Maryland state election board sign in?"

She looked through her paperwork. "Here he is, sir. Utz, right?"

"That's him."

Damn, Clairborne thought. He was going to have to report this one up the food chain.

23

The pundits and pollsters were all over the Sunday talk shows, less than forty-eight hours before the polls opened in most of the country. CNN's Rick Hoglan stood in front of the "Magic Board," the computer-generated electoral map the network used to post results as they came in county by county across the nation.

"This is how things turned out when America woke up the day after the 2016 election," he said, tapping the lower left corner of the screen. "Trump won 306 electoral votes to Clinton's 232. But look what happens if you take those same numbers as a base line, and just Pennsylvania and Florida go Democrat." He tapped the right side of the screen and flipped the two states from red to blue. "This puts the Democrats over the top with 281 electoral votes to Trump's 257. Now if North Carolina also flips, which the polls show is quite likely, that gives the Democrats 296 electoral votes. And don't forget, you've still got tight races in Arizona, Wisconsin, and Michigan, all of which went for Trump in 2016. If those all break for the Democrats, you're looking at a 333 to 205 vote Democratic electoral college blow-out."

"How likely do you think that is, Rick?" Keith Cobb asked. Cobb was the designated anchor for the network's election coverage. Sober, slow to arouse, he worked hard at conveying an aura of impartiality, which for CNN was an accomplishment.

"It's still two days before voters go to the polls. But I think it's a safe bet that the Democrats win Florida, where Governor Tomlinson has maintained a three-point edge in the polls for the past six weeks, and where activist groups have been harvesting absentee ballots for several weeks. If all the other states vote the same as in 2016, that puts Democrats at 261, just nine votes shy of victory. They don't even have to win Pennsylvania to get over the top. Any one of these rust-belt states," Hoglan said, flicking first Wisconsin, then Michigan, then Ohio, from red to blue, "would put them over 270. So would North Carolina, or even Georgia, which almost went Democratic in the 2018 governor's race, as you recall."

"That's right, Rick. We'll be having the Democratic candidate in that race, Stacey Abrams, on the show a little later to tell us how Governor Tomlinson fares in the Peach Tree state."

On *Fox News Sunday*, Matt Hall was holding up a whiteboard showing a Trump re-election victory with 284 votes. A professional pundit who plunged into the weeds of election statistics, he was also an amateur history buff and loved to dig out obscure comparisons from elections past. Host Benjamin Bryant had paired him on the Sunday panel with Galen Beaty and Kristina Brower, co-anchors of the network's election team. Beaty was standing in front of the Fox News version of the "Magic Board." He had the chiseled good looks of a movie star, playing a journalist on TV—and a good one, at that. While not devoid of humor, he had a boyish sincerity about him.

"I don't have to tell you, Matt," Beaty was saying, "if just a couple of these swing states go the other way, the election goes to Governor Tomlinson and the Democrats."

"Sure. Just start with Pennsylvania and Florida. If they flip just those two and win all the other states that Hillary won in 2016, they're at 281. They can even afford to lose Nevada's seven votes, which Clinton won in 2016, and come out with 275, or five more than they need for victory. I just don't think that's going to happen."

Hall went on to explain that the early voting numbers in Florida and Pennsylvania weren't showing a big run-up in voter turnout for the Democrats, which they needed if they were going to flip them. "Governor Tomlinson needs sixty-five percent African-American turnout in Philadelphia if she's going to have any chance of winning the state, and so far we just aren't seeing that," he said. "Remember, unemployment in the African-American community reached the lowest level in history last year under President Trump, and it's recovered well from the coronavirus recession. Down in Florida, early voting in the Democrat strongholds in Miami-Dade, Palm Beach, and Broward Counties has been anemic, so I'd have to say things look pretty solid there for the president as well."

"Alright," said Bryant, the show host. "So now it's time to put your money where your mouths are. This will be the last time this year we'll be playing election sweepstakes on *Fox News Sunday*. Where do you place your hundred dollars. Matt?"

"My money is going on Trump, Benjamin. I'm all in."

"All one hundred?"

"That's right."

"Well, that's saying something. How about you, Kristina?"

"I'm going to hedge just a little bit, Benjamin. I'm putting sixty-five dollars on Trump, and thirty-five on Tomlinson."

"Galen?"

"I'm going to join Kristina with sixty-five on Trump. But I'm only putting twenty-five on Governor Tomlinson and the other ten as our good friend Charles Krauthammer used to do."

"Ah yes," said Bryant. "On wine, women, and song."

"Which this year means a contested election, Benjamin. We're forty-eight hours away, and if history teaches us anything, it's that the only poll that counts is the one on Election Day, and I'll wager that one's going to be very close."

Granger had been watching the shows in the study of his Georgetown mansion. *What does this guy know?* he wondered. He made a note to call Navid on the blue line. There mustn't be any fingerprints. And no leaks.

24

elson Aguilar was still clearing the dishes from breakfast at 7:30 AM on Monday morning when the doorbell rang. Brady had left for the bus a half hour earlier and planned to join him at campaign headquarters later that afternoon with a couple of friends from Wheaton High School—not wearing his hat as IT manager, but as high school recruiter. Camilla Broadstreet, the campaign's volunteer coordinator, was always eager to get more high schoolers engaged in the campaign. If they talked up the candidate at home, there was a greater likelihood their parents would vote for him, she said. Even in Democrat households.

It was way too early for the Crocodile or Annie to show up. Even if Annie came across on the InterCounty Connector, she still had that horrible stretch on I-270 from Urbana down to Gaithersburg, which was jammed from 7:00 AM until 9:00 AM. The Crocodile also lived up I-270, but on the other side of Frederick. Even though tomorrow was Election Day, both of them waited until after the morning rush hour to head down to Montgomery County.

As he turned into the living room, he saw the unmarked white Ford Fusion parked outside before he saw the two men at his front door. When he opened the door, both of them had badges in their hands.

"Mr. Aguilar? Special agents Jim Clairborne and Tyrone Masterson, sir. FBI. Do you have a minute? We have a security matter that's come to our attention we'd like to discuss with you."

"Sure. Sure. Of course," he said, ushering them inside.

The two men were giants. Both of them were wearing shoulder holsters that made their suit jackets appear even tighter than they were, and when they sat down they carefully unbuttoned them and pressed down the lapels to keep their weapons out of sight. They wore blue jeans beneath the suit jackets, and the one called Tyrone was wearing jogging shoes. Neither one of them wore a tie.

Clairborne did all the talking. As a political candidate, Aguilar was aware that U.S. elections had attracted quite a bit of attention from foreign actors, including some with impressive computer skills. They hadn't detected any breach of his campaign—yet, he said. But they wanted to put him on notice and urged him to hire a computer security specialist if he hadn't already done so.

"I've got one," Aguilar said. "One of the best."

"Do you mind if you put us in touch with that person?" Clairborne said. "Perhaps we could sit down with them later this morning?"

"I'm afraid that won't be possible," Aguilar said. "It's my son. He's in high school until three PM."

Aguilar didn't like the look the two agents shared at the mention of Brady. Something about this visit didn't smell right.

"Is this about the spear-phishing emails?" he asked. "Brady mentioned that last week, but I didn't pay it much mind."

The two FBI agents exchanged another glance, this one verging on disbelief, as if they suspected him of trying to mislead them.

"Actually it was something else we wanted to discuss with you," Clairborne said. "We've received a complaint from the State Board of Elections about an attempted computer breach of the state voter registration database. When we ran a trace on the IP address, it resolved to a server in this neighborhood."

"Is everything okay?" Aguilar said. "You know that early voting ended last Friday. As far as I know, there haven't been any reports of irregularities."

"So far, we are calling this an attempted break-in. Not an actual breach. It may have been carried out by a foreign actor, or by an activist in the neighborhood. Whoever it is, they need to know it's a class three felony to tamper with the voter rolls."

Aguilar was starting to get indignant. "Why are you telling me this?" he asked icily.

"We'd like you to put the word out that we are onto it," Clairborne said. "You know teenagers these days…"

"Teenagers, what?" he said.

"They think that just because they are sitting at home behind closed doors that no one can see what they are doing."

"Are you making an accusation?"

"No, no, Mr. Aguilar," Clairborne said. "But kids like that tend to know each other, even if they've never met face-to-face. If Brady puts the word out, we're hoping these efforts will stop before any harm is done."

"Thank you, Mr. Clairborne," Aguilar said. "I will be sure to raise this with my campaign people later this morning. Now if you'll excuse me, I must get ready to leave. I go on air in thirty minutes."

He showed them the door, and watched them go down the steps to their car before he let it fall shut. *This is outrageous,* he thought. *Do these guys really think I'm afraid of the law, that they can intimidate me like that? What century are they living in?*

25

The Aguilar campaign headquarters took up two whole floors of a corner building, just across the street from the Wheaton mall. Before they had moved in, a year earlier, the space had been rented out to Provident Bank. Aguilar owned the entire six-story building and declared the rent to the Federal Election Commission as an in-kind contribution. It gave the campaign instant visibility and a large, street-level space where the curious could walk in to meet the candidate.

Aguilar had summoned them into the conference room to explain the visit he had received that morning from the FBI, and when Brady understood what had happened, he burst out in tears.

"Dad, it wasn't me!"

"I know that, *chico*."

"No, seriously, Dad. I'd never be so dumb as to do that kind of thing from home. Mom would be rolling over in her grave."

The evocation of Graciella made Aguilar laugh. "His mother was chief of network security for PDVSA before she left Venezuela," he said, pronouncing the name *peydey-besa*. "That's the state-owned oil company. Once she came here, she had to start all over again and got degrees in computer science from College Park, and later, from Johns Hopkins. I guess she was very good at this kind of thing."

"She was the best, Dad. Still is."

Aguilar crossed himself and said a silent prayer. Annie had wrapped an arm around Brady and could feel him grow calm again.

"So what do you think happened?"

"I've been spoofed. Somebody spoofed me, impersonated my computer, my IP address."

"Is that possible?

"It's not easy, but it's possible if you get access to the root servers in the area."

"Ken, what do you know about this kind of thing?" he asked the Crocodile.

"Whoa, boss. You're looking at the expert," he said, indicating Brady.

"What are root servers?" he asked Brady.

"It's basically the internet backbone. The big computers that handle all network traffic and assign domain names to smaller providers. It's kind of like a gigantic telephone switchboard."

"So it's the telecoms?"

"No, Dad. It's the government. Our government. Somebody got into the root server and pretended to be me. I bet it was the same Russian server that sent the spear-phishing emails to the campaign."

"Oh my God," Annie said. "This is all my fault."

"What do you mean?" Aguilar said.

"I told Gordon about the spear-phishing emails. That got him running system tests on the state voter database. And *that's* when he found they had been penetrated—or at least, that someone was trying to penetrate them—and he went to the FBI."

The Crocodile smirked. "So it's not just a guy."

"I never said he was," Annie said.

"So this *Gordon* works on computer security for the state board of elections?"

"Yes. Actually, he is in charge of computer security for the state."

Annie explained as best she could what Gordon had told her about the computer intrusion, and the fact that the intruder had also spoofed the IP address of his computer to make it look like it was coming from somewhere in Wheaton when actually it resolved to a dot RU address. "That's Russia," she said.

Brady jumped up. "That's the same thing that happened to us, Dad! The spear-phishing emails resolved to a dot RU address."

Aguilar was troubled by what he thought he understood of what they were saying.

"So if you could see that someone from Russia had spoofed their IP address, and Gordon—right, Annie? Gordon?—could see that, too, why couldn't the FBI? Why did they say that the hack on the state voter database came from a local IP address? Is their technology so backward they couldn't see what you all could see?"

"Sure, boss," said the Crocodile. "I'll believe that when the Chesapeake Bay turns into peanut butter."

"I sure don't like this," Aguilar said finally. "*Quis custodiet ipsos custodes.*"

"Ha!" snorted the Crocodile. "I studied Latin like three generations ago. It's probably the most famous quote there is, outside of the opening of Caesar's *Gaul*. Who is watching the watchers."

"*Quien vigilara a los vigilantes,*" Aguilar said.

"So did this bent FBI agent leave a card?" the Crocodile asked.

"Actually, no," Aguilar said.

"If it's the same guy Gordon saw, he's like a deputy assistant director or something," Annie said. "Pretty high up."

Aguilar was puzzled. Why would the FBI resort to such trickery with him, a mere congressional challenger? Wasn't their job to *protect* people such as himself, not play games with them?"

"Look what happened to Trump in 2016," the Crocodile said. "Nobody thinks for an instant that he rooted out all the bad apples after Comey, McCabe, Page, and Strzok."

"I can't believe that," Aguilar said. "I won't believe that. We believe in the rule of law."

If the FBI really was playing this kind of game, America had become a banana republic. What was he to say to his supporters then? For the past year, he'd been preaching rule of law. He'd been arguing with families who were worried their loved ones were going to be deported that they should follow the law, and that law-breakers deserved to be punished, because without the law they were no better off here in America than they had been in Guatemala or Salvador.

"My advice, boss, is that you hold onto that thought. Keep it to ourselves for the time being. And that all of us, especially young Brady here, go into a heightened state of alert."

PART II

THE ELECTION

26

It's a truism in American politics that you can find a pundit for anything and its opposite. Take Election Day weather. Some said that the high pressure zone that brought beautifully clear autumn skies to the East Coast, from Maine to Florida and into much of the Midwest would increase voter turnout because elderly voters who might otherwise be deterred by bad weather would show up at the polls. But naysayers made just the opposite argument, that the beautiful weather would deter working-age voters, in particular tradesmen and construction workers, who would take advantage of the good weather to put in a full day's work outdoors. Or that soccer moms might neglect to vote, staying to watch their children's outdoor sports practice. In the end, it was probably a wash.

In today's highly charged partisan environment, whenever the president made a comment on Twitter, you knew that most of the national media would immediately charge in the opposite direction. So when President Trump tweeted on the morning of Tuesday, November 3rd, that the beautiful weather augured well for a fair election, just about every commentator denounced him for attempting to suppress the minority vote. He and Melania flew from Andrews Air Force Base to Palm Beach International that morning on Air Force One, then drove by presidential limousine south on I-95 and crossed the Intracoastal to Manalapan Town Hall, some seven miles south of Mar-a-Lago, where they cast their votes amid a media circus. Governor Tomlinson actually beat them to the polls, casting her vote in Chicago at 8:00 AM local time.

At Aguilar campaign headquarters, the candidate called together his staff and volunteers early that morning to pray. More than a hundred people had packed the open floor to get final words of encouragement from the candidate. They linked hands and bowed their heads.

"God tells us that if his people will repent of their evil ways and call on his name, he will hear them and save them from destruction. Because that is what we are facing my friends— not in my race, no, but in the race for the presidency. Just as in 2016, America is at a crossroads. Do we want socialism, which means slavery of free men to the state? Or do we want to remain sovereign citizens who acknowledge that our freedoms come from God, not government? So join me in calling on our father God to save us from self-destruction. In his glorious name we pray, amen."

"Amen," they said.

Richard August, who had played a modest role in the local congressional race when he had moderated the Aguilar-McKenzie debate many weeks ago, continued his service to our nation's democracy by volunteering as an election judge in his home precinct at the Ashbury Methodist Village in Gaithersburg, Maryland. The judges worked in pairs in every precinct, one Democrat, one Republican. August got along well with his Republican counterpart, Dick Burbridge, a math teacher at the Shady Grove campus of Montgomery Community College—and an Aguilar supporter. They both knew the rules and understood that challenges could come from any quarter. Given the heavily Democrat demographic of this part of Montgomery County, August saw his main role as providing a credible guarantee that his precinct would not engage in the type of ballot stuffing that had made Baltimore infamous in years past. "Democrats are going to win big anyhow, so let's all play by the rules," was his motto.

So when he overheard Burbridge talking with a disgruntled voter shortly after 10:00 AM, Richard August came over.

"Damn it, Dick," the gentleman was saying. "I'm telling you. Somebody has scrubbed me from the voter rolls."

"Good morning, sir. I am the chief election judge. What seems to be the problem?" August asked.

"I'm not able to vote," the man said.

They were blocking one of the check-in desks, and the line behind them stretched out into the hallway. This precinct had a high number of retirees so there was no drop-off in turnout after the morning rush.

"I told him there was no one with his name at that address," said Margie, the check-in volunteer.

"Here's my driver's license. See, this is my address," the man insisted.

"Sir, please," Margie said, putting a hand in front of her eyes. "I am barred by Maryland law from looking at anyone's ID."

"Of course you are," August said, all smiles and bonhomie. "Let's see if we can fix this. Did you vote in the primary, sir?"

"I most certainly did," the man said.

"So do a query under his name of the State voter database," August instructed the poll worker.

She typed in the name and came up blank. "How did you say you spelled your last name again?"

"Brock," he said. "B-R-O-C-K."

"And your first name?"

"Anthony."

"I'm very sorry sir, but I don't see you here."

"Ma'am," Brock said. "I voted in the *Republican* primary."

"Oh," she said. "That's a different query. Let me check."

She retyped his information, scowled, and retyped it again.

"Let's have a look," August said, moving behind the check-in table so he could see her computer screen.

The page displayed the State Board of Elections logo, with the stylized yellow, black, and red Maryland flag. But instead of data, there was a message: "The page you have requested is temporarily unavailable."

"It looks like that database is currently off-line," August said. "But that's okay. You can vote a provisional ballot. I'm sure it'll clear up by the end of the day."

Brock was fuming. "Everyone knows you toss more than half of the provisional ballots," he said. "I'll come back later."

"No he won't," Margie muttered under her breath.

An hour later, the same thing happened with another Republican voter, and a half hour after that with two more. And still, the State database with the primary election results, which could have provided a back-up of the Republican registrations, remained off-line.

"I'm going to file a report," August said.

"I already have," Burbridge said, indicating his cell phone. He wasn't really supposed to use a cell phone inside the polling area, but given the circumstances, August said nothing.

27

Carroll County was Republican country. During the 2018 election, Carroll County voters re-elected Republican Governor Larry Hogan and Lieutenant Governor Boyd Rutherford by nearly a six to one margin, well beyond the 54 percent the Hogan-Rutherford ticket won statewide. The county was so heavily Republican that the chairman of the local central committee told Nelson Aguilar he shouldn't waste his time campaigning there but should focus on the battleground precincts in Montgomery County to the south.

Turnout had been brisk at South Carroll High School during the early morning hours, but slowed to a trickle by 11:30 AM. Normally, it would pick up from noon to 1:00 PM, slow down in the afternoon, and pick up again after 5:00 PM until the polls closed at 8:00 PM.

Republican chief judge Richmond Hall saw a lot of MAGA hats as people parked their pick-ups and strolled into the school, and he stationed himself outside to politely inform them they had to take them off. "State law doesn't allow any campaign material within one hundred feet of the polling place," he told them. He knew most of these voters by name.

Shortly before noon, he heard the familiar voice of one of the Trump supporters, apparently arguing with a poll-worker.

"I voted Trump," he said.

"Sir, please don't tell me how you voted," the poll-worker was saying.

"You don't understand. I voted Trump. But when I pressed on the button to review my ballot, it said I was voting for Governor Tomlinson."

Hall tapped the poll-worker on the shoulder. "I'll handle this," he said quietly.

He explained to the voter that this type of thing used to happen with the old touch-screen voting machines, usually with women wearing fingernail extensions. But since the state had shifted to paper ballots and scanners, it was virtually impossible. He had probably bent his ballot when he inserted it into the scanner without realizing it. "As long as the scanner hasn't actually tabulated your vote, we can discard it and you can try again," he said.

He took out his key card and inserted it in the machine to clear the current ballot, which emerged a rumpled mess, then blocked off the machine until the voter had filled out a fresh paper ballot.

"Make sure you insert your ballot holding it with both hands until the scanner accepts it," he said. "Now I'll just stand back while you review your ballot. If it shows up correctly this time on screen, then you press the button to cast your ballot, and you're good to go. Second time is a charm."

An hour later, the same thing happened with another Trump supporter on the same machine. An hour after that, it happened a third time. Hall called up the State Board of Elections. They told him to shut down the machine for the rest of the election and place it under seal. A Board technician would examine it the next day. It was probably just a calibration issue. They would tabulate the results of that machine separately and segregate them along with the provisional ballots, so as not to contaminate the results.

28

nd it wasn't just happening in Maryland.

At 4:00 PM outside Coral Terrace Elementary School southwest of Miami International Airport, an angry crowd was beginning to gather. They had come out one by one from the polling place, unable to vote, and as they began to compare stories, their numbers swelled until now more than two hundred people had formed into a sweaty mass. "Where are our ballots!" they chanted.

This particular part of Miami was located within the 10th city commission district. It was heavily Cuban and heavily Republican. For years, they had voted for Ileana Ros-Lehtinen, one of their own, as their member of Congress. But today, due apparently to a glitch with the precinct printer, poll workers had run out of ballots.

Domingo Alcazar, the chief judge, came out onto the pavement to explain that they were working on repairing the printer, but if that failed, they had already called into the County Supervisor of Elections to use a backup printer to issue more ballots. Because each election district had different local races, none of the ballots were standardized, so there wasn't some large stock-pile of blank ballots they could draw from. They actually had to be printed for each district, tallied, numbered, and sealed in numbered blocks.

"If you come back by 6:00 PM, we'll have the problem solved, and we'll keep the polls open until everyone who wants to vote has had a chance to vote," he said.

But it was obvious that many of the working-age men and women would not be coming back. They had come to vote for the president and for their Republican candidate for Congress. But they would not make the trip twice.

Navid turned from the bank of computer screens he was monitoring when he noticed his phone vibrate on the blue line. He recognized the number instantly.

"Where are you calling from?" he asked.

"The Netherlands," Granger said.

"Okay. Hold one."

Navid switched to the TunnelBear mobile app and scrolled through the list of countries they could select to host their virtual private network (VPN) until he found the Netherlands and selected it. Then he returned to Signal, which was the end-to-end encrypted voice and text application they used for all communications between them. Using Signal on top of the VPN gave them an added layer of protection. When the metadata from the call reached the NSA's massive computers, it would show up as an encrypted communication between two phones in the Netherlands and get set aside for future decrypt, if needed—unless, of course, the NSA had flagged the IMEI numbers of their phones and put them on a watch list. That could only happen if NSA had obtained a Foreign Intelligence Surveillance Act (FISA) warrant against them, which they could not get without a detailed application by the Justice Department to a special FISA court, a procedure that was far less likely today after the Obama administration got caught red-handed using that procedure to spy on the Trump campaign in 2016. So they felt pretty confident about security on the phone.

"Go ahead, boss," he said.

"What in Sam Hill are you doing?"

Navid was taken aback. "Exactly what we planned, if that's what you are referring to."

"Miami-Dade County?

"Oh, yeah. We win big."

"Well, you'd better turn on CNN right now," Granger said.

"Hold one."

Navid put his phone on mute and went out into the fish tank to look at the TV screens.

A CNN correspondent was reporting from Miami Gardens, a heavily Democratic area of the city, where a very different demonstration was taking place from the one at Coral Terrace Elementary. Protestors carrying placards in Spanish had gathered on the sidewalk outside of a school in a sea of political signs, demanding to be allowed to vote.

"Who are these guys?" Granger asked.

"Heck if I know," Navid said. "From the signs it looks like they have been organized by some voter's rights group."

"That's right. CNN is reporting that they were sent voter registration cards by an outside group and told to report to several precincts in Miami Gardens to vote, but when they got to the polls their names were not on the voter rolls."

"We had nothing to do with that, boss."

"The voter registration group apparently sent the ID cards to former convicted felons, which in Florida is now legal," Granger said. "Also to undocumented immigrants, minors, dead people, even pets. CNN reported on one elderly Jewish guy who'd received a voter ID card in the name of Gold Fysch."

"Hey, what can I tell you? Stuff happens, Granger. When you've got so many birds in the air, somebody's going to get poop in their eye. Hahahahaha. But I can guarantee you one thing: We're going to win Florida, and win it well beyond the margin of error. Or recount."

"We'd better," Granger said. "The turnout in Michigan and the Philly suburbs hasn't been going our way."

"Don't you worry about that," Navid said. "That's all going to change before the polls close."

29

Gordon Utz had been prepared for problems on Election Day, but the sheer scope and frequency of the calls his office had been receiving from polling places all over the state was overwhelming. By 11:00 AM, it became clear that the central voter database had been hacked. Maryland, like many states, allowed voters to register online and to verify the status of their registration online as well. So the whole system was accessible to the hacktivists who could penetrate it using free tools downloaded from the dark web. Within forty-five minutes, Gordon had isolated the threat in cyber-quarantine where it couldn't infect other systems and restored the voter database using a secure backup he kept on the internal server they used for all sensitive operations, including the election night vote counts and system patches.

"We need to put out a statement," he told Lisa Rasmussen, the State supervisor of elections.

She had the television in her office tuned to *The View*. Gordon thought he detected a lingering scent of acetone—nail polish remover.

"Have you drafted something?" she asked airily.

"Ma'am, I've been a bit busy just putting out fires. We've got machines that are down in multiple precincts and a major data breach. The important thing is to tell people: one, that we have identified the problem with the voter registration database that prevented people from voting earlier in the day, and two, we have restored the database so they should return to the precincts to vote. We should also make it clear that we have vigorously pursued reports of defective voting machines in Carroll and Montgomery counties and have isolated those machines for further review."

"That sounds pretty dire," she said. "Don't you think that's going to create panic?"

"It's better to be honest than to let people imagine the worst," he said.

"In that case, your statement should explain to people why they can feel confident that their votes are secure, and that these problems were minor. Our systems are not under attack."

Gordon couldn't believe what he was hearing.

"Uh, ma'am, our systems *are* under attack. We have isolated the attack and restored all services."

"No," she said. "Our cybersecurity team responded to isolated calls relating to a publicly accessible database and to technical glitches in a handful of voting machines. That's the message we need to get out. Our system is secure."

An hour later, she emailed him a draft one of the toadies had prepared. It was titled, "Rumor Control: Just the Facts, Please," and began with acknowledging the Election Day glitches.

"Maryland voters need to know that their voting system is secure. It includes built-in redundancies and has been subjected to rigorous security testing by an accredited national laboratory.

"Our new system includes a paper record of every vote cast. These ballots can be retabulated if needed. Voting equipment, including the tabulators citizens encounter at the polling place, are never connected to the internet. Physical access to the network is restricted and limited to election officials, all of whom have had a security background check. Furthermore, all network transactions involving the transmission of votes and tabulated results occur over a private network that is not connected to the internet. These transactions are all encrypted and logged to ensure there are no intrusions.

"As for the temporary distributed denial-of-service (DDoS) attack on the state's voter database that occurred this morning, Maryland voters need to know that their personal data is heavily encrypted and secure. The network is constantly monitored, so no unauthorized third party can access their information. Indeed, it was precisely because of the effective security procedures we have in place that the DDoS attack was detected, isolated, and eliminated earlier today."

The words sent a chill down Gordon's spine. All is well, kiddies. Sleep well. Your votes are secure. Nothing can go wrong here.

He knew it was a lie and suspected that the problems he had corrected that morning were just the beginning.

30

ranger was with Governor Tomlinson and vice presidential nominee Bellinger in the Chicago war room, a top floor suite at the Langham overlooking the Chicago River and the Wrigley Building, an art deco masterpiece in the center of downtown. The hotel had set up two big screen TVs tuned to Fox News and CNN and four smaller screens on a credenza along the wall of windows showing the other networks. The campaign had booked the entire twelfth floor. The only inconvenience was that the war room overlooked Trump Tower. Governor Tomlinson couldn't take her eyes off it, as if somehow its proximity brought her political opponent into the room with her.

By 5:00 PM, Granger was starting to rant. "Where are those big numbers we're supposed to be racking up in Detroit and Philly?" he said to no one in particular. "Where's Palm Beach County? Where's Broward? Where's Miami-Dade?" So far, his people on the ground were telling him that turnout had been hovering around 60 percent in those heavily Democratic areas. Meanwhile, the exit polls showed Trump racking up big numbers in rural counties, as Rick Hoglan was reminding him.

"It's still early, Keith," the CNN numbers man was saying. "There's always a surge in turnout when the polls close. But I'll bet you the Tomlinson camp is watching those turnout numbers just as we are. They've got to be paying particular attention to Philadelphia and to Montgomery and Delaware counties in the Philly suburbs, where Obama won big in 2012."

Hoglan touched on each of the counties on his "magic wall" to contrast the 2012 and 2016 results.

"If the governor is going to pull this off, she's going to need better numbers than Mrs. Clinton had in these deep blue precincts to counter the strong Trump turnout we're seeing in the exurbs and the more rural counties. Right now, it's trending in the low sixties. They need seventy-five, seventy-six percent if they're going to win Pennsylvania—and with it, the presidency, Keith."

Turnout didn't always work in favor of Democrats, Granger knew. In the 2016 election, when Trump won Pennsylvania by 44,292 votes, Hillary came to within 70,000 votes of Obama's score and conceivably could have equaled it, if Trump hadn't surged his base and hauled in 300,000 more votes than the Romney-Ryan ticket in 2012. Even in downtown Philadelphia, where CNN and other "mainstream" networks were holding out for more Democratic votes for hours after the polls closed in 2016, Trump won 12,000 more votes than Romney-Ryan won in 2012. His "What the Hell do you have to lose" mantra to the black community had hit home. Indeed, it arguably put Pennsylvania in his corner.

Four years later, with black unemployment rates at a historic low—nearly 200 percent better than under Obama!—Trump's approval numbers with African-American voters had gone up dramatically. They were so high—well over 30 percent—that the media stopped reporting on them a year before the election.

They'd just report the top-line number and scream out the headline—52 percent of voters disapprove of President Trump! Forty-nine percent support impeachment and removal from office!—and neglect to tell their audience the rest of the story.

The rest of the story is why Granger had been so worried going into this election, and why he had hired Navid. His IT guy was supposed to pull the "Secret Switch" before the first hard results were announced, although Granger wasn't quite sure what it was. They had agreed on target states, and the overall state numbers; the how of it he left up to Navid. But if voters didn't turn out, how could Navid work his magic? Where was that big inner-city turnout they were all expecting?

At 6:00 PM eastern time, Keith Cobb cocked his head to listen to a voice in his earpiece. He held up a hand, then looked toward the camera. He never smiled. He never scowled. He worked hard at looking impartial and he did so now.

"CNN is prepared to make the first projection of this historic election night," he intoned. "Polls are now closed in most of Kentucky and Indiana. Let's go to Rick Hoglan at the Magic Board," he said.

"Keith, CNN is ready to call Indiana and Kentucky for Trump. That's not a surprise, and I've got to caution our viewers, these are very preliminary results, with just one percent of precincts reporting. But our exit polls give us confidence to call both states for the president and vice president."

"Any states for Governor Tomlinson, Rick?"

"We've got pretty firm exit poll data from a number of blue states, Keith, but as you know, our policy is not to call a state until its polls have closed. Everyone still remembers the Florida debacle during Bush-Gore in 2000, when we and most of the other networks called Florida for the Democrats at 7:00 PM, when voters were still lined up to vote in the heavily-Republican Panhandle, which sits in a different time zone."

"Right," Cobb said. "None of us want a repeat of that. So what comes next, Rick?"

"Check back in one hour, Keith, when we will have the next round of poll closings. Until then, we'll continue to monitor turnout, and if there are any surprises, we'll let you know."

At 7:00 PM, CNN called Vermont and New Hampshire for the Democrats and South Carolina for Trump. Virginia and Georgia were too close to call. And Floridians in the Panhandle were still voting.

Keith Cobb brought on a young female correspondent, Allie Esfandiari, who had breaking news to report from the floodlit grounds of Mar-a-Lago in Florida.

"Keith, CNN has learned from a close advisor to the Trump campaign that they have become increasingly pessimistic with the numbers they are seeing from these early states. They had been hoping to win Pennsylvania and Florida with decisive margins and so far that hasn't happened. And while they were prepared to lose Virginia, Georgia is a must-win and they now see that state going to Governor Tomlinson."

Cobb was a pro, and he showed zero emotion as he resumed his broadcast after this stunning information. He was hoping for a report from inside the Tomlinson camp shortly, he said. The next hard numbers should be coming at 7:30 PM, when polls in North Carolina, Ohio, and West Virginia closed.

31

At 8:00 PM, Congressman Hugh McKenzie sat with Willie, his wife, and their two college-age children, Katie and Jack, around a TV in the suite his campaign had rented at the Bethesda North Marriot Hotel and Convention Center on Rockville Pike. Morton Nash was ticking off the wins for the Tomlinson-Bellinger ticket.

"North Carolina, boom!" he said. "That's a huge win. That's fifteen electoral votes Hillary didn't win in 2016. And look at the numbers. The DNC's get-out-the-vote effort is bearing fruit. If Pennsylvania goes for us, we're just three votes shy of 270. And that leaves so many other states in play, we can win this big."

"But they're only reporting two percent of the precincts in Pennsylvania," McKenzie said. "And CNN and all the networks have called Ohio and West Virginia for Trump."

"They're pros, Congressman. They've had so much egg on their faces in prior elections, they won't be making calls unless they've got real solid exit polling. Watch Georgia, Arizona, Florida, and Michigan," he said. "And there's no way Trump's winning Wisconsin again. Seriously? Our people are *engaged!*"

Results from a ton of states started trickling in. Maine split two for two, just as it had in 2016, and Democrats predictably won Massachusetts, Connecticut, Rhode Island, New Jersey, Delaware, and Maryland. Trump won Tennessee, Oklahoma, Missouri, and Kansas and was projected to win Texas and the Dakotas. At 8:30 PM, CNN called Arkansas for Trump. But without races called in Pennsylvania, Florida, Georgia, or Michigan, no network was ready to hazard predicting a winner.

It would be another half-hour at least until they had results in the only race that mattered: Aguilar's surprisingly strong challenge to McKenzie's re-election effort. After nearly a year of campaigning, where they measured progress month by month, week by week, and finally day by day, now it was just a matter of minutes before voters would decide McKenzie's fate—and those minutes seemed to drag on interminably.

32

"Turn to Fox 45 in Baltimore," the Crocodile said. "They're going to be watching the Maryland races."

Aguilar campaign headquarters was packed, and the candidate was roaming amongst groups of volunteers, stopping to press an arm here, kiss a cheek there, bump fists with the *chicos* who had taken off work in late afternoons and weekends to go door-to-door with him in the high rises below Wheaton Mall. Camilla Broadstreet made sure they had several tubs full of ice, beer, and wine, but no one was celebrating yet.

"There it is!" the Crocodile shouted. "It's on the chyron."

The Fox 45 commentator was talking about the presidential race, but at the bottom of the screen numbers for Maryland's congressional races were rolling. Republican Andy Harris, in CD-1, was projected to blow away his opponent. With only 6 percent of precincts reporting, he was showing 76 percent. Nothing yet in CD-2 north of Baltimore, but John Sarbanes in CD-3 was only at 52 percent so far. In the western Maryland district, CD-6, incumbent Democrat and former businessman David Trone was neck and neck with his Republican challenger, a former journalist. But the big surprise was CD-7, the inner city Baltimore neighborhoods hit by the Freddy Grey riots, which Elijah Cummings had represented until his untimely death the year before. Cummings had been returned to Congress reliably for decades with over 70 percent of the vote, sometimes well into the 80s. Once, in 2006, he ran unopposed and won 98.1 percent of the vote, only missing a perfect score because of 3,147 write-ins for other candidates.

The chyron showed Grady Jones, his hand-picked successor, running in the high 50s. Trump's campaign against Cummings for neglecting Baltimore seemed to be paying off. African-American voters were turning to Trump in bigger numbers than anyone had imagined.

"There's a sign for you, boss. If Grady Jones is not walking on water in the Elijah Cummings district, you're going to be the next Congressman for the eighth district."

The room went deadly silent as the CD-7 numbers finished scrolling by, and the chyron began to spell out Aguilar. The candidate lifted his gold cross to his lips and kissed it. And then, the room erupted in cheers.

The Crocodile actually jumped into the air as he called it, displaying an enthusiasm and agility no one had believed him capable of. "Look at *that*!" he said. "Sixty-two percent. Sixty-two percent, boss! That's better than even we had predicted."

Aguilar did not share his enthusiasm. At least, not yet. "It's just four percent reporting," he said. "No one is calling the race."

Annie went out into the hallway and called Gordon on his cell.

"I saw that announcement earlier," she said. "Everything under control?"

"Won't know for a couple of hours."

He explained the procedure for closing the election. It was way more complicated than people imagined. The chief judges needed to close out each voting station individually, the Republican and Democrat together, take out the memory card, note its serial number in the precinct book, then reseal the machine and the detachable ballot boxes and seal them with tamper-proof tape. Each tamper-proof seal had a number, which the judges noted in the precinct logs. If anyone tampered with the seals, the words *VOID VOID VOID* would replace the number. Then the election judges placed the memory cards in the precinct tabulator and uploaded the result using the on-board modem connected through a VPN to their county boards of elections. Even if someone intercepted those votes—near nigh impossible, since the VPN was like a tunnel drilled through the core of the internet, with only one entrance and one exit ("think of it like *Stargate,* or a wormhole," he said)—tonight's results were not official. Tomorrow they would run the image files through separate tabulators in Annapolis and add in the electronic votes from the DRE machines. Only if there were no discrepancies with tonight's totals would they announce official results. Any significant discrepancies and Gordon and his team would step in. They had an elaborate system of redundant security checks to guarantee the accuracy of the vote. But those procedures took time.

"Your guy seems to be doing well," he said. "But we're getting results mainly from Carroll and Frederick so far, where he ought to be doing well."

"No Montgomery precincts have reported yet?"

"Only a handful," he said. "Less than one percent. We post them as we get them."

"What about early voting?" she asked.

"We'll be releasing that at 9:30 PM, since all those machines were tabulated last Friday."

"Can you have a look?" Annie said.

"You know I can't do that."

"We should do well there," Annie said. "We got amazing responses at the polling places we visited last week. Even the Silver Spring Civic Building that normally runs heavily Democrat."

As she was talking, Gordon pulled up another screen on his left-hand monitor and whistled.

"Oh, my. You will want to look at this."

"Gordon, stop! You're killing me!" she said.

"We're releasing the numbers in another fifteen minutes, so no harm no foul. You need to look at them carefully. Carroll and Frederick early voting are showing big numbers for your guy. But MoCo is way out of the norm. Seventy-four percent McKenzie."

"Huh?"

He caught a glimpse of his supervisor, Lisa Rasmussen, walking down the hallway toward his office.

"Hey, gotta go!"

Annie was stunned. Their internal polls showed Aguilar winning with 68 percent in Carroll County, 62 percent in Frederick, and 47 percent in Montgomery County. The problem, of course, was that Montgomery County alone had three times the voters of Carroll and Frederick combined. So if that early vote total was real, they were in big trouble.

She needed to warn the Crocodile.

33

As soon as his supervisor had returned to her corner office suite, Gordon pulled up the early voting results from Montgomery County. Overall, they showed that 74.4 percent of early voting had gone for McKenzie, and just 20.8 percent for Aguilar. That just didn't track with the Election Day results the State board had just posted. He wanted to see the individual breakdowns from all eleven early voting places in the county, since they were in areas with different demographics.

For example, the Silver Spring Civic Building, while in a deeply Democrat part of the county, should have shown a healthy result for Aguilar. First, there were large numbers of Hispanic voters in that area, plus he had campaigned there virtually every day. Same thing for the Mid-County Rec Center up on Layhill Road and the one at the Catholic school in Wheaton. Aguilar should also be doing well up in Damascus and Burtonsville, which were more Republican-leaning anyway.

McKenzie should have better results in downtown Rockville, where voting took place at the Executive Office Building, and in the traditional Democrat strongholds of Kensington, Chevy Chase, Bethesda, Potomac, and Gaithersburg.

It took a while to extract the data from the spreadsheets, since there were so many different elections and candidates. Before the initial gerrymander, in 1999, all of Montgomery County was grouped into a single congressional district, which made sense. Now, twenty years later, Montgomery County voters were spread out over four. Most people never went through the data, but if they did, they'd be surprised to discover there were usually around a dozen presidential candidates on the ballot, in addition to all the congressional and local races. So there was a lot of data to eliminate.

Next, he had to separate out the Election Day results, so only the early voting columns appeared. And then he had to run a percentage calculator on each of the eleven early voter centers, not just on the total number.

As soon as he configured the calculator, the result leapt off the screen.

McKenzie was running between 62 percent and 78 percent in all eleven early voting centers in Montgomery County. Not a single one showed that Aguilar had made inroads during the campaign. It was as if all the votes had been thrown into a common bin and counted with no distinction for demographics or geography.

That was statistically impossible.

He ran a printout of the results and took it to the office of the State administrator of elections, Lisa Rasmussen. He practically threw the printout onto her desk.

"We can't put out these numbers," he said all in a rush.

"Gordon, calm down. What are you talking about?"

He explained what he had found, and why it made no sense.

"But these *are* the numbers, correct?"

"They are the numbers that have been reported to us, yes."

"Then unless you have some reason to think there has been an error—"

"But they can't be correct," he said.

"That's just your hunch. Or perhaps, a bias? Have you seen this type of discrepancy in any other congressional race?"

"Actually, yes," he said.

He hadn't told Annie about this earlier, but there were other things going on that heightened his suspicions that there could be a problem with the Aguilar race.

"Look at the numbers in CD-7. Congressman Jones is running in the low fifties so far."

"And?"

"Elijah Cummings used to win that district by well over seventy percent, and Grady Jones is his hand-picked successor."

"What does that have to do with the McKenzie-Aguilar race?"

"Don't you see? If Grady Jones is doing poorly—and in that district, the mid-fifties is not good—that would suggest that minority voters are not voting for the Democrat in the huge numbers we've seen in earlier elections. If that's the case in Baltimore, which is over eighty percent minority, it ought to be happening in District 8, which has thirty-five percent Hispanic voters."

"But it's not. Is that what you are saying?"

"That's right. There are also the precinct numbers from Wheaton and from Kemp Mill, an Orthodox Jewish community that is very conservative. Early returns there show that McKenzie is winning both areas with over seventy percent as well."

"Put out the numbers, Gordon. Just as you received them. Tonight's results are unofficial anyway, you know that. We'll have all the memory cards tomorrow so you can run a full audit."

34

It was just after 9:15 PM when Keith Cobb brought on Jeff Greystone, the CNN correspondent embedded with the Tomlinson campaign.

"Keith, senior sources inside the Tomlinson camp are telling CNN they feel increasingly confident as these new results come in. Nobody doubted the Democrats would win New York and New Mexico. Voters are still at the polls in Nevada, but the Tomlinson camp feels confident from exit polls earlier today that they will win there and possibly also in Arizona. As of right now, they see several roads to 270 for their team, and very few for the president."

Granger smiled to himself. He had just returned from spinning Greystone in their media suite, and he was regurgitating it almost word-for-word. *Good boy*, he thought.

Cobb turned from the giant display where he'd been watching Greystone and looked over to Rick Hoglan at the Magic Board. "So, Rick: What more does Governor Tomlinson need to become president-elect?"

"Well, Keith, there are many ways this could happen, as Jeff was just telling us. As it stands now, with North Carolina in the Tomlinson camp, and the West Coast and Hawaii almost certainly going to the Democrats, they need to flip just forty-six more votes out of the 131 from states currently too close to call. In one scenario, Governor Tomlinson can abandon the rust-belt states to Trump except for Pennsylvania, then win three of the five remaining states up for grabs. With Nevada, Arizona, and Georgia, she's at 277. If she loses Georgia and wins Virginia, she's at 274."

"So what about Pennsylvania?" Cobb asked.

"As you can see, the president is predictably winning the rust-belt counties in western Pennsylvania, but with lower numbers from 2016, and he's holding his own in the Philadelphia suburbs, where Mrs. Clinton won in 2016. The key is going to be the African-American vote in downtown Philly. So far, only forty percent is reporting."

"So we'll keep our eyes on that," Cobb said. "What about Florida?"

"That remains the big one, Keith. The panhandle has gone big for the president as expected. But they are still counting the votes down in Broward, Palm Beach, and Miami-Dade counties."

"What if Trump wins both Florida and Pennsylvania. Is it all over then for the Democrats?"

"No, Keith. Governor Tomlinson can actually lose both Florida and Pennsylvania. But then she's got to sweep the table of all the other states that are still up for grabs, and that means winning Nevada, Michigan, Georgia, and Virginia."

"Alright. CNN's Rick Hoglan, thank you for that update."

35

G ranger muted CNN when he saw the Fox News alert on the screen: something about crowds of people still trying to vote in Detroit, Milwaukee, Minneapolis, and Scottsdale, Arizona, even though the polls had closed in all of those states.

"Fox News is receiving multiple reports of problems at the polls and, apparently, problems with the vote counting as well," Galen Beaty announced. "In Michigan, election officials are telling Fox News they have discovered an anomaly with the touch-screen voting machines they continue to use, as do many other states, for voters with disabilities or who otherwise have problems reading and marking their ballot. Scott Ramsey from our affiliate, Fox2 Detroit, has the details."

The young reporter was standing in front of a rundown brick building with a crowd of people lining up behind a twisted metal fence to get in.

"Galen, it's chaos out here. Election officials here in Detroit are telling us they have had to shut down more than a dozen of the touch-screen machines they use for disabled voters. Michigan switched to paper ballots in 2018, but because of the Americans for Disabilities Act, they are required to maintain systems accessible to these other voters. But problems arose when thousands of people swarmed inner city polling places demanding to use the touch-screen machines because they could not read the paper ballots. These machines have a function that can speak the ballot to the voter in their own language over a headset.

"You also need to understand, Galen, that Michigan is a voter ID state, and some of these voters didn't have ID. Now normally, they would be allowed to cast a provisional ballot that would only be counted once election officials have been able to verify their identity. Republican poll watchers have been complaining that there is no mechanism with these touch-screen machines to segregate provisional from regular ballots, so when the results get reported, all those votes will be included in the final count with no way of separating them out later on."

"I guess this is not the first time Detroit has had problems on Election Day."

"That's right, Galen. Everyone still remembers 2016 when more than sixty percent of the Detroit precincts had more votes counted than people who came out to vote. It was so bad they couldn't do a recount."

"And yet, Michigan still went for Trump," Beaty said.

"It did, Galen. And all the exit polls show that it will go for Trump again tonight—unless of course these problems with the voting machines become more widespread."

Granger made a note to call Navid about Michigan. This wasn't part of the plan. *Perhaps it was just local activists flooding the zone,* he thought.

In heavily Republican Scottsdale, Arizona, they had run out of ballots, so lines of increasingly angry voters had formed at the polls. Granger needed to ask Navid about that as well. Arizona *was* part of the plan. But he had always assumed that Navid was operating under the radar, not with such obvious gimmicks.

"Galen, we're getting reports from South Florida of a massive turnout for Governor Tomlinson," co-anchor Kristina Brower said.

Granger leaned forward. This he wanted to hear.

36

The Fox News co-anchor turned to the display where Tammy Dayton of Fox affiliate WSVN was standing in front of the Broward County Government Center in Fort Lauderdale, Florida.

"So, Tammy, what are you hearing?"

"Kristina, the Broward County supervisor of elections is reporting a massive turnout for Governor Tomlinson. So far, and this coincides with exit polling from earlier in the day, it would appear that Broward is going to give Governor Tomlinson a big leg up against the president, perhaps even enough votes to put her over the top in the state of Florida. Now as you know, Democrats out-register Republicans here by almost two to one, and this area is home to one of the most liberal members of Congress: Representative Alcee Hastings.

"You're talking about the former federal district court judge who was impeached for bribery by the House of Representatives by a vote of 413-3 and subsequently removed from office by the U.S. Senate," Galen Beaty said.

"That's right, Galen. Representative Hastings was first elected to Congress in 1992 just three years after his impeachment as a federal judge and has been returned to office with overwhelming margins ever since. His congressional district contains the heaviest concentration of African-American voters in Broward County. And it seems tonight that they came out *en masse* for Governor Tomlinson."

Yes, Granger thought. *Navid is the man*!

"Now behind me you can see a group of protesters—these are actually Republicans. They are protesting because their poll watchers took photographs of the run-sheets from the precinct tabulators that were released a little more than an hour ago and posted them on the internet. Here's an example of what they found."

The camera zoomed in on the printer tape, which looked like a cash register receipt, showing a total of 2,146 votes cast.

"The problem, Kristina, is that this particular precinct only has 1,856 registered voters who are eligible to vote."

Granger jumped up and slapped his hands on the table. This was *not* how this was supposed to play out. It was supposed to be quiet, no waves, nothing noticeable. He switched his VPN to Belgium and punched in Navid's number.

"Navid! Turn on Fox News. Now!" he barked.

"Country?"

"Who gives a—. Belgium," he said.

"Right. What's the problem? Things are going as planned."

"Did you plan to have more votes cast than eligible voters?" Granger asked.

"Of course not. That would be an immediate red flag. I mean, that would be, like, voter fraud! Hahahahaha."

"It's not a joke, Navid."

"Sorry. Of course not. It's just, there's a lot of crazy stuff going on tonight. Stuff that has nothing to do with us."

"You think the Russians are interfering with the election results? Hacking the touch-screen machines?"

"No way. They are too dumb."

"I thought they were the best hackers in the world."

"They're good at remote access, sure. But with the DREs, you've got to have boots on the ground. You need physical access to the machines. You need somebody to actually open them up to insert a Trojan. The Russians don't have that."

"So what's going on in Broward County?"

"What's going on in Broward County? Are you kidding me? What always goes on in Broward County! You have a lot of highly partisan Democratic operatives who all want to do their part for God and Country."

"Freelancers?"

"You could say that, yeah."

"What if their actions trigger an audit?"

"I wouldn't worry about that."

"Why not?"

"Have faith, my friend. Have faith. Does Navid deliver, or does he call for Chinese takeout? Hahahahaha."

The Fox News anchors now turned to another WSVN reporter, Ainsley Westerrupp, in Delray Beach.

"Galen, Palm Beach County is reporting enormous numbers tonight for Governor Tomlinson. Turnout among registered Democrats is at historic highs, and these voters have come out for their candidate."

"But are you getting hard numbers? We don't have them yet up here on the board."

"Not yet, Galen. But the word we're getting from Democrat party poll-workers is that their people showed up at the polls. Look at this."

They aired bits of an interview Ainsley had done earlier just as the polls were closing with an ecstatic middle-aged woman, Marie Schneiderman, who was explaining the reasons for their success. "I gotta tell you, we've been working all day long. We get the list of voters who haven't yet voted, we send it out, and in ten minutes we've got a team at their door. Even in the nursing homes. You wouldn't believe the enthusiasm our voters are feeling for an opportunity to just say no to Donald Trump. It's a rich harvest," she said.

Granger heard Navid typing rapid-fire on his keyboard and hung up. He preferred this news to what he'd been hearing earlier.

37

The Crocodile couldn't believe the numbers that were scrolling across the screen. Grady Jones was still hovering below 60 percent in the Elijah Cummings district, with nearly half of Baltimore precincts reporting. But when the Aguilar-McKenzie race scrolled across the chyron, it showed McKenzie had overcome his early deficit and was now winning with 52.4 percent.

"Boss, this is unbelievable. It's like somebody just flipped a switch," he said.

"And that's with sixty percent of precincts reporting," Annie added. "It doesn't look good. But why?"

"Something is very, very wrong here," the Crocodile went on. "Boss, you remember that young gal from the Cameroun at the Civic Building in Silver Spring?"

"How could I forget her," Aguilar said with a smile. "She reminded me of Graciella. So happy to vote for the first time, she was literally jumping up and down."

"She was a registered Democrat, remember?"

"Yeah, she was waving her voter registration card at anyone who would look. Casa de Maryland automatically registered her as a Democrat when they greeted her at the Baltimore citizenship induction center," Aguilar said. "It's what they do."

"But she told us how happy she was to be casting her first vote as an American for you, the son of immigrants, remember? You were her dream come true. She wanted her son to be able to grow up and run for Congress, maybe president."

"That's right. And why not?" Aguilar said.

"And when she came back out, she wanted a selfie with you wearing her 'I voted' sticker."

There had been so many people like that woman, the Crocodile reminded them. All the young Latinos who listened to Aguilar's daily radio commentaries; they, too, were registered Democrats and had told them proudly they had voted for Aguilar.

"I'd really like to see the numbers on this one, boss. Where are the under votes? The Republicans who voted for Trump and blank for Congress? And the split votes: the Dems who voted for you and for Mrs. T?"

"We're not going to be getting that kind of granular detail until tomorrow, at least," Annie said. "But the state board of elections has just posted preliminary breakdowns. Look, in Elijah Cumming's old district, bluest of blue, Trump is winning thirty-six percent of the vote. That's more than Romney and McCain combined," she said. "Or Trump 2016 and Romney."

She showed them the state's numbers for their district. Aguilar was still winning Carroll and Frederick Counties with predictably high margins, 68 percent and 62 percent respectively. But down in Montgomery he was under 30 percent. That was catastrophic. Their projections showed they needed to win at least 43.5 percent in Montgomery to win the district, based on the 2016 turnout and results. In off years, with no president on the ballot, turnout was much lower so it was possible to flip the seat with fewer votes.

"Campaigning matters, boss," the Crocodile was saying. "Voter contact matters. If these results are real, it means that nothing we did made any difference. None of the ads, none of the rallies, none of the door-to-door and polling place contacts. You must have shaken hands with 5,000 voters at the Silver Spring Civic Building alone, out of what, around 8,300 votes cast during early voting? What are those numbers now?"

"McKenzie wins 73.4 percent of the Silver Spring Civic Building, and between seventy percent and seventy-five percent of all the others," Annie said. "It makes no sense."

"Boss, you can't do all that campaigning without having an impact. It's just not possible. That's what politics is all about. These results are basically a carbon copy of the way these areas have voted traditionally."

"They are also in line with the Governor's Redistricting Advisory Commission by around one-tenth of one percent," Annie added.

"Boy, I'd love to hire statisticians like that to run my retirement portfolio," the Crocodile said.

"Good luck," Aguilar said. "Nobody gets results like that. No prediction ever holds true to that degree of accuracy. There's always a standard deviation."

Aguilar wanted to hear from Brady, to see if he had detected any more anomalies. Meanwhile, Annie went out to talk with Gordon. None of this smelled right.

38

"It's all my fault," Gordon said when Annie finally got him on the phone. "When I first examined the attempted intrusion into the voter database, I must have triggered a Gh0st RAT."

"A who?"

"It's a what, actually. A time bomb, if you prefer. Hidden code triggered to release its package into the Montgomery County voter database at 7:00 AM on Election Day."

"How do you know that?"

"I was able to reconstitute a few lines of code from one of our backups. These guys were good. When I started sniffing for malware, it must have triggered an exploit that altered the hash so our virus protection software and even the ALBERT system didn't detect the intrusion."

"The hash?"

"Yeah. That's a summary number of all the code in a particular program. If it's off by a single digit, you know that someone has altered the code. So the Gh0st RAT replaced the hash files and substituted its own hash for ours. When our virus detectors sniffed the program, the current hash matched the one on file. So they came back with, nothing to see here, move on."

"But the one on file had been altered."

"Right."

"And so the time bomb. What was that?"

"That was code that randomly erased ten percent of all registered Republicans from the voter rolls and erased the primary returns as well so we couldn't confirm their registration against the primary vote."

"That's why we had so many complaints of voters who were unable to vote."

"Yes. We instructed the precincts to allow them to vote provisional, so eventually their votes will be counted."

"Still, even if it worked throughout the District, that would only lower our total by three percent, since we have thirty percent registered Republicans district-wide."

"Actually, it would have even less impact, since it only hit Montgomery."

"So that doesn't explain the results."

Gordon was silent.

"Gordon?"

"You're right. That doesn't explain the results," he said. "There has to be something else I've missed."

Gordon was scrolling through the results in Montgomery County and there were a lot of things that made no sense.

"We're going to be posting precinct by precinct results in a few minutes," he said. "You need to take a close look at them. I am assuming you have polling data down at that level?"

"Of course," Annie said. "We had a pretty good idea exactly where our votes were coming from."

"Would you be willing to share that with me on the QT for Montgomery?"

"Sure. Well, let me ask the boss. But I'm sure he'll say yes."

When she sent him the data files a few minutes later, Gordon knew exactly where to look. There were two areas in Montgomery County where Aguilar had been campaigning hard and that he expected to flip from the Democrats in order to win the district. These were the heavily Hispanic precincts around Wheaton and Silver Spring, and the Orthodox Jewish neighborhoods in Kemp Mill. Wheaton and Silver Spring normally went around 75 percent to 80 percent Democrat, and that's exactly what the combined results from early voting and Election Day on his screen were showing. But Aguilar's polls showed exactly the opposite, with him winning between 58 percent and 63 percent in those areas. His polls also showed him surging new voters in those precincts, so their numbers contributed to his overall win. What happened?

The Kemp Mill precincts should be even more telling. There were a handful of Orthodox synagogues that ministered to a heavily Orthodox Jewish population. If you drove through the neighborhood on Friday evening or Saturday morning, you would see families walking together to shul, the men wearing hats and the women covering their hair with nets. It was like a piece of old Europe, or of a West Bank Jewish "settlement," transplanted to suburban Maryland. Since Bush 43, an increasing number of these voters had become Republicans. While Democrats still won the precincts, it was by much smaller numbers than in the traditional white liberal strongholds in Kensington, Bethesda, Chevy Chase and Potomac. So how was it that McKenzie had won these precincts by over 70 percent? What was going on? The same with Trump and Governor Tomlinson. He would have expected Trump to get at least 45 percent in Kemp Mill because of moving the U.S. embassy to Jerusalem, which no previous president had agreed to do. Instead, he was hovering around 28 percent to 30 percent.

He needed ground truth, and he knew where he could get it.

He called Rabbi Yonni Paz, a long-time political acquaintance of his mother's. What was going on, he asked him.

"What's going on? You wanna know what's going on, Gordy? I'll tell you: Somebody is playing tricks. Nelson Aguilar is a mensch. He spoke in my shul. Everybody loved him. And he loves us. He has a heart for Israel."

"I'm sure he loves your money," Gordon said.

"Don't be cynical. We don't have money. All of us are broke, everybody knows that. Those are the Potomac Jews you're thinking of. We just have lots of children, and that's better than money.

"Those Potomac Jews. Look. The more Trump does for Israel, the more they despise him. Because they despise themselves for their betrayal of Israel. They put Israeli flags in front of their synagogues and banners saying United for Israel. But that's just for show. They are self-hating Jews. You wanna know how they are united? They are united against Trump. And probably against our boy Nelson, too. You know, I gave Nelson a nice green embroidered kippa when he came to speak on Shabbat. I see he wore it whenever he went into shul, even with the lefties. So the visiting goy was covered, and those kosher *beheymes* were not."

"So what do you think of the election results? According to our numbers, your precinct voted for McKenzie overwhelmingly, more than seventy percent."

The Rabbi exploded. "You're telling me what?"

"Those are the unofficial results," Gordon said.

"There is no way my people voted for that *momzer* McKenzie. We despise him! He claims he is for Iron Dome and David's

Sling and Arrow 3 and you name it. And then he goes and votes against the appropriations bills every single time. Not a single penny has he voted that would help Israel! And Gaza, who can forget that! That *schlump* signs a letter condemning Israel with the Council on American-Islamic Relations, the U.S. branch of Hamas. The self-hating Jews who support him have no family in Israel. No skin in the game. They don't worship Elohim but the great god abortion. That is their religion."

"So Rabbi, tell me how you really feel," Gordon said.

"Ya, Gordy. You're a good boy. You go figure this one out. Will ya?"

"I'll do my best, sir."

39

At 10:30 PM, the major networks called Nevada and Virginia for Governor Tomlinson and with that, the online predicators upped the odds of a victory by Governor Tomlinson and Senator Bellinger to over 75 percent. Even though the networks had also just called Wisconsin for Trump, most of the anchors and their guests were now treating Governor Tomlinson and her running mate as the next president and vice president of the United States. The reason was simple: Governor Tomlinson had racked up such an impressive lead in Florida that it now seemed insurmountable. It didn't matter that Michigan, Minnesota, and Arizona were still up for grabs. If the governor won Florida, it was game over.

CNN played its dramatic breaking news music, and in the Langham Hotel in Chicago, Granger sat forward on his seat. Keith Cobb picked up a piece of paper and, doing his best to suppress a smile, appeared to read from it. "It is now 10:40 PM here on the East Coast, and with eighty-five percent of precincts reporting down in Florida, CNN is projecting that the Sunshine state goes for Governor Tomlinson."

Governor Tomlinson's suite erupted with hoots and cheering and clapping and hollering, and Granger leapt to his feet and turned to the governor, who had remained in the sofa, next to her reverend husband, calmly watching the results.

"Madame president-elect," he said, bowing to shake her hand.

"Not yet, Granger. It's not yet official," she said. "And we don't yet have Pennsylvania in the bag."

"Don't worry, we will. We've got our guys working on your acceptance speech. Wonder when Trump will give you a call?"

"I'm not holding my breath," the governor said.

"And so once again, as goes Florida, so goes the nation," Keith Cobb was saying, trying to be profound or at least quotable. He turned to Rick Hoglan at the Magic Board to explain why CNN was making the call.

"Keith, it's a combination of things going on here," Hoglan said.

He explained that turnout in some heavily Republican areas, including Nassau County in the north and the Florida Panhandle, had been a bit lower than expected. That gave Trump a voter deficit from which he was never to recover. Meanwhile, down in the heavily Democrat counties of Palm Beach, Broward, and Miami-Dade, Democrats showed up in record numbers, beating even the score racked up by President Obama in 2012. The end result, with more than 85 percent of precincts reporting, was an overwhelming victory by Governor Tomlinson. "We're looking at a victory margin of over 180,000 votes, Keith. That goes well beyond the margin of error and makes our projection desk feel confident in calling Florida for Tomlinson. With Florida, Virginia, and Nevada in the bag, that gives her 266 electoral votes, just four shy of victory."

From here, Hoglan said, Governor Tomlinson had to win just one of the five swing states that were still too close to call: Arizona, Pennsylvania, Michigan, Minnesota, or Georgia.

"With the numbers we are seeing, it's easy to imagine her making a clean sweep of all five, Keith. That would give her 339 votes, an electoral college blow-out. But all she really needs at this point is just one of them. If Trump's popularity in the rust belt is confirmed as most of the exit polling suggests, he could still win Michigan, and perhaps even Pennsylvania. After all, he just eked out a win in Wisconsin, which he won by 22,000 votes in 2016—the first Republican to win the state since 1984. Georgia is trending Democratic and could be a surprising pickup for the Dems this year, but with only forty-five percent of precincts reporting, it's still too early to call. And don't forget that Minnesota has not voted for a Republican presidential candidate since the Nixon landslide of 1972. Even Hillary Clinton won Minnesota in 2016."

"So you're saying there are multiple pathways to 270 for Governor Tomlinson. What about for the president?" Cobb asked. "Is there any way he can still pull this off?"

"I've gotta tell you, Keith. That is looking increasingly unlikely. The president would have to sweep the table of all the states that remain too close to call. He'd have to win Minnesota, which we just discussed. He'd have to win Georgia, where you know there has been a very successful effort over the past eighteen months by the Democrats to register new voters—over 100,000 new voters, by latest count. He'd have to win Michigan, where as you can see, he's running neck and neck with Governor Tomlinson—basically a tie, each of them at 49.2 percent. With just fifteen percent of the precincts left to report, and with some of those precincts in downtown Detroit, a heavily Democratic area, a win there looks unlikely for the president. And he'd have to win Pennsylvania, where the president is leading by 16,000 votes but you still have precincts in Philadelphia and suburban Delaware and Montgomery counties that have yet to report. So lots of African Americans and lots of soccer moms whose votes still need to be counted. Not Trump voters, Keith.

"And then, there's Arizona," he said.

Hoglan explained that Arizona had been trending purple for a number of years as Democratic voters fled California's high taxes and over-crowded schools and moved to Phoenix where the economy was booming. "Arizona has been on the radar for Democrats ever since 2018 when Democrat Krysten Sinema beat Republican Martha McSally by more than 50,000 votes for the U.S. Senate seat that opened with the retirement of Jeff Flake. That was an electoral margin of 2.4 percent."

"So where does Arizona stand now, Rick?"

Hoglan worked the Magic Board and explained that even though the overall numbers in Arizona were showing Trump ahead, there were large numbers of Democratic precincts that had yet to report in: Coconino and Apache counties in the north, and Pima and Santa Cruz counties along the Mexican border. These areas were going to be giving big numbers to the Tomlinson campaign and, quite probably, enough to frustrate the president from winning the state.

"So without Arizona, President Trump will be a one-term president, is that what you are saying?"

"That's right, Keith. That is certainly one scenario."

While the other networks began debating what a Tomlinson-Bellinger first term would look like, the visibly embarrassed anchors at Fox News brought on a panel to rip apart the refusal of their election desk to call Florida for Tomlinson. Granger had to chuckle when both Democrats and Republicans squirmed, unanimously embarrassed by the election desk fence-sitters.

For a good ten minutes, they debated whether President Trump would announce his concession on Twitter, without even calling Governor Tomlinson, or issue a White House statement.

They had won, and won big. It was time for the blowhard to bow out.

Navid is the man, Granger said to himself. *Navid is the man.*

40

atherine Herrera, supervisor of elections for Nassau County in northeast Florida, didn't understand the numbers on her screen. What in the world had happened to John Rutherford?

Rutherford, a two-term former sheriff of neighboring Duval County, had been elected to Congress with more than 65 percent of the vote since 2016. But tonight, his numbers were in the mid-50s. It just didn't make sense.

Trump was also running in the mid-50s. In this heavily Republican county, where the president practically walked on water—and there was a lot of it in Nassau County surrounding Fernandina Beach and Amelia Island—that was incomprehensible. Did people just stay home?

Her turnout screens suggested not. Of the 68,415 active registered voters, 76 percent (or nearly 52,000) had cast ballots—paper ballots, she was happy to say. Herrera was first elected to her post in 2000 and had watched in horror the Bush-Gore recount and the hanging chads. The punch-card ballots were long gone by now, and most Florida counties had switched to a system of paper ballots that voters filled out by hand and fed into scanners that tabulated the votes. In Nassau County, the precinct election judges took out the memory card from the precinct tabulator and fed it over the private VPN to her office, where the results were again tabulated, all of it under the watchful eyes of security cameras and election judges from both political parties. The precinct tabulators also kept image files for each paper ballot, and tomorrow morning the precinct judges would hand-deliver the backup memory cards from the tabulators and she would do a 100 percent audit of those image files, retabulating them to determine if there were any significant discrepancies with the totals showing up tonight.

Of course, the low Republican vote could have a perfectly legitimate explanation. Perhaps there had been some last minute political scandal she had missed, some mailer that had gone out, that had shocked Nassau County voters. But if so, she hadn't seen it.

Or it could be over-votes, where people mistakenly filled in more than one circle per race. But why would they do that in the presidential race? And how likely was it that those same voters would also over-vote in the congressional?

Highly unlikely.

Actually, no, she thought. *It's statistically impossible.*

Something was wrong. Could her voting machines have been hacked? But how? They had so many layers of security, it was hard to imagine how anyone could have accessed them all across the county and its fifteen precincts. To upload a virus to the tabulators, someone would need physical access to the machines, since they were air-locked from the public internet. She wasn't worried about the ones in government buildings and community centers, which she could lock down. But others were located in churches and sports complexes where just about anyone could come in. They would have to unlock the machines—okay, that wasn't so hard, since they all had the same key. Break the tamper tape. Also possible, using nail polish remover: an old trick. Then access the operating system to upload some form of virus.

Catherine Herrera wasn't a computer whiz and didn't pretend to be one. But she was naturally suspicious by nature—much more so than the geeks who ran operations in most of Florida's counties. How many state-wide conferences and seminars had she attended where the geeks pooh-poohed the security concerns she raised? "We're in charge," they liked to say. "We designed these systems. And we are the best. Don't you worry your pretty li'l head about what's gwon'on inside."

Well, she did worry what was inside. Black box voting, everyone remembered that! And who wanted another scandal like the one in Wellington in the last election where a manual recount totally reversed the election night results? Council members announced as victors by twenty or thirty votes wound up losing by several hundred because the tabulators had been calibrated to switch columns, attributing votes for the winning candidate as votes for the loser. It was a nightmare—just the type of nightmare she wanted to avoid.

She was going to check the tabulators first thing in the morning and then do her 100 percent audit of the paper ballot images. If that didn't explain the numbers she was seeing tonight, then they had a real problem.

A truly huge problem.

A problem so big they might never find its cause.

When she got back in the next morning, she planned to call Milford Gaines, her colleague in Okaloosa County in the strongly Republican Florida panhandle. If he had the same issues, then they could be assured this was no accident. Someone had broken into their systems.

41

At 11:00 PM, the polls closed on the West Coast, allowing the networks to officially color in California, Oregon, and Washington for Governor Tomlinson, and Montana and Idaho for Trump. Fox News called Georgia, Michigan, and Minnesota for Trump, but unlike CNN and the other networks, they still were not calling Florida.

That made them the only network claiming that the election remained too close to call, and it was clear that both Galen Beaty and Kristina Brower felt increasingly uncomfortable with that decision. They brought Allison Wright, the Fox News reporter assigned to the Tomlinson campaign, on air every ten minutes or so to report on the elation that was now filling the ballroom at the Langham Hotel in Chicago, where more than 10,000 Tomlinson supporters had gathered to celebrate.

"When are they dropping the balloons, Allison?"

"If the celebrations get any louder, those balloons are going to drop on their own, Galen."

Governor Tomlinson announced that she would not appear in public before her supporters until she heard from the president. There was a lot of clucking and nodding from the talking heads at her announcement, so wise and so humble from the challenger.

"We've been told by Fox News correspondent Mandy Baz at Mar-a-Lago that we should be expecting a statement any minute now from the Trump campaign. We don't know if the president will weigh in on camera or via Twitter, or whether we'll be getting a written statement. But stay tuned," Beaty said.

"Our viewers need to take a good look at that electoral map," Kristina Brower added. "With Michigan, Georgia, and Minnesota going for President Trump, the president now has 241 confirmed electoral votes. If the other networks are right, and Florida with its 29 votes goes to Governor Tomlinson, that puts her at 266, still four votes shy of 270. She still must win either Pennsylvania or Arizona. There's no way around it, Galen. Those are her only remaining pathways to 270."

"And as you say, Kristina, the Fox News election desk continues to consider all three of those states too close to call. If the president is declared the winner in Florida, he wins his second term with exactly 270 electoral votes. A squeaker, for sure. But victory all the same."

"So, Galen. This election is still too close to call."

As they waited for more definitive results, Fox News updated reports from earlier in the day of election incidents across the country.

In suburban Bucks County, Pennsylvania, election officials had discovered an unusually high number of over-votes from what appeared to be Republican voters. As they examined the results from the tabulators that counted the paper ballots, nearly 10 percent of them were disqualified because voters had selected President Trump and the Libertarian candidate.

"And so how do we know these are Republican voters," Beaty asked Mark Enderwood with Fox affiliate WTXF, reporting from Newtown.

"Simple, Galen. Election officials here tell me that their ballot marking systems have a feature that allows voters to vote a straight party ticket. So the ballot should have been marked automatically for President Trump. The only explanation they can come up with is that the machines made an error, or that a large number of ballots had been placed into the machines with the Libertarian candidate for president already selected."

"That would be fraud, wouldn't it," Beaty said.

"Or an unbelievable mistake by precinct or county officials, Galen."

"Remind our viewers how these particular machines work, Mark."

"Well, as we've been reporting, Galen, Pennsylvania is one of several dozen states that replaced their old touch-screen voting machines with a new generation that produces paper ballots. Several different systems went into service for this year's election. In Bucks, Delaware, and Philadelphia Counties, the new system still has a touch-screen interface with the voter, but instead of directly recording the voter's selection electronically, it marks and prints out a paper ballot that the voter must feed into a scanner to be tabulated. So it would appear these voters never thought to verify their paper ballot, since they had voted a straight Republican ticket."

Beaty exchanged a glance with his co-host. "Really?" he said. "Ten percent of Republican voters never thought to check their paper ballots to see if they were accurate?"

"That's what we're being told, Galen."

Granger called Navid.

"Please tell me you are watching Fox News, not just our own networks."

"Sure, boss."

"So what's this about over-votes in Philadelphia, Bucks, and Delaware Counties?"

"Again, boss. Not us. Those are the old touch screens. Okay, new touch screens, ballot marking systems, but still. We don't touch 'em. Too obvious. Before 2016, that's why Obama won Pennsylvania twice. Now state officials are wise to that game."

"So who is doing this?"

"Dontcha love it?"

"No, I don't love it, Navid. I want to see the results we discussed. I don't want to see all this uncertainty."

"Chaos, Granger. Chaos!"

"What do you mean?"

"Chaos is our friend. We didn't do it. We aren't responsible. Ain't no trace back to us."

"So how many votes are we talking about here?"

"The Republican over-votes in those three counties?"

"Yeah. Bucks, Delaware, and Philly."

"Hold one," Navid said. He swiveled down his long narrow desk and clicked on a separate keyboard commanding a dual monitor.

"Ballpark, boss: Ten percent of Republicans in Bucks: 15,000. Delaware and Philly: 10,000 each. So 35,000 altogether."

"And so, out of six million votes cast, what does that make?"

Navid did a quick calculation.

"A little less than zero point six percent, boss. Just squeaking out of audit range."

"Please tell me, my skanky Parsee friend, that you actually are banking a larger margin."

"Hahahahaha, Granger. How many times I gotta tell you: I pull the switch, we get the results. Nowhere near the margin of error."

"You got a real number?"

"Pennsylvania? 120,000 votes. That's two percent."

"So even if those 35,000 votes are counted against us, we still win."

"You got that right, boss. Hahahahaha!"

42

att Hall and Aaron Duffy were the only two Fox News analysts who didn't appear to be swept away by Tomlinson fever. Hall had done a deep dive into county-by-county returns in western Pennsylvania and compared them to the way the same counties had voted in 2016. Trump was actually winning fewer votes in the Pennsylvania rust belt than he had in 2016, nearly ten percent fewer, in fact. A similar trend was occurring in the purple counties close to Philadelphia, although the numbers were much smaller. Overall, Trump was down about 120,000 votes in Pennsylvania from where he had been in 2016.

"Kristina was right earlier to point at the electoral college map," Hall said. "This thing is far from over, Galen. I think you're going to have election officials working over-time into the wee hours of the morning double-checking their tabulators, because these results just don't add up."

He pointed to the high enthusiasm levels in neighboring West Virginia and Ohio, where Trump was pulling in higher margins than he had in 2016. And then, not only had he won Michigan and Wisconsin—again, with bigger margins than 2016—but he had picked up Minnesota by a margin of 21,000 votes.

"So you've got to ask yourself, Galen. If the president is doing so well in those other states, how can it be that he is under-performing in western Pennsylvania, which has many of the same kind of voters? It just doesn't make sense."

Hall saw a similar thing going on in densely populated urban areas, which tend to have a high proportion of African-American voters. In Wayne County, Michigan, which includes Detroit, you had 392 precincts in 2016 that recorded 95 percent of votes cast for Hillary Clinton, and only 3 percent for Trump. More than half of the precincts in Detroit had more votes counted than people who actually turned out to vote. And still Trump won the state by 10,000 votes. Flash forward to tonight: Trump won 25 percent of the vote in those same inner city Detroit precincts. The same thing in Milwaukee.

"So if African-American voters are surging for Donald Trump in Michigan and Wisconsin, how come they aren't showing up for him in Philadelphia? And yet, that's what we've been seeing tonight," Hall said.

"I've got to tell you, Galen. This is beginning to look an awful lot like the kind of election shenanigans we've been told to expect from the Russians or some other foreign player, seeking to create chaos across this country. And I haven't gotten started on Florida, where Palm Beach County is using a whole new voting system for the first time this year, after the disastrous recount fiasco they had in 2018."

Kristina Brower saw something on her monitor and put up her hand.

"Sorry to cut you off, Matt, but we've got some breaking news here," she said.

The Fox News Alert logo flashed on the screen. Beaty turned to the camera and squared his jaw, putting on his game face.

"It is now midnight here on the East Coast, and polls have closed in Alaska and Hawaii and all across the country. The Associated Press election desk, which as our viewers know is coordinating the state-by-state results of this historic 2020 presidential election, has now called Pennsylvania for Governor Cheryl Tomlinson, and with that win, they have designated the governor the president-elect of the United States. While we at Fox News generally follow the calls the AP makes, this puts us in an unprecedented situation because our own election desk has not called Florida for Tomlinson. And without Florida, the Pennsylvania win puts her at just 257. She needs a clear win in Florida for her to become president-elect."

Kristina Brower jumped in with a statement just issued by the Trump campaign, refusing to concede defeat. The president was concerned with widespread reports of election incidents across the country, almost all of them involving Republican voters. His campaign was in touch with election officials in Florida, Pennsylvania, and Arizona, and was being told that results in all three states were still too close for them to call a winner. All three states intended to begin mandatory recounts later this morning, the day after the election. The president was sending teams of campaign lawyers to assist their efforts and expected Governor Tomlinson to do the same. The president had already communicated his decision to the governor and asked her to join him in exercising restraint as they awaited results. "Americans engage in a long, grueling election campaign every four years," the statement concluded. "We can afford to wait another day or even more if necessary to learn the true results."

"Wow," Beaty said, after he had read the statement to the Fox News audience. "I am speechless. Matt?"

"I can only say this, Galen. Half the people who voted today are going to bed believing the president was re-elected and the other half believing Governor Tomlinson is president-elect. Things could get very nasty out there."

Granger had watched the president-elect's face go from jubilation, when the AP called Pennsylvania and the election, to a knowing smirk when her aide announced the call from President Trump, to downright alarm after she picked up the phone and the president's message sank in.

"Navid?" he shouted into the phone. "Will we survive a recount?"

His Asian whiz-kid just laughed at him.

"That's actually a question, Navid."

"Sure, boss," he said, once he had recovered. "Ninety-nine percent."

"What's the one percent?"

"Hahahahaha."

"I'm paid to know these things, Navid. You're paid to tell me."

"Okay. Ninety-nine point nine percent."

"And?"

"It's not going to happen."

"What's not going to happen?"

"An actual recount. They're going to be auditing the digital image files. Like, man, we *own* the digital files."

PART III

THE RECOUNT

In his arrogance the wicked man hunts
    down the weak,
who are caught in the schemes he devises…
He says to himself, 'God has forgotten;
He covers his face and never sees.'

PSALM 10: 2; 11 (NIV)

43

Most Americans, even political junkies who stay up until the TV anchors have called it quits, believe that the mechanics of elections stops on election night. Unless they work in an election office, or as an election judge, they would never suspect the number of gears thrown in motion the very next morning, regardless of the results of the night before. Elections are supposed to present closure. They are supposed to be the final result, the end of the political campaign, when America votes and determines winners and losers and then gets on with her business. But in fact, it's not until the day after the elections that official results are actually tabulated. And in many cases, it's not for another two or three weeks—and sometimes longer—before those results are certified and declared immutable.

Few Americans outside of Floridians paid much attention to the 2018 recount fiasco when officials ultimately threw up their hands after ten days of riotous recounting and declared Republicans Kirk Norton and Rick Scott the next Governor and U.S. Senator. And while Democrat Party gubernatorial candidate

Stacey Abrams in Georgia wanted Americans across the country to pay attention to her claims that somehow Republicans had prevented African-Americans from voting—and thus, presumably, denied her victory—no one outside of a faithful inner circle or party wonks paid her much heed. The Georgia turnout numbers had been sky high, especially in black communities.

The morning after this year's election was no different. Most Americans woke up believing that Governor Tomlinson had been elected president with 286 electoral votes and that any protests by Donald Trump of problems with the Election Day vote tallies were sour grapes. Adding to that impression were the unofficial results from Arizona, which put Governor Tomlinson ahead by a 2 percent margin. Meanwhile, election judges and precinct captains from across the country were congregating at canvassing centers, hand-delivering the sealed ballot boxes and the precious memory cards from the precinct vote tabulators so they could be re-tabulated by county officials on separate machines. While each county had slightly different procedures and equipment for carrying out the official morning-after vote count, almost all of them involved physically transporting the memory cards, because of the widespread belief—reinforced by warnings from the FBI and DHS—that data transmitted over the internet was easily subject to hacking. And while the national media duly reported on the president's 10:30 AM tweet that he had just instructed the FBI and the Department of Homeland Security to investigate potential interference with the nation's election systems, nobody took it seriously. Americans had gone back to work.

@POTUS: I applaud the efforts by FBI and DHS over the past 18 months to harden our election systems. Unclear results in Florida, Pennsylvania, and Arizona

*require a full investigation into outside interference,
which I have ordered FBI and DHS to begin.*

Shortly before noon, Nelson Aguilar's campaign team reassembled at his headquarters across from Wheaton Mall. The volunteers and the well-wishers were gone. Now it was down to just the three paid campaign workers: Annie Bryant, the Crocodile, and Camilla Broadstreet. No one had gotten much sleep and all of them had red eyes. Aguilar welcomed them into the conference room and led them in a brief prayer. "Lord God, we can aspire to no higher calling than to be instruments of your glory and recognize it's not up to us to determine how we achieve that," he prayed. "Lord, make your will known and we, your humble servants, will obey you."

The final unofficial results from election night, with 100 percent of precincts reporting, were still up on the whiteboard. The numbers were devastating.

District 8:

Nelson Aguilar, Republican:	131,411	36.16%
Hugh McKenzie, Democrat:	220,506	60.67%
Jason Levin, Green:	11,543	3.18%

The Crocodile was urging Aguilar to call McKenzie to concede.

"It's still not too late, boss. I think you should have done it last night."

"I know. So you told me," Aguilar said. "Annie, what do you think?"

Annie's secret was now out in the open. They all knew she was dating Gordon and knew what Gordon did for a living. So, she was now their in-house expert on the election results—not on what they meant politically, that was the Crocodile's job. But on their actual validity.

"The numbers are not right," she said.

"Ya, I know we don't like the results. But how much not right," the Crocodile said.

"A lot not right," she said. "Like perhaps, upside-down."

"This is what Gordon told you last night?" Aguilar asked.

"Not in so many words. But yes," she said.

Gordon hadn't actually come home until 3:00 AM and hadn't woken her when he crept into her bed. Only later, when they shared a coffee at around 7:00 AM, did she quiz him on the election night results.

"He was absolutely convinced they were not right. But exactly how, and why—"

"He didn't know," the Crocodile said, finishing her thought.

"He's got some ideas he needs to work on today," she said. "A working hypothesis."

"Involving…?"

"He wants to run the numbers from the Montgomery County early voting sites again, zeroing out the votes from the touch-screen machines. It's just a hunch for now. But he thinks that will give him data he can use to get to the next step."

"Oh come on, AB. How long are we going to let this thing drag out? Nelson's going to look like a sore loser if he doesn't call McKenzie to congratulate him. McKenzie beat him three to one in Montgomery County, for crying out loud! It's time to end this thing and keep our powder dry for the next time. Nelson is now a former congressional candidate who waged the best campaign ever against McKenzie. He can hold his head high."

"He's right," Aguilar said. "These numbers are so big…. Unless we have something absolutely solid, I've got to concede."

"Our people are going to be devastated," Camilla said. "You can't concede, *jefe*."

"Yes, I can," Aguilar said. "And if Gordon comes up with something solid, I can also say later that new information has come up to make me withdraw my concession."

"It wouldn't be the first time," Annie said.

Young Brady swung by the campaign office shortly after three, once school had let out. He had slept less than the rest of them, getting up at 6:50 AM to make his 7:05 AM bus, and was still running on adrenalin.

"Everybody knows what happened last night," he blurted out, pointing to the whiteboard with the election results. "Every kid in my school knows something fishy happened. All their parents voted for you, Dad."

"Not every one of them, *chico*," Aguilar said.

"Just about!"

School had been tough that day. Brady found himself replaying the movie of election night all day long, starting with the moment of victory shortly after the polls closed and the first results were announced, and then the stunning reversal when McKenzie jumped ahead.

"The election was hacked!" he said.

"We don't know that, and you shouldn't say that to your friends until we do."

"But Dad, there is no other explanation. You know that's true!"

Annie gently pulled him aside and took him into her office. She felt badly for him and wanted to offer him some consolation.

"You know, I have a friend," she began. "He works for the State Board of Elections, doing their IT. He agrees with you that the election was hacked. But he can't prove it, either."

"Everyone knows those touch-screen machines can be hacked," he blurted out. "I could write the program in half an hour if I wanted."

"I'm sure you could—and I'm glad you didn't," she said, trying to get him to laugh.

"I bet those FBI types aren't helping, either," he said.

"Actually, we haven't heard from them since before the election."

"What does your friend think?" he asked.

"He's got a theory," Annie said. "He thinks it's got to be either the touch-screen machines or the precinct tabulators."

"To hack the touch-screen machines, you have to gain physical access," Brady said. "That's actually the hardest part. An eleven-year-old kid can write the script—two of them actually did at DEFCON two years ago. Once you're in, you change the tabulation algorithm, and because the machines are daisy-chained, it spreads to all of them almost instantaneously. But getting access to the machines, that's something else. That would take, like, real criminal intent."

"It's crime enough, Brady, to change the vote count, don't you think?"

"What I mean is, like old-fashioned criminals. People that break into banks, not cyber. That's not what hackers do."

"The other option is the precinct tabulators. Gordon says that's a lot harder."

"Aren't they air-gapped?" Brady asked.

"You mean, separated from the internet? Yes."

"So somebody would have to be inside the air gap. That means it's probably somebody in his office or on the Montgomery County board of elections. That would be, like, whoa. Super criminal. Isn't that what the FBI is for?"

"The FBI likes to chase Russian ghosts," Annie said. "And teenage hackers. But you're right. That would be, like, super criminal. It's hard to imagine McKenzie doing such a thing."

"Well, yeah!" Brady said. "He's a politician!"

"What's that supposed to mean? Your dad is a politician, too."

"But he comes from the real world. McKenzie is entitled."

"What makes you say that?

Brady swept the question aside, already onto the next thought. "Did you pay any attention to his social media campaign? I don't think he's got a computer guy smart enough to carry off an SQL injection behind a VPN. That'd be quite an exploit."

Hmm, she thought. *That's exactly what Gordon said.* She liked this kid and didn't want to see him get hurt.

"I'll let you know what I hear," she said. "But don't go snooping around. You don't want to be drawing attention to yourself."

44

Gordon Utz didn't have much time to work on his theory of what might have gone wrong on election night. He had twenty-three county supervisors of elections to deal with, plus Baltimore City, and they began trickling into the main election center in Annapolis at 8:00 AM that morning. Each came trailing a Republican and Democrat election judge, and several bag carriers—or more accurately, ballot-box handlers, entrusted with the sealed and numbered ballot boxes from each county. The supervisors themselves carried the memory cards from the 2,162 ADA-compliant touch-screen machines, one per precinct and early voting site, which Gordon and the IT team would tabulate separately, as well as another 2,162 USB drives from the paper ballot tabulators. The county IT guys had already uploaded the tabulation files and the PDFs of the ballot images for the second time over the state board of elections VPN earlier that morning. These, too, would be tabulated a second time using special auditing software, not the county tabulators.

Redundancy was key to election security. If you could reproduce the same results on different equipment, you could feel confident in releasing the results to the public. They operated under the general principle, inculcated to election officials all across the country over the past eighteen months by roving DHS security teams, that anything driven by software was vulnerable to hacking. Conversely, it was statistically unlikely that two separate, air-gapped systems would be hacked in the same way. That was the message Lisa Rasmussen put out on the BoE website that morning in the latest edition of her "Rumor Control" feature. Over the past four years, Maryland had taken extraordinary measures to upgrade and modernize its election systems, so citizens could feel confident in the election results.

But Gordon didn't feel confident in the results. Nor did he feel confident in confiding his doubts to Rasmussen. He needed more to go on than just the early voting stats or the Aguilar campaign polling data. He needed hard facts, hard evidence of a breach.

By 4:00 PM, his team had completed the audit, and the re-tabulated state-wide results matched those uploaded over the VPN on election night, except for the DRE machines in Baltimore—naturally. There, a surge of individuals not appearing on the voter rolls had voted provisionally on the DREs, and inevitably their votes got commingled with those of legitimate voters.

"So you're saying it was fraud?" Lisa Rasmussen objected when he raised the issue with her privately.

"Yes."

"Are you blaming the Baltimore city supervisor of elections?"

"I'm not blaming anybody at this point. But those votes should have been walled off until we could verify the identities of the voters."

"Did it change the results of the election?"

"No," he admitted. "It just made Grady Jones look somewhat less bad."

"Excuse me?"

"Without those votes, he was at 59.3 percent. With them, he topped sixty percent. Sounds better to say you were re-elected with over sixty percent of the vote, doesn't it?"

"That is not sufficient reason for me not to release the official results. Unless, of course, you've got other problems."

Gordon caught himself. "No, ma'am," he said finally.

When he got back to his office, he pulled up the spreadsheet of the Montgomery County early voting centers he had set up last night and, using the new data sent down this morning, separated out the DRE votes from the paper ballots that went through the tabulators.

Once again, the numbers jumped off his screen.

At all eleven early voting centers, McKenzie won exactly 73.4 percent of the paper ballots. Regardless of the number of votes cast, the percentage remained constant. That was statistically impossible. With the touch-screen votes included, McKenzie's percentages varied from a low 62 percent in Wheaton to a high 78.2 percent at the Silver Spring Civic Building, both of which were Aguilar's home turf. What did that mean, Gordon wondered? He made a note to conduct a logic and accuracy test on the DRE machines from Silver Spring, but if they had been hacked, it was likely the hacker would have written his RAT to deactivate and erase itself after the polls closed. That left the stunning results from the Dominant Technologies paper ballot tabulators. Someone or something had breached the VPN and injected the fixed percentage result, taking advantage of the tabulator's ability to count fractional votes. But how? He himself had downloaded all the patches and updates from the manufacturer and posted them to the counties over the State's FTP site, itself protected behind a VPN. No one he had not personally authorized could get into the network.

He checked the access logs and found nothing out of the ordinary. Most of the IT guys at the twenty-three counties and Baltimore City had downloaded the patches within twenty-four hours of his notification that they were available. He sent out the last one on September 29, he saw. No one had actually accessed the State's FTP site after October 2—except for the failed attempt to penetrate it he had taken to the FBI.

There had to be something with that last patch, he thought. There was no other logical explanation.

45

ight people were shot dead on the streets of Chicago over election night, two of them children under the age of fourteen. It was just another night of random gang violence in the Windy City, but the ballroom of the Langham Hotel looked like the aftermath of a high school prom, littered with red-white-and-blue streamers and overturned chairs and the brightly colored husks of thousands of balloons, stuck in gooey clumps to the floor. There were so many champagne corks lying about that one member of the clean-up crew, Estelle Estaban, tripped and broke her leg. But while Chicagoans celebrated the election of the Illinois Governor to the highest office in the land, down in Lauderhill, Florida, angry crowds had gathered waving large envelopes. They were chanting, "Count our votes! Count our votes!" Many of them carried Tomlinson/Bellinger signs. They were trying to drop off vote-by-mail ballots the morning after, but the deadline had been 7:00 PM on election night.

Under Florida law, county boards of elections had four days to report official election results, and Broward, Palm Beach, and Miami-Dade County officials were in no hurry to rush the canvassing. Memories of the 2018 election recount were still fresh, and everyone was hoping the election night results, which showed Governor Tomlinson winning by a 2.1 percent margin, would hold so they could avoid the messy process of recounting the paper ballots by hand.

The Reverend James Dupree, who ran a nation-wide voter registration group on behalf of the DNC, had mustered around 300 demonstrators in front of a stately government structure in Tallahassee. The open esplanade had no shade, and the late morning sun made Reverend Dupree's dark forehead glisten with sweat as he exhorted his followers.

"Certify now!" he coached them. "Certify now!" they chanted.

They wanted the state supervisor of elections to announce the official results, which everyone knew meant that Governor Tomlinson was now the president-elect.

"Call the vote!" the Reverend urged his supporters. "Call the vote!"

"Call the vote!" they echoed.

Up at the Yulee Government Center, Catherine Herrera, supervisor of elections for Nassau County, was on the phone with Milford Gaines, her colleague in Okaloosa County in the Florida panhandle. Like her, he was not an IT specialist and had a healthy distrust for the security geeks. Whenever they told him their system was 100 percent secure, tight as a drum, his nose told him they had a problem. A former Navy SEAL, he was used to things blowing up on calm days.

"It's just not possible, Ford," she said. "There have been no indicators that John Rutherford would come in at anything less than seventy percent, and zero reason why Trump should have lost ten percent of his support in this election."

Both of them had done their 100 percent audit run early that morning, and in neither county were there any discrepancies between the precinct vote tallies from election night and the retabulation.

"Remember, we are just retabulating what the computers have in their memories," Gaines said. "Garbage in, garbage out."

"What do you mean?"

"We are tabulating the ballot images, not the actual paper ballots."

"But the images were created by the ballots. I mean, they are the scanned images of the ballots."

"Right. But they are *electronic* images. When the voter puts his ballot into the scanner, the software in the machine generates the PDF file. And so our tabulators are merely recounting those same software-generated ballots, not the actual ballots themselves."

"I knew we had to talk," she said. "I knew something was wrong but couldn't put my finger on it."

Florida law only required a recount of the paper ballots if a race was decided by less than one-half of a percentage point. With the unofficial results showing Governor Tomlinson winning by 2.1 percent, that was not the case. But it also gave the county supervisors of elections twelve days to certify the results, and wide latitude to do their own examination of the tabulation of the ballots to determine if it was accurate. This procedure was generally called a "risk-limiting" audit, and meant choosing at random 2 percent of their precincts, breaking out the paper ballots, and feeding them into the precinct tabulators again.

"That's not going to help," Gaines said. "If the tabulators gave us a bad result first time around, they're going to do the same thing if we just repeat the same process. We need new tabulators, from another state."

"How are we going to do that? What's the justification?"

"There is none," he said. "In my former life, we called it extreme ownership. You are in charge, you take responsibility. Two of our guys wrote a book about that. If need be, you can ask for forgiveness later."

Each county supervisor of elections office had a discretionary budget reserved for post-election audits and recounts. Normally, they wouldn't have to dip into it this year because of the apparently clear result. But they resolved to break into the piggy bank. Gaines knew where to go.

"Nebraska," he said.

"Why Nebraska?"

"Melissa Black down in Miami-Dade brought in tabulators from Nebraska for the 2018 recount. Let me give her a call."

It was their best shot. The clock was ticking, Herrera knew.

46

When it became clear that Governor Norton wasn't going to immediately certify the election results, Granger ginned up the party apparatus. Calls went out to teams of lawyers who had signed up during the campaign and were on stand-by for just such an eventuality. By the close of business on Wednesday, the day after the election, Granger had lined up some 200 volunteer lawyers to accompany him down to Florida and hired the venerable Washington, DC, white shoe law firm of Myers, Ogilvy, Pantazis, and Pugh to lead the legal effort to get Florida to certify the results.

Granger flew down to Fort Lauderdale early Thursday afternoon and set himself up on the top floor of the Ritz Carlton on Beach Boulevard, where he had requested a suite overlooking the Intracoastal and the city, better to keep an eye on things. He'd be damned if he was going to hunker down in the cramped sweaty headquarters of the Broward County election office in Lauderhill. It was located in a mall, for crying out loud! He resolved to avoid the pool and its magnificent bar that at nighttime appeared to be suspended over the Atlantic until he had a better grip on the recount process. As things turned out, he wasn't going to be spending much time at the pool.

The Trump campaign predictably followed suit and sent teams of lawyers to Doral, where the Miami-Dade canvassing board met, and to Riviera Beach in Palm Beach County, in addition to Fort Lauderdale. The Trump effort was led by Trump's personal attorney, Ivo Silander, a former federal prosecutor who had put away terrorists and big name mobsters. Granger knew he was a formidable opponent and found it mildly amusing that Trump had put him up at his Doral golf resort. He could have gone to the Trump Sunny Isles beach resort, but then Trump would have had to shell out hard cash, as it was independently managed. And why not Mar-a-Lago? Maybe Trump had already rented all the guest suites. For all his love of bling, Trump remained Scottish to the end.

On Friday morning, Granger settled down to watch the canvassing boards, which he did in turns, by calling the chief Democratic lawyer sitting with the election observers and getting him or her to turn on their cell phone video. What surprised him the most was the inactivity. They had just one more day to complete the election night vote tally and no one seemed in a hurry. The tabulators they had set up were much larger than he had imagined. Propped up on long desks, they dwarfed the election staff. For now, no actual ballots were in sight. The counting was going on electronically, inside the machines.

"Tell me that is a good thing?" he asked Navid. "And what in the world are those gigantic machines?"

"You must be looking at the 486 tabulators," he said.

"Thanks for that intelligence, but I need *information*."

"Those are the central tabulators. Don't worry about them machines. They will give the same result as the precinct tabulators did on election night, hahahahaha."

"How's that?"

"The 486 is just a jacked-up version of the model 48 precinct tabulator, you know, the ballot scanner that voters see. But under the hood, they are the same. Same logic board, same patch."

"So as long as we stay with the scanned images, we don't care about an audit."

"That's right."

"And what if someone calls for a risk-limiting audit of the paper ballots?"

"Hahahahaha!"

"A serious answer, please."

"So, they run the paper ballots through the same tabulators running the same patch they were running on Election Day. They get the same result."

"That's what I wanted to hear, Navid."

Navid is still the man!

Governor Norton gave a 5:00 PM press conference in Tallahassee, along with Secretary of State Shelley Hughes, who administered the elections, and Attorney General Craig Romero. The three of them comprised the Elections Canvassing Commission. It was a stacked deck from the start, Granger knew. Norton was explaining why the State had asked the counties to take their time in compiling the initial vote tally. It was a tortured explanation that immediately made Granger sit up, because clearly something was going on that Norton wasn't saying. He repeatedly made reference to chapter 102-141 of State election law as justification for the decision of the Commission to hold back on certification.

"Are you watching this?" Granger asked Johanna Weaver down in the Lauderhill Mall. "What in the Sam Hill is chapter 102-141 of State election law?"

"Hold one, sir. Let me get to a more private setting."

The lawyer put Granger on hold—dead silence over the muted line—then reappeared to the sound of a truck grinding its gears.

"So. Chapter 102-141 governs the duties of the county canvassing boards," she said. "Basically, what the governor is saying is that he is deferring to the counties to tell him when they are ready to send in their final count."

"Why would he do that?" Granger said.

"He isn't saying why. He's just slow-rolling this."

"I don't like it."

"By law, the counties actually have until noon of the twelfth day after the general election to certify their results. They are supposed to send in an 'official' tally four days after the election, but under 102-141 they can delay that for just about any reason."

"He must know something," Granger said. "You need to find out what he knows."

Granger made another call to Governor Tomlinson.

"Time isn't our friend," he said. "We need to push hard to certify now."

The governor's fund-raising team had already launched a Florida Recount Appeal. Granger suggested they transfer an additional $400,000 cash payment to Reverend James Dupree to step up his Tallahassee protests. "Every Democratic talking head on every show in the country needs to repeat that twice in every sentence," he said. "'Certify now!' That's our call sign. I don't care if people get tired of hearing it. Certify now."

"Certify now," she said softly. "I like it."

Wasn't it sweet irony for them to be calling the law to their side, Granger thought. It was time for him to head down to the poolside bar.

47

Gordon Utz was fighting a rear-guard battle against his boss, elections supervisor Lisa Rasmussen. Absent any serious election-day mishaps, and with no candidates or voters filing complaints, she saw no reason why they shouldn't convene the board of elections to begin the process of certifying the Maryland election results.

On a lark, he called Jason Barber, his counterpart on the Montgomery County Board of Elections, and spelled out the discrepancies he had found between the actual vote count and the pre-election polls, as well as the unusually low re-elect numbers of Grady Jones in Baltimore. He also mentioned the statistically impossible numbers from the early voting sites. Barber liked to call himself a graduate of Hacker U, the Chaos Computing Club at the College Park campus of the University of Maryland. He was one of the elite, masters of the digital universe.

"Dude, like, we are *secure*. We've got protocols."

"So what do you think happened at the early voting sites," Gordon said.

"What do you mean what happened?"

"How is it that when you remove the votes from the touch-screen machines, every single early voting site comes up with the identical percentage of votes for Congressman McKenzie?"

"What are you talking about, man? I've got numbers all over the charts."

"I don't mean numbers of votes. I mean percentages. McKenzie got 73.4 percent—exactly 73.4 percent—from the tabulators in all eleven early voting centers."

"Impossible."

"I agree. Take a look."

Gordon could hear him clicking on his keyboard and assumed he was pulling up the numbers. Then the clicking stopped, and Jason groaned.

"Oh man, this can't be happening," he wailed.

"That's exactly what I was saying. So why *did* it happen?"

"It's a fixed percentage—an algorithm."

"Only possible answer. And where do the tabulation algorithms come from?"

"Dominant Technologies."

"Right again. Every time they make an update to the software they send out a patch. The last patch they sent out I received on September 29, and you installed sometime between then and October 2. Right?"

Jason didn't answer.

"Right?" he asked again.

"I can't believe this," Jason said finally.

"I'm glad you're starting to agree with me." Gordon laughed.

"Dude. Like, you don't understand. I must have fallen for it."

"Fallen for what?"

"The last patch."

Jason went on to explain what had happened. Around three weeks ago, he had received an email from a guy at the Dominant

Technologies state support division, with a link to the most recent patch.

"You mean you clicked on a link in an email from a guy you didn't know?"

"Hey. It came in over the VPN. The guy had the correct naming protocol and digital signature."

"Did you actually check the signature hash?"

"Dude, like, would you ever do that? To email coming in over the VPN?"

"Hey. I'm not blaming you. Just tell me exactly what happened."

"So the link reffed the Dominant Technologies FTP site—"

"You mean, something that looked like the Dominant FTP site."

"Yeah. And there was a whole list of patches, and they all matched up to the earlier ones we had installed, except for the newest one right on top. So I downloaded it and installed it onto our machines."

"Okay. So that patch must have included the tabulation algorithm that affected the early voting sites. Now we need to see if they had a similar algorithm for Election Day ballots. We need to rip open that patch and go over it line by line."

Barber called back a half-hour later with more bad news.

"I found the email. It came in on October 24. It was so close to the election I figured they were trying to be helpful by reaching out to us county techs directly."

"Does the guy who sent it have a name?"

"Eric Figueroa. But the link is dead."

"How about the disk image from the backup drive?"

"Already checked. Wiped. Dude, like, with a cloth. Hahahaha."

Damn, Gordon thought. *These guys were good.* They must have inserted a rootkit deep inside the system that contained a routine to wipe the backups whenever they were called. If you were going to steal an election, better not to leave any fingerprints behind.

He asked Barber to try a cold exfil of the operating system from one of the early voting tabulators, although he didn't give it much chance of success. If the hackers were as good as they seemed, they would have coded the algorithm to erase itself if anyone attempted to debug it without the correct permissions.

The only way they were going to catch them was by a manual audit of the paper ballots. But Lisa Rasmussen would never go for that. The results of the election were not even close, so what was the point?

That's why this hack was so brilliant.

48

Marcie had made herself at home in Annie's townhouse in Urbana. It was Friday night, and she knew the two of them were still hungover from the election, so she called Annie and offered to make dinner.

"Let's just make it an evening," she said. "You two need some comic relief. I promise I won't stay too long."

She made them meat loaf with a mix of ground pork, veal, and lamb with a mushroom cream sauce, and it was to die for. Gordon brought several bottles of old vine Zinfandel. And, as promised, Marcie kept them laughing for several hours.

"This morning when I left the house, I placed my Remington 12-gauge semi-automatic shotgun right in the doorway. You know the one, right, Gordon? You learned to shoot skeet on it."

"Right, Mom." He rolled his eyes.

"I know what you're thinking, honey. Just wait. So I left six cartridges next to it, propped the door open, and went out."

Annie nearly choked on her wine but did her best to hide it. She had heard this one before.

"While I was gone, the mailman delivered the mail, Mr. Schumacher's son from across the street mowed the lawn, just about everybody in the neighborhood walked their dog, and cars stopped at the stop sign in front of the house.

"When I came back an hour later, I checked on the gun. It was still sitting there, right where I had left it. It hadn't moved itself. It hadn't killed anyone. It hadn't even loaded itself."

"I know you like guns, Mom," Gordon said. "Your meat loaf is great, too."

"But Gordon, don't you watch TV or read the newspapers? My gun was supposed to have killed people! Committed mass murder! All by itself! I must have the laziest gun in the world! Don't you know that the United States is the gun murder capital of the world? My gun didn't kill anybody!"

Gordon still didn't get it, and Annie couldn't stop from chortling.

"Gordon, you'd better get rid of the spoons in the kitchen," Marcie said. "I've heard they're supposed to make you fat."

Later, once the wine took the edge off his battles in Annapolis, Gordon started to explain what had happened with the election. Lisa Rasmussen had wrapped him in knots. Legally, there was no way he could call for a recount in CD-8 where Nelson Aguilar had lost inexplicably to Congressman McKenzie. And yet, he was convinced that the vote had been rigged by malware injected into the voting machines through a patch sent from the manufacturer or someone impersonating them.

"And by an extraordinary coincidence, the same manufacturer, Dominant Technologies, supplies voting machines to all of the states that Governor Tomlinson flipped this year. Florida, Pennsylvania, North Carolina, Arizona. And a few others she won by bigger margins than anyone would have thought. How do you like that?" he said.

"What's a patch?" Marcie asked.

So Gordon explained. All the voting machines used a standard commercial operating system, just like any computer. But because the machines were proprietary to the companies that sold them, only those suppliers—not the software giants—could send out security updates or "patches" to protect them from known viruses and other glitches. What if, under the guise of sending a security patch, the manufacturer sent out a sub-routine that altered the way the voting machines tabulated the votes and did it in such a way that no one would ever see it?

"That would make the Russia collusion look like a tea party in a doll house," Annie said.

"Which it was, by the way," Gordon added.

"You said Dominant Technologies. Right, dear?" Marcie said.

"Yes."

"That's the same Dominant Technologies that's based in Dayton, Ohio?"

"How do you know that, Mom?"

"Because everyone on my Facebook knows how evil they are. Didn't you know they were bought out by Richard Foreman Hall in 2017?"

"*The* Richard Foreman Hall?" Annie asked.

"The one and only. Billionaire hedge fund investor from San Francisco. Big Democrat donor. And all-around scumbag," Marcie said. "He not only wants to take Trump down. He wants to take America and all of our friends down. He has spent billions of dollars around the world to undermine pro-American governments and support socialists and Antifa and all kinds of anti-American groups. This man is seriously evil."

Gordon gripped his forehead with a hand. His mom came up with such weird information at times, most of it from Facebook. Normally, he didn't pay it any attention.

"You've heard of this guy?" he asked Annie.

"Oh, yeah."

"And this is for real, not the fever swamps? Like he owns Dominant Technologies?"

"That's pretty easy to confirm," she said, getting out her phone.

Ten seconds later she showed him her screen, with the Dominant Technologies investor information webpage.

"Look here, under institutional investors."

The link showed that the hedge fund owned by Richard Foreman Hall controlled 23.5 percent of Dominant Technologies stock, and that a Hall crony sat on the DT board.

"I'd say that would give them the inside track," Annie said.

"So conceivably, Hall—through his nominee on the board—could get the company to hire someone who might do something contrary to the company's best commercial interests," Gordon said.

"But that something would be virtually invisible," Marcie added. "How would anyone figure out what he had done?"

"So there would be no risk," Gordon said. "Or little risk, at any rate."

"And if anyone ever found out, they burn the guy. Or he just disappears."

"Expendable."

It was perfect, Gordon thought.

But he had one advantage over Richard Foreman Hall: He knew the name of the someone who had sent the patch. Or, at least, he knew the name that someone had used on an email. Now he had to document what the patch had actually done.

"You should go to the FBI," Annie said.

"No way!" Marcie almost shouted.

"Why not?"

"Are you kidding? After what they did to our president? Who can trust the FBI?" Marcie said.

"Mom's probably right," Gordon said. "I've gotten no help from them so far. And every time I've gone to them, bad things have happened."

He had to pursue this alone. Quietly. With little talk on the phone or by email. He had to assume that any electronic communication could be monitored.

But was the FBI really interested in him?

Hard to believe.

49

Officials in Phoenix, Arizona, completed their canvas over the weekend and declared Governor Tomlinson and Senator Bellinger the winners of Arizona's eleven electoral votes. That put the Democratic Party nominees at 297 electoral votes, if you included Florida.

But without Florida—which Governor Norton still refused to call—they were at 268. If Florida went to Trump, he would win re-election in a squeaker: 270-268.

Granger made the rounds of the Sunday talk shows, pounding out the party line.

"There is just no way the president is going to win Florida," he told CNN's Keith Cobb. "We are ahead by more than 186,000 votes, just over two percent. Frankly, I don't understand why he insists on putting the nation through this type of trauma all over again. He's just a sore loser. It's time to certify now."

On *Fox News Sunday*, he ridiculed Florida governor Kirk Norton. "I don't know where the governor learned his 'rithmatic, Benjamin. It must have been that fancy law school he attended. This election is nowhere near the margin of error. It's time to certify now."

Former Obama White House official Jarrett Herr introduced Granger's segment on *This Week* with an attempt at irony. "And so once again, the fate of America hinges on how a handful of officials in Florida decide to count the votes. Here's the president tweeting just an hour ago:

> @realDonaldTrump: *The great state of Florida is right to take its time to make sure every legal vote is counted. I have instructed the Dept of Homeland Security to provide every assistance Governor Norton might require to determine the accuracy of election night vote counts.*

"What can the president possibly be talking about, Mr. Granger?"

"That's a great question, Jarrett."

And while Granger played along with the effort to ridicule the president, he was actually very worried by the president's words and his actions. How could Trump possibly believe he could beat a 2 percent lead by his opponent, the same margins, by the way, Tomlinson had racked up in North Carolina, Arizona, Nevada, and Pennsylvania? And why was he focusing on Florida and not any of those other states? Could he possibly know something? Suspect it?

He was still puzzling over Trump's odd behavior the next morning when he got a call from Congressman Hugh McKenzie.

"We have a problem," McKenzie said.

He explained that his Republican opponent had just filed a petition with the Montgomery County Board of Elections, demanding they conduct a machine recount of the paper ballots using tabulators brought in from other Maryland counties.

"What possible justification could he have for doing that?" Granger asked.

"Apparently some kid with the State board of elections did a test run on one precinct using a tabulator from Carroll County. The results were completely upside-down."

"On whose authority? The state supervisor?"

"No, I just called her. Lisa Rasmussen says it's a firing offense. He just went ahead and did it without asking. But if she fires him now, the optics won't look good."

"I hope you got some of our money left over in your campaign account," Granger said. "Because you're going to need it. I'm going to send you Harvey Simon. He's one of the best election lawyers we've got. You're going to need him. And he's not cheap."

"He's holding a press conference at 5:00 PM."

"Who's that?"

"My opponent."

"Well, let's make sure we have a lot of friendlies in the crowd who are well-briefed on Maryland election law. I'm going to call Harvey now and tell him you'll be calling him in five minutes. Your future depends on this, Hugh-boy."

Granger maintained his composure long enough to call Harvey Simon and briefly explain the situation. He had to do everything—whatever it took—to prevent the recount in the Maryland congressional race. Yes, this was more important than Florida, at least for now. No, the retainer would not be coming from the presidential recount fund but directly from McKenzie's campaign.

And then he exploded. He threw his phone against the sofa and started pounding a fist against the coffee table until it jumped across the rug. *Damn Bellinger!* They were all going to jail because of him. If he hadn't had a soft spot for that pathetic excuse of a congressman from suburban Maryland, none of this would be happening.

But Granger was not one to wallow in a dark mood. He poured himself two fingers of Maker's Mark, no ice, and as he sipped the whiskey, he knew that Navid would have a solution. He couldn't possibly have left traces in Maryland that would point to the national campaign. Those were the orders: no fingerprints.

50

Granger was getting a live feed of the Aguilar press conference from one of Harvey Simon's attorneys jammed in with the crowd outside the Montgomery County board of elections in Gaithersburg. It was a low brick building, set on a hill, so Aguilar stood naturally higher than the reporters in the parking lot. Simon and his team had worked hard over the past few hours, Granger could see. These reporters were loaded for bear.

"Mr. Aguilar!" the *Washington Post's* Darcy Macintosh called out. She was a lamp post of a woman, with a head of long dark curls dripping with grey. But because she was from the *Post*, the local reporters deferred to her. "Mr. Aguilar, what legal basis do you have for calling on the county board to do a recount?"

Aguilar exchanged a glance with AB, who had already briefed him on what to expect. "As I set out in my prepared statement, Darcy, State election law does not specify which contest shall be audited, nor does it establish any timetable for the audit, except that it must be completed within 120 days of the election."

The reporter had expected this. "Section 11-309 of the Election Law Article, sir, sets out parameters for a two percent *state-wide* audit and gives specific instructions for how one precinct from each county is to be selected at random."

"I will defer to my attorney for a specific answer to your question—that was a question, wasn't it, Darcy?" he said. The local reporters who had been following the race for the past three months laughed. "But let me just point out that in the Wheaton precinct where the paper ballots were recounted by a clean tabulator—"

"—Are you saying that the tabulators used on election night were somehow tainted?"

Aguilar nodded to Gail Copeland, a Frederick County attorney who volunteered with the Republican Lawyers Association and had immediately answered Aguilar's call for help over the weekend. Granger thought he detected a smirk on the face of the Hispanic businessman. Did he know something?

"We cannot draw any conclusions at this point about the accuracy of the precinct tabulators used for the election night count," she said. "That is precisely what the audit will determine. As for Section 11-309 of the Election Law article, you are correct: It sets out parameters for a state-wide audit, not for the purpose of determining the accuracy of the election night vote count, but merely to determine *in general* the accuracy of the new voting machines. It passed the General Assembly during the 2018 session amid widespread misgivings about the new machines. We do not base our request on 11-309 but on Section 11-307, which states—"

She pulled up the reading glasses suspended around her neck and opened her binder.

> *"'If a board of canvassers determines that there appears to be an error in the documents or records produced at the polling place following an election, then it immediately shall investigate the matter to ascertain whether the records or documents are correct.'"*

What the FGB Duck was that? Granger wondered. It sounded like an open door for McKenzie's opponent to do whatever he liked with the recount. Surely Harvey Simon's people had thought of that, no?

"We assert that the results of the verification audit conducted on the paper ballots cast in Precinct 13-44, which is Arcola Elementary School, demonstrate in and of themselves that there 'appears to be an error' in the election night results," Copeland went on.

Aguilar called on a tall male reporter in the back who was holding a legal pad.

"Clifford Lucas, Mr. Aguilar, of the *Legal Times*."

"Please go ahead, Cliff," Aguilar said.

"I think, sir, my questions are more appropriately addressed to Ms. Copeland, if you don't object."

Atta boy, Granger murmured. He could detect the not-so-subtle hand of Harvey Simon and his team.

"Ms. Copeland, you say you are basing your petition on 11-307 of the Election Law article."

"That's correct," she said. "We also note that Section 2-202(b)(8) empowers the County boards to 'make determinations and hear and decide challenges and appeals as provided by law.' So we have addressed our appeal to the Montgomery County board."

"Well that gets to my question," Lucas went on. "As provided by law—in this case, Section 2-301(6)(b)(1), subparagraph ii—no employee of the state board of elections shall 'use the individual's official authority for the purpose of influencing or affecting the result of an election.' Isn't that precisely what the employee who conducted the unauthorized audit of the Wheaton precinct did? Used his official authority to affect the result of an election?"

Brilliant, Harvey. Absolutely brilliant, Granger thought. *Attack the messenger, discredit the message.*

Aguilar chuckled. "Good thing you work for the *Legal Times*, Cliff, and not the *Post*. I have a hard enough time reading the *Post* as it is. Gail?"

She was scribbling something in her binder and didn't join in his mirth.

"Once again, we assert that the result of the initial precinct audit speaks for itself, and no attempt to discredit the manner in which the audit was conducted, or by whom, can erase that fact," she said.

"Let's give them the actual numbers, Gail? What do you think?" Aguilar said.

"That's up to you, sir."

"On election night, that precinct was called for my opponent with 73.4 percent. When the state election board official ran the paper ballots through the clean tabulator, I won the precinct with a bit over sixty-two percent. So the real result is literally upside down from the results declared on election night. I believe the people of District 8 deserve to have their votes counted as they cast them, not as some computer software made them appear."

The actual numbers got the reporters humming, and they pulled out cell phones and started frantically calling their news desks to report. The press conference had ended. Aguilar was ecstatic.

"Gail, you did it!" he said.

"It's only beginning, sir. And you can bet they're going to oppose us every step of the way."

"Hey, where's my *cocodrilo*?"

They looked around and couldn't find the Crocodile. At some point, he must have tucked in his head and sunk away in the crowd.

"Strange," Aguilar said. "Just when we are getting traction, our Crocodile disappears."

Later, as they were preparing to leave, Annie drew the attorney off to the side and cupped her hand over her lips in case anyone was watching.

"Do you think Gordon is in trouble for having conducted that audit?"

Gail shrugged. "Too early to tell. We'll have to see how dirty they want to play," she said.

51

The next morning, Tuesday, a brilliant autumn sun licked the skies over the Atlantic with streaks of fire that woke Granger in his top floor suite even through the blackout curtains. He had barely finished shaving when his phone rang. It was Chuck Myers, the lead attorney for the Florida certification effort.

"Are you watching the morning news?"

Granger groaned. "It's barely 7:00 AM."

"Turn it on," Myers said.

"Any particular channel?"

"Unfortunately, no."

He went out to the sitting area and turned on the remote. It was still set to MSNBC, and host Sondra Veil was interviewing the local NBC affiliate reporter after her stand-up in front of the state election office in Tallahassee.

"So what does this recount mean, Krissie?" she asked.

"Well, it's too early to know what they will find when they actually examine the paper ballots. But I can tell you, the

Tomlinson team is absolutely steamed. They are doing every-thing they can to shut this down, Sondra."

"I sure hope you are," Granger said into the phone. "What recount?"

"The Nassau and Okaloosa County supervisors of elections filed notice about a half hour ago that they would be doing a recount of the paper ballots. The law requires a forty-eight-hour notice, so we're looking at Thursday morning," Myers said.

"Isn't that bumping up to the deadline to certify the vote?"

"Thursday is nine days after the election. By law, the coun-ties have until noon on the twelfth day to certify their results. That's Sunday."

"If they find something—and that's a big if—it's going to take them all day. That only gives them three more days to do the rest of the state. Tell me that's not possible. Right?"

"Nassau and Okaloosa are small counties. Sixty-some thou-sand registered voters each. So it shouldn't take them more than an hour. And they are heavily Republican."

"We didn't win them, anyway, so why are they doing this?"

"That is the $64 million question, Granger."

Why would Republican supervisors of election go through the effort, let alone the expense, to conduct a recount of paper ballots if their guy won anyway, he wondered. There could be only one reason: They suspected something.

"Can you slow them down?"

"By all means at our disposal."

"So if we make it through Sunday, we're clear?"

"Politically speaking, yes."

"What's that mean?"

"Legally, the losing candidate can still file a petition to con-test the election with the circuit court within ten days after certi-fication by the state. But they would have to have awfully good grounds to do so. Losing by two percent statewide isn't going to cut it with public opinion. Or the courts."

After a half hour of laps in the pool, and a sturdy breakfast of grits, local sausage, and eggs, Granger's day started to look better. Harvey Simon called in from Maryland to tell him that the McKenzie campaign had just filed an injunction with the Montgomery County Circuit Court to prevent the recount of the Aguilar-McKenzie race.

"All three judges are Democratic appointees," he said.

"That's good news."

"It's Maryland. We'll get two of them."

"Why not all three?"

"Because the third judge sees himself as some kind of Zorro in black robes. He actually campaigns for re-election. Styles himself as the 'people's advocate.'"

"Does he have a name?"

"Jorge Alvarez."

"Plus, he's Hispanic."

"There's that, but you'll never hear me or one of my lawyers make the mistake of mentioning it. We expect him to carry the ball for Aguilar, but our two guys will win the day. We will argue that because of the intervention of the state election official, who conducted a recount of the paper ballots of a Montgomery County precinct with no representatives of the parties present, that the election results have been hopelessly tainted. Chain of custody of the ballots has been compromised. Different tabulators were used, without county certification. The official's actions were illegal. Indeed, we will assert they constitute a felony. Our opponents will seek to convince the court that if the recount were conducted again under proper legal authority, it would achieve the same result. But we assert that this is unknowable—and irrelevant. Because the election results have been tainted, they could count them a thousand times and it wouldn't make any difference. The county must certify the election night returns."

"Not bad for a lawyer," Granger said.

"We try," Harvey said.

52

For Annie, it had been a bad day all around. It began with news of the injunction, then the 2:00 PM emergency hearing where the circuit court over-ruled their objections and, in a two to one vote, ordered Montgomery County to certify the initial results. Their hopes of getting the county board of elections to actually count the paper ballots were dwindling and would require an appeal to more Democrat-appointed judges. And now, Annie just got word from Marcie that the FBI had come to Gordon's office in Annapolis to arrest him.

She was distraught. She felt guilty for pushing Gordon to act on his suspicions, and now he was the one paying the price, not her.

"We've got to get him out," she said to their volunteer attorney, Gail Copeland.

"I'd be careful about that if I was you," the Crocodile said. "Don't forget you're dealing with the FBI."

"We should pray on it. Come on, Ken," Aguilar said to the Crocodile. "Give me your hand. If ever we were in need of prayer, it's now."

The four of them joined hands in a small circle in front of his desk.

"Father God," Aguilar began. "We acknowledge our smallness before you. We acknowledge that we are in your hands, and that we are but vessels of your will. Inspire our sister Gail with your holy spirit as she argues before the courts today. Give courage to our brother Gordon as he suffers oppression. Keep him strong in the knowledge that justice is not in the hands of men, but in your hands, Lord. And whatever happens, let your will be done. In the name of Jesus, savior and creator, Amen."

"Amen," they joined in.

"Do you really think God intervenes in the affairs of men?" Gail asked.

"I do," Aguilar said. "In big ways and in small. But especially in big."

"How so?"

"Just look at us here in this room. Who would have thought that a son of immigrants would be able to raise $4.6 million on his first political race and win a seat in Congress? God has blessed me. He has blessed each of us. And so it is right that we give him thanks and praise."

"Gordon could use a little divine intervention right now," Gail went on.

"And that is why we have prayed for him. And we will keep praying for him," Aguilar said.

"It was a gutsy move on the part of the FBI to actually arrest him, especially on state felony charges."

"We've had dealings with that particular FBI agent," Aguilar told her. "Jim Clairborne."

"You mean the head of the FBI's elections division?"

Gail was visibly shocked. Clairborne was not some low-level agent. He was the public face of the FBI's entire effort to reassure voters and election officials that our election systems were secure.

"That's him."

"And he's actually going out in the field to make an arrest, not handing that off to one of his squads?"

"From what Gordon told his mom, yes," Annie said.

"Wow. That's kind of like Peter Strzok going to the White House in person to interview Mike Flynn in January 2017. Line agents should have conducted that interview, not a supervisor."

"What do you mean?" Annie asked.

"Look, when the FBI is doing its job, it's got thousands of employees who line up shoulder to shoulder to get it done. When someone is off the rails, or conducting political espionage, he or she flies solo or with a trusted partner in crime. I'm not a criminal defense attorney, but I know a couple we can call. I can't imagine them being able to hold Gordon more than a day or so for arraignment. They'll have to release him on bond."

"Don't bet on that," the Crocodile said.

53

At night, the Antifa thugs all looked alike. They were dressed in jeans and black hoodies and black bandannas covering their faces and had inked out any bright spots on their running shoes. They emerged out of the darkness of the giant live oak trees in knots of four or five, suddenly charging in total silence until they found their target. They first hit the broad bay windows of the Florida Chamber of Commerce, shattering them with baseball bats, then went next door and attacked the Florida Health Care Association. Another band emerged from the darkness of Kleman Plaza and swung their bats at the front window of Andrews restaurant, then ran across South Adams street and smashed shop fronts. They had reached the brick and glass-fronted FEA building when the owner of the Andrews caught up with them.

"Stop where you are or I'll shoot," he shouted at them.

He was half in a crouch, legs spread wide, two hands gripping the 9mm Beretta in front of him. The last of the four kids turned to face him, gave him the finger, and started to whirl around to run away with the others when he fired and the kid went down.

Andrew Santiago, the restaurant owner, flicked on the safety and stuffed the handgun in his belt. Then he pulled out his cell phone and dialed 911 to report the incident.

The next morning, Santiago was all over the local news. Some were calling him a hero for standing his ground against the Antifa thugs; others called him a cold-blooded murderer and demanded his arrest.

The crowd in front of the elections office just a few blocks away from the shooting incident had swollen to over 1,500. Many of them had been camping on the grass just off the plaza and the esplanade was littered with bottles, food wrappers, dirty towels, diapers, and human excrement. The Reverend James Dupree arrived promptly at 9:00 AM in a convoy of two black Cadillac Escalades, the first for himself and an aide, the second with his bodyguards. The TV cameras were waiting for him.

"Reverend Dupree, Mr. Santiago is claiming that the young man he shot last night, twenty-two-year old Alvin Lambert, was part of your organization. Is that true?"

The Reverend hauled himself up to his full five-foot-six height, smoothed his shirt front, and buttoned his dark suit jacket.

"That is an absolute slander," he said.

"Santiago claimed he had seen him and the others earlier here in the square."

"That is a figment of the sick imagination of Mr. Santiago."

"What will you do if Nassau and Okaloosa counties go ahead with the recount?" another one asked.

"We will continue to demand that the governor uphold the law and certify the vote. It's time to certify now!" he said.

Milford Gaines and Catherine Herrera watched the live interview with Reverend Dupree on local television as they waited to
speak with Lula Rowe, the elections division director at the secretary of state's office. Their plan was simple. Now that the state
Supreme Court had upheld their recount notice, they would
conduct the recount of the paper ballots tomorrow morning on
the tabulators imported from Nebraska. The bizarre election
night numbers led them to suspect that the results of the recount
would be surprising, significantly different. How different, they
had no idea.

At 9:06 AM, Rowe brushed by them and waved them with
her into her office. She was a tall, imperious, impeccably dressed
woman in her early forties, of an indefinite mocha hue.

"Thank God you did this the right way, not like that poor
kid up in Maryland," she started off.

She was referring to the forty-eight-hour notice, which was
required by Florida law.

"They have tougher statutes up in Maryland," Gaines said.
"They basically need a demonstrated violation and a close election in order to recount the paper ballots. Here our law is more
vague and leaves the county administrators more discretion."

"So walk me through this. You do your recounts tomorrow
morning and find that they tally with the election night results."

"Then we announce it and our confidence, as a result, to
certify," Catherine said.

"And what if the recounts show a tiny discrepancy? A couple
of hundred votes? Not enough to change the outcome?"

Catherine exchanged a glance with Ford.

"Same thing, Lula," he said. "We announce it and our confidence, as a result, to certify."

"So obviously, neither one of you expects those scenarios. What *do* you expect?" she asked.

"I don't know, really," Catherine said. "Not actual numbers. But I would expect the actual result to be closer to previous elections. There is no reason why Trump should be losing ten percent of his base after four years in the White House, with all that he has accomplished in their eyes."

The director was doodling on a yellow legal pad, drawing infinity signs and attaching them like dominos.

"So both of you run small counties. If the Trump vote is off by ten percent, that's roughly another 10,000 votes for him between the two of you. For the sake of argument—and only for the sake of argument—let's say that what happened in your counties happened in all the other counties using the same tabulators. That's Miami-Dade, Palm Beach, Broward, and a bunch of others—what kind of numbers are we looking at?"

"Actually," Ford said, "nearly three-fourths of our sixty-seven counties use the same tabulators, including some—but not all—of the larger ones. So if Trump got 3.4 million votes in those counties and his numbers are off by ten percent, you're talking another 340,000 votes for Trump."

The director's eyes widened. "You're joking. Please, tell me that."

"No. This election could be completely upside-down. Statewide, instead of a two percent win by Tomlinson, we could be looking at a three percent win by Trump, maybe more."

"How is that possible?" she whispered.

"We don't know that yet." Ford said. "It may take weeks or months or even longer to find out. But we will know the *what* in a matter of days. For now, that's the most important thing."

"Are we going to look stupid, or what?" Lula said.

"I don't think so," Catherine said. "We had suspicions. We took action. We discovered we'd been hacked and we took all the necessary steps to walk it back."

"We are merely doing our job," Ford added. "Administering the elections so that Floridians can feel confident that every vote legally cast was counted accurately."

"But still," Lula said. "We got hacked. That's on us."

"And so we own it. And we correct it—in time," Ford said. "Better that than sit back and allow someone to steal the election. You need to bring in enough clean tabulators so that all the big counties can get to work by tomorrow afternoon. We will release the Nebraska ones to you, but they won't be enough."

"So where are they going to come from—assuming that my boss and the governor sign off on a state-wide recount?"

"Kansas. Ohio. Michigan," Ford said. "All of those states had clean results, and all of them use equipment that is certified in Florida."

"So nobody can make the argument we are using uncertified equipment."

"Oh, they'll make the argument. I can guarantee you that. They just won't win in court."

"I've got to take this to Shelley today," Lula said, referring to the secretary of state.

"You have our support, one hundred percent," Ford said.

54

"**D**id you really have to use the handcuffs?" Gordon said. "They hurt."

"Poor baby," Clairborne said.

Rone was driving up Route 50 from Annapolis toward Washington, DC. Clairborne was fiddling with his phone and declined to look up to acknowledge his back-seat prisoner. Both of the G-men had rammed their seats back as far as they would go, so Gordon's knees came up to his chin.

"You did a great job notifying the press," Gordon went on. "I bet there's no better perp walk on *Law and Order*."

"Just doing our job, kid."

"What about doing your job when I came down to see you in DC?" he said.

Clairborne turned to his partner. "Can you tell the kid to shut up before I get angry?"

"Kid, you'd be wise to put a lid on it until you get a lawyer," Rone said.

They hit traffic on the Beltway, so Clairborne flipped the switch on the recessed blue lights at the top of the windshield of the unmarked Ford Fusion and turned on the flashers. With the powerful strobe lights hitting drivers from behind, cars gave way to them so they could navigate the break-down lane. Once they had worked their way through the Georgia Avenue bottleneck and hit I-270, it was smooth sailing until the HOV lane traffic jams began to form. They got off at Montrose Road west, crossed 270, and then took a right onto Seven Locks Road to the Montgomery County Detention Center.

"Welcome to your new home, kid," Clairborne said.

It was a nondescript building in low-slung government brick, set behind trees. It didn't scream out *jail*, Gordon thought. Small blessings.

Rone helped him out of the back seat, since he was unable to use his bound hands, and they followed Clairborne inside, where he showed his FBI badge to the intake officer.

"You got our paperwork ready for us, chief?" Clairborne said.

"It's right here, Mr. Director," the older man said.

They had Gordon put his belt, his phone, his watch, his wallet, and a couple of coins and scraps of paper from his pockets into a tray. The intake officer noted each item down on a form, counted the money in the wallet, then had Gordon sign for his belongings.

"We're going to need a private screening room to do a search," Clairborne said.

Gordon couldn't believe what was happening. He was the one who had discovered that a crime had been committed, and now he was the one being punished for it. How do they get away with this stuff, he wondered? This is America!

"I'd like to see my lawyer," Gordon said.

"You'll have plenty of time to see a lawyer, kid," Clairborne said. "Nobody's going to prevent you from retaining counsel. Let's go."

The intake officer led them down a corridor to a steel door he opened with a key from a ring on his belt. Set on the table were a plastic basin, a pair of latex gloves, a jar of Vaseline, and a bottle of water.

"Thank you, Officer McKinney. I'll let you know when we're through," Clairborne said.

McKinney closed the door behind him with a finality that shocked Gordon. It wasn't just the hollow metallic echo, but the exiguity of the examination of room, and the two large men whose intentions were becoming clear.

"What do you think you're doing?" he asked Clairborne, as he pulled on the latex gloves.

"Rone, will you remind the kid of his situation here?"

"The boss wants to search you."

Gordon jumped back. "What for?"

"For whatever you're hiding from us, kid," Clairborne said.

"You have no authority to do such a thing."

"Wanna bet? Now take down your pants. And your underwear."

They stared at each other for an instant. Clairborne was smug, confident in his power. Gordon realized suddenly that nothing he could possibly say or do would have any impact on what was about to happen. These two large, powerful men were going to humiliate him just for the fun of it.

Clairborne dipped his gloved index finger into the jar of Vaseline and indicated for Rone to hold the prisoner, clearly enjoying himself.

"Hey, brother. You really don't have to do this," Rone said quietly.

"Rone, we already know he tampered with election equipment. He's head of IT, remember? He could be hiding a USB stick up his ass with the hacker's code."

"Why don't you let the judge order the search. It doesn't look good."

"Because I have no guarantee that's going to happen. Besides, the kid's gotta learn."

"Are you a complete moron?" Gordon shouted. He wasn't taking down his pants. If they wanted to forcibly search him, that would be on them. But he wasn't going to assist.

"You can hear this, right?" he shouted to Rone. "You hear what he is saying? This guy is completely out of control. You know it. You've seen it before!"

It was true: Rone *had* seen prisoner abuse before. In Iraq. He didn't like it then, and he didn't like it now. He and Clairborne had even spoken about it years before when both of them were detailed to the same FOB in Afghanistan, where Clairborne had been part of a counter-terrorism team detailed from the FBI.

"Brother, you need to chill. I'm going to open the door, and we're all goin' back to intake and deliver the prisoner."

"Right. Of course," Clairborne said. "Just a bad joke."

Some joke, Gordon thought.

55

t 10:06 AM on Thursday, nine days after the election, Granger read President Trump's tweet and groaned.

@realDonaldTrump: Recount in two Florida counties shows dramatically different results from those reported on election night. My numbers go up by 10%! Governor Norton must order a state-wide recount NOW. Thankfully Florida has paper ballots!

The networks were reporting that Governor Norton would hold a press conference at 4:00 PM that afternoon to announce his next steps. *It was like watching a train wreck in slow motion*, Granger thought. They were tied to the tracks and the engine was approaching. They could scream all they wanted, but it just kept coming.

The November sun was already high and reflecting off the Intracoastal Waterway, shimmering in a thousand mirrors from the high rises of the city beyond. Granger's first call was to Chuck Myers. He and his legal team had to pre-empt any effort by Norton to order a recount. Surely they controlled enough judges in this state to do that?

"We've already been to the state Supreme Court. And we lost," Myers said.

"What about these tabulators? Doesn't the election law prevent them from using equipment that is not certified in Florida?"

"Absolutely. And my guys are filing a motion as we speak."

"I hear a but."

"But, we're going to lose. If the elections division director has half a brain, she will bring in equipment identical to that used in Florida."

"Come on, Chuck. It's not *Florida* equipment."

"We're going to try. But don't hang your hat on it. That would assume that Florida certifies every individual piece of equipment. They don't. They certify the class."

"Okay, so you know that. They know that. But the judges don't know snot from Shinola."

"Twelve hours at the most. That's all it will give us."

"I'll take twelve hours. And then twelve more. And twelve more."

"I'm telling you as your attorney, Granger. Don't hang your hat on it."

How did they know to bring in out-of-state tabulators? That's what he really wanted to know. If they just did a recount of the paper ballots using the Florida tabulators, they'd would be fine. That's what Navid had said. So how did they know? And how much did they know?

His next call was to Vinnie Bellinger. He and the vice president-elect shared a long and mostly secret relationship. For six years, Bellinger had co-chaired the powerful Senate Select Committee on Intelligence, and during that time he made a point of touring foreign outposts run by the CIA and Joint Special

Operations Command, JSOC. Of course, he came to show the flag, to let these secret warriors in the fight against the amorphous, transnational extremist threat know that he was their Uncle Vinnie and he had their back. But he was also identifying potential allies and promoting them inside the intelligence community. We need some of those allies now, Granger said. He suspected Bellinger's hand in the arrest of the kid in Maryland, who had come dangerously close to exposing the secret switch. They needed to create a distraction, catch the Florida election officials off guard. Cause them to focus on staying out of jail, rather than conducting this recount.

"We need dirt," he told Uncle Vinnie. "Enough dirt to stop them in their tracks."

"I know just the man to call," Bellinger said.

At 4:00 PM, Governor Norton convened his press conference at the secretary of state's office, with the other members of the state canvassing board. Also joining them were the two county supervisors who had conducted the recount, Catherine Herrera of Nassau and Milford Gaines of Okaloosa.

"This morning, Nassau and Okaloosa counties conducted an audit of the paper ballots using the authorities granted them under Section 102.141 of Florida election law," Norton began. "We now have the results of that audit. In both counties, the results of today's count were significantly different from the results reported on election night. While we don't know yet why the results differ so substantially, we have full confidence in the numbers resulting from today's audit and recount, which both counties have now certified as the official results. Before I get into the steps that the state canvassing commission has decided to take in furtherance of a complete, transparent count of all legal votes cast in the recent election, let me call on our county officials to give us a few details."

Catherine Herrera explained that the election night results got her attention because both the president and Representative John Rutherford's scores had gone down ten percent relative to 2016. That would be an interesting political phenomena, but she couldn't see what had caused it. It was way beyond any sort of statistical anomaly. So she decided to consult with some of her colleagues across the state to see if they were witnessing similar results.

"And that's where I come in," said Milford Gaines. After introducing himself to the media, he picked up the thread. Results in his county were almost identical to those in Nassau. "Just like Catherine, I saw a significant shift of support from the president to Governor Tomlinson and knew that it went beyond any statistical anomaly. In our case, it was around six percent. The potential that we had made an error in tabulating the ballots was something we had a duty to examine. As elected officials, we are accountable to the voters of our counties."

He explained the legal procedures involved, the forty-eight-hour notice, and the presence of both Republican and Democrat election judges and campaign lawyers during the recount they had conducted early this morning. Gaines went on to explain that they had decided to bring in tabulators from out of state, because they did not trust the ones used on election night.

Governor Norton called on a reporter from the *Tampa Bay Tribune*.

"Are you telling us, Governor, that you are ordering a statewide recount on the basis of reports from two Republican county election supervisors?"

There were grunts of approval from the crowd of reporters.

"No, Dean. That's not what I'm saying. I am saying that we are ordering a state-wide recount because we have credible evidence that the election night results were wrong."

NBC News had sent its national political correspondent to Tallahassee to cover the recount. She stood up without being called on.

"Governor Norton, don't you see the optics here? Nine days ago, the people of the United States voted to elect Governor Tomlinson the next president. She won your state by two percent, way beyond the margin of error. Way beyond the legal requirement for a recount, too, which is half a percent. So how can you stand up here, in front of a national audience, and tell us that you have the right to change the outcome of the presidential election?"

Norton covered his mouth to stifle a chuckle. "Thank you, Laura, for what I guess is a question. I am responsible to the people of Florida, not to the people of New York, or California, or Hawaii. It is my duty to certify the results of last Tuesday's election after ensuring that all legal votes were counted accurately as they were cast. I don't know what the result will be. Neither do you. Or do you, Laura?"

"But why else would you be having this press conference? It's crystal clear what your motive is here. You are trying to prepare the American people for a different result."

"That might be your opinion, Laura. But those are not the facts."

A reporter from the *Miami Herald* asked about the out-of-state tabulators.

"I understand that Governor Tomlinson's legal team has filed an injunction to prevent you from bringing in this equipment from out of state. Why did you decide to do this?" she asked.

"The legal issues involved should be clarified within the hour, if they haven't been already," Norton said. "Election officials—and here I am speaking for Secretary of State Shelley Hughes and our elections director, Lula Rowe—have been very careful to identify equipment that is identical to that used in the overwhelming majority of Florida counties, fifty-one of our sixty-seven counties, to be exact. Lula, would you care to address that?"

The elections director looked down at her clipboard and read from what appeared to be a prepared script about the model and make of the scanners and tabulators the state was bringing in for the recount. The fifty-one counties the governor mentioned would be able to begin the recount by 6:00 PM today, she said. Her office expected to have found sources for the equipment in the other sixteen counties shortly.

Norton took another couple of questions, all of them hostile, then asked if someone had a question for anyone else on the podium.

Clyde Norris, a reporter from BuzzFeed, raised his hand.

"Sure, Governor. My question is for Secretary of State Shelley Hughes-Jackson."

Florida's secretary of state was the official with overall responsibility for running the elections, although she delegated most of the operational duties to the director of elections. Hughes-Jackson had been appointed by Governor Norton shortly after he took office two years earlier. She was a political neophyte who had previously worked as a Florida mermaid after graduating from college. (Yes, the state of Florida actually hired young women dressed as mermaids to promote the state's spectacular beach fronts and communities.) She also had a law degree from Florida Atlantic University and had served as a campaign lawyer for Norton.

"Go ahead, Clyde," Norton said.

"Ms. Hughes-Jackson, are you aware that your husband, Charles Aloysius Jackson, who represents numerous—uh—transportation—uh—interests in South Florida, has been cited in a rape complaint that was turned over to the FBI earlier today by the office of Congressman Alcee Hastings?"

"Oh, my, my," Granger said out loud as he watched her response on live television. *That is absolutely precious. The proverbial deer in the headlights.* No. Blonde *deer in the headlights. Good for you, boy.*

56

The state-wide recount began promptly at 6:00 PM that afternoon. Election officials had just two and a half days to complete the tabulation of the paper ballots to meet the statutory deadline of 9:00 AM on Sunday, twelve days after the election. The previously sleepy scenes at county election buildings in Palm Beach, Broward, and Miami-Dade counties were quickly replaced by swarms of election officials who seemingly emerged out of thin air. Hundreds of badged workers stacked numbered and sealed boxes of ballots before the 486 tabulators, with election judges and party officials checking them off on clipboards and iPads. There were hundreds of boxes at each location, massive walls of boxes, like blocks of furniture stacked for auction. It was hard to see how they would ever finish on time.

Making the process even more confusing were the campaign lawyers who occupied two rows of folding chairs directly in front of the tabulators, and the national media who had set up their TV cameras behind them. Chuck Myers, chief counsel for Governor Tomlinson, instructed his lawyers to demand that officials verify the seal and number on every ballot box in front of witnesses before the ballots were removed and fed into the tabulator. Every time one of the tabulators spit out a ballot as unreadable, they demanded that officials stop the count to examine it. Clearly, they were stalling for time.

At 6:14 PM, President Trump tweeted out:

> @realDonaldTrump: Thanks to Gov. Norton, Florida is now counting the paper ballots filled out by voters. The American people will know the truth—unless Democrat election lawyers succeed in running out the clock. The future of our country is at stake. It should not be a race against time!

The state elections director, Lula Rowe, had called on Milford Gaines to apply some of his military skills to ensure that the larger counties had enough tabulators to meet the deadline. Gaines devised a rule of thumb: If each tabulator could rip through 300 ballots per minute, they could process 144,000 ballots in an eight-hour day. He rounded that off to 100,000 to account for set-up time and the lawyers. That meant that the overwhelming majority of Florida counties—forty-two by his count—could finish the recount by 7:00 PM on Friday with just one machine each.

He gave Brevard, Lee, and Polk counties, each with between 300,000 and 400,000 votes cast, three machines each. Duval, with its 500,000 votes cast, got five. So did Hillsborough, Orange, Pinellas, although they were closer to 600,000. But as always, it came down to the Big Three—Miami-Dade, Palm Beach, and Broward. This was where the campaign lawyers were focusing. This was where the media had set up camp. This was where they would have the most problems. He gave them six each but held a half dozen machines in reserve. He was especially worried about Miami-Dade, where more than a million people had cast ballots. With six machines, he estimated it should take around nine hours of run-time to process the ballots. But that was not counting for the lawyers.

He knew it was going to be close.

At 7:00 PM on Thursday, just one hour after the recount began, lawyers for Governor Tomlinson obtained an injunction from the circuit court to halt the canvassing so they could examine "out-stacked" ballots. These were under-votes, which seemingly contained no choice for president, and over-votes, which contained more than one. The tabulators spit them out of the queue on a separate off-ramp, along with ballots that had been mutilated or marked in ways that prevented them from being electronically counted. The court order required the counties to halt the automatic count each time a ballot was out-stacked so that lawyers and election officials could determine the intent of the voter.

Attorneys for the president filed an appeal and requested an immediate hearing, which the chief judge agreed to convene at 9:00 PM. By that time, election offices across the state had shut down.

Secretary of State Shelley Hughes-Jackson left her office just before the injunction went into effect. By that point, fifteen of the smaller counties had already finished the recount. All of those using the 486 tabulators showed an increase in votes for the president, sometimes eight or nine percent, sometimes just one percent. But all of them showed different results from the election night count. Those using other equipment had the same count they had reported on election night.

Her fifteen-year-old daughter, Kaylee, was chatting with a friend over Messenger when she got home at 7:30 PM.

"How am I ever going to school tomorrow?" she said before even saying hello.

"You, young lady, are going to hold your head up high. And thank God for all your blessings. You know very well that your father has done nothing wrong."

"That's not what *they* are saying," she said, nodding at the TV.

Shelley sighed. "How many times do I have to tell you, don't ever believe what they say. Not ever. About anything."

Her teenage daughter suddenly smiled and gave her a hug, her enormous head of dark, tightly curled hair slapping against her cheeks.

"I bet Dad was quite the thing back then," she said.

"Kay-lee!" her mother said.

Then they both laughed. "I guess he was," Shelley admitted.

Later, after dinner and a couple of glasses of wine, she called him over Facetime. He was still at the computer in his Miami office. He looked wrung-out, old sweat congealing on his forehead, his eyes bloodshot from anxiety or drink.

"Have you been drinking?" she said.

"What do you think?"

"I think you are still the most handsome, most desirable man I have ever met."

"You're a good liar, Shelley. Always were."

"You know I thank God every day for bringing us together. You know I do."

"I know that, baby."

"How serious is this?"

"Are you joking? This is a career-killer. This is like an atom bomb going off in my kitchen."

"Do you recognize the woman?"

"Hell, no. And nobody I've called does either."

"So what is this all about?"

"You haven't figured that out yet? They want *you* to pull the plug on the recount, that's what."

"And saying that I can, which I don't think is the case. Then what?"

"Then this all goes away. Alcee Hastings says he forwarded it to the FBI. They say they investigated and decline to prosecute."

"And if I don't? Or if I can't?"

"That's it, baby. No more Beemers, no more bubbly. No more Sandals holidays. Maybe you go back to being a mermaid."

"Charles Jackson!"

"What?"

She gave him a look that made him chuckle despite himself.

"I thought you rather liked me as a mermaid."

57

helley Hughes-Jackson was pleasantly surprised when she drove past her office at 8:00 AM on Friday morning. Several hundred pro-Trump supporters were standing outside, without saying a word, holding up hand-written signs that said, "Count My Vote." They were surrounded by a sleepy mob of anti-Trump protesters; but with the early hour, and the lingering effects of whatever substances they had ingested the night before, they didn't fully grasp what was happening. She went around the corner to park in the guarded lot.

Upstairs, she saw on the TV in the reception area that similar crowds of pro-Trump supporters had gathered outside the canvassing centers in Doral, Lauderhill, and Riviera Beach. And then she saw her husband's face on the screen, bleary-eyed, drunk, twenty years ago, just after they'd graduated from law school. The dog-whistle was clear: Here is the black man who raped the white woman. It didn't matter what they said on air. That was the conclusion anyone could be expected to draw from the images and the chyron explaining that the FBI had taken over the investigation of Miami attorney Charles Jackson for allegedly raping a fellow student twenty years ago at Florida Atlantic University.

What investigation? she thought. It was all a hoax. Fake news.

The whole phony story was aimed at one person: herself.

And they—whoever *they* were—wanted her to shut down the recount and then all of this would go away. *Really?*

Did they really think she was as dumb as that?

They could never undo that photo or that headline. They might have the power to make the FBI go away, but they could never undo the damage they had already done to her and her family.

She was going to make sure the recount proceeded even faster than before. She had an idea she thought the Governor would approve.

Gordon Utz, released on bail from the Montgomery County Detention Center, arrived at the courthouse in Rockville that Friday morning at 10:00 AM, accompanied by Stan Erins, his criminal defense lawyer. Erins, a short, stocky man with a shock of sandy blonde hair, did his best to button his suit jacket as they made their way up the steps. He had come to Gordon through the Republican Lawyers Association, the same group that provided pro-bono campaign lawyers to candidates around the country and had mobilized some two hundred lawyers for the Florida recount, just as they had during Bush-Gore in 2000. In his day job, he handled white collar crime for the DC firm of Norton, Diaz, Gutierrez, and Knight.

They were meeting with Grant Maldonado, the state's attorney for Montgomery County, to make a proffer. He ushered them into a tiny interview room, not his office. That was a bad sign.

"Under Section 104.30 of the election law, your client is looking at a felony of the third degree," he said.

"And we're going to argue that you are prosecuting under the wrong statute," Erins said.

They went back and forth arguing the law, with Erins making a series of arguments why Gordon could not be prosecuted for tampering with voting equipment or interfering with the election process or its results, as 104.30 required.

"Besides, if you really think you're going to trial on that, we're going to demand discovery. And then you'll have to open up the voting machines and everyone will see that they were hacked. And you're going to look like an old fish that's been left in the sun for three days. My client should receive a commendation from the Governor, not prosecution."

Maldonado was not impressed.

"Who do you think is going to grant you discovery?" he said.

"The judge, of course."

"And I'm going to oppose. And I will win."

"What about Judge Alvarez?"

"What about him? He can't do it alone. There are two other judges on that panel, and they will agree with me. So. No discovery, no facts. No facts, no defense. My side will be controlling the facts. And don't think you're going to the media, either. I've just obtained a gag order until we finalize your client's proffer."

Gordon was lost in all the legal speak, but he understood enough to sense this discussion was not going well.

"We're going to ask for five years jail time."

"What?" Gordon said. "I just saved all of you from perpetuating a fraud!"

"What my client is trying to say," Erins interjected, laying a hand on Gordon's wrist, "is that you may have obtained a gag order against us, but there are plenty of other parties who witnessed the risk-limiting audit he conducted and who are aware of the results. You're not going to be able to keep this out of the press."

Again, Maldonado was not impressed. "We'll be arguing that his actions constituted an aggravated felony, because of premeditated intent."

"You have no proof of intent."

"He disobeyed a direct order from his superior not to do this."

"I never asked her," Gordon interjected.

"That's not what she tells us," Maldonado said.

Erins decrypted the coded language as they drove to Wheaton, where they planned to brief Aguilar and his team.

"They're playing hardball," Erins said. "They apparently have deposed Lisa Rasmussen, and she has told them that she ordered you not to conduct the audit."

"But that's not true," Gordon insisted.

"It's going to be your word against hers. So now let's take a close look at how much they know, how much they know we know, and figure out what we know that they don't so we can get that information out. Got that?"

"I do," Gordon said. "And I've got the answer, too."

"What's that?"

"Eric Figueroa," he said.

"Who's that?"

"I'll explain," he said.

58

nnie burst into tears when Gordon came through the door. It was the first time she had seen him since his arrest.

"This is all my fault," she sobbed, throwing her arms around him, all pretense of their "non-relationship" gone.

"No, it's not," Gordon said.

They had kept him three nights in the Montgomery County Detention Center. The first night he had shared a cell with a homeless man infested with lice; the second with a pair of drunks. The third day had been the longest, with no one coming or going, and no one to talk to. Despite all the efforts by Erins to get him out on bail and public calls by Aguilar, the judge refused to bring him up for arraignment until that morning.

"It's good to meet you, sir," he said to Aguilar, offering his hand. "And thank you for all you did. But with all due respect, I didn't do this for you, or for Annie, or for any political reason. I did it because it was right."

"It's because of people like you that this country is still great," Aguilar said. "Bless you, and thank you. Do you mind if I say a prayer?"

"No, please," Gordon said.

They joined hands and formed a circle in front of his desk.

"Father God, you are our rock, our fortress, and our deliverer. We thank you for releasing your servant, Gordon, from the snares of his oppressors. Let the wicked fall into their own nets, and your people pass by in safety. Give us wisdom, Lord, as we deliberate on the path we must take today. In your name we pray, amen."

"Amen," they said.

Erins filled them in on his discussion with the state's attorney.

"So he's imposed a gag order," Gail Copeland, his colleague from the Republican Lawyers Association, said.

"That's right. Gordon is not allowed to speak in public—or theoretically, in private either—about the risk-limiting audit or the results."

"So it's as if it had never happened," Gail said.

"Unfortunately, yes."

"Can't we petition the Governor to order a recount?" Gail wondered. "I mean, for crying out loud, he's a Republican."

Aguilar exchanged a glance with the Crocodile. "I'll go out on a limb and make a prediction," he said. "Governor Huber may be a Republican, but he walks two paces behind the Senate Majority leader down in Annapolis. He wouldn't even endorse me during the campaign. He won't lift a finger now. He's a fox. Congenial, but cunning."

"It's true," the Crocodile said. "You'll get no support from that quarter."

"What about all your supporters?" Camilla said. "All those thousands of volunteers we recruited. We could bring an army into the streets. All you have to do is say the word."

"We're not Antifa," the Crocodile said.

"Antifa doesn't have a monopoly on street protest," Aguilar said.

"No. But it's not the Republican way."

"Oh, come off it, Ken! There is no Republican way. Trump would do it!"

"He hasn't yet."

Why was the Crocodile getting so defensive, Aguilar wondered?

"That's because he hasn't needed to," Erins broke in. "Do you have any idea how many lawyers have descended on Florida to work this thing?"

He gestured toward the TV, which was on mute. It was showing live footage of the paper ballots running through one of the giant tabulators.

"All those people whose faces you can't see are lawyers. Theirs and ours. And it's the same thing in all the big counties that haven't finished the recount."

"We have no legal basis to file a recount petition now that Montgomery County has certified the vote," the Crocodile said. "Isn't that right, Gail?"

She shrugged, unsure.

"You don't, yet," Erins said. "Gordon, tell them what you just told me."

And so Gordon told the story of his counterpart at the Montgomery County board of elections who had been contacted over the secure server by Eric Figueroa from Dominant Technologies.

"He pretended to be the tech in charge of sending out the latest patch. The Montgomery County guy fell for it, downloaded the patch, and installed it into his scanners and tabulators. That's why, when I brought in a tabulator from Carroll County that hadn't been infected with the patch, we got the correct vote count."

"Who knows about this?" the Crocodile asked.

"Just the five of us. And whoever ordered Figueroa to send the malware."

"If you know an honest reporter in Washington, DC, give it to him," Gail suggested.

"Assuming Figueroa is a real person and can be located," Erins said.

"Don't do it, boss. Your fingerprints will be all over it," the Crocodile said.

Aguilar took Gordon aside and asked him to tell him as much as he knew about Figueroa and to provide any documents he had about the patch. He had an idea whom they could approach—not because he was honest. But because he was probably involved.

59

Aguilar called Jack Riley, the son of a Fox News anchor he had gotten to know up in New York who was now the network's chief congressional correspondent, and laid out the story. He promised to get him a copy of the incriminating email so he could run a trace and call the company for comment. He was just a kid—couldn't be more than twenty-five or twenty-six—but he was sharp.

"You realize the email's probably a dead end," he said.

"You're right," Aguilar said. "The links have already gone dead."

"But maybe we can do an archive search on that FTP site. Even if it was shielded behind a VPN, there might be something. I know a guy who's pretty good at that."

He thanked Aguilar for the lead and promised to get back to him with what he found out.

Aguilar's next call was to Clifford Lucas, the reporter from the *Legal Times* who had tipped his hand at the press conference in front of the board of elections. He was the one who had suggested that Gordon's risk-limiting audit might violate Maryland statute—the precise allegation that had led to his arrest. It was too specific a claim to be based on intuition or even a good knowledge of the law.

Lucas pretended to be apologetic.

"I'm sorry about what happened to your guy," he said.

"If you mean the kid from the board of elections, he's not my guy."

"It's just, I've been doing these kinds of stories for years, and it leapt out at me."

"You're a smart guy," Aguilar said. "There's nothing wrong with that."

"So why are you calling me?" Lucas said. "The guy's now out on bail from what I understand and is going to cop a plea."

"I just got a call from a reporter from Fox News who apparently has been following the story."

"Okay."

"He thinks there's more to it."

"Like what? Some kind of conspiracy at the FBI? Fox loves that kind of thing."

"No. He didn't mention the FBI. He was asking me for comment on Dominant Technologies."

"The voting machine manufacturer?"

"The same."

Lucas might think he was smart, but Aguilar was an old pro. He actually enjoyed stringing it out, leading him along by the nose.

"It seems there was malware in the patch."

"You mean, like a software patch? Don't they send them out all the time? Aren't they checked and triple-checked by people who've been cleared by the FBI?"

"That I don't know," Aguilar said. "I'm no expert. But I'm sure you can find out. It seems that Fox has the name of the guy who sent out the bad patch and they're going after him."

The line went suddenly dead. It didn't cut off—Aguilar could see they were still connected. But Lucas went silent for nearly a minute, as if he had put his phone on mute.

"Sorry about that," he said when he came back on. "I had another call coming in. So do you have the name?"

"He mentioned it to me, but you know I can't share that. It's pushing it right up to the edge giving you a tip-off like this."

"Yeah, sorry. I get it. Thanks," Lucas said. He rang off with Aguilar and returned to the other call.

"So what are you offering me?" he said. "That's big time."

"You just get me that name, boy. Then we'll see. It ain't worth nothin' without a name."

As soon as Granger hung up with Lucas, he rang Navid on the secure line. He was seething, but not with anger. Fear gripped his stomach like a hand slowly clenching into a fist.

"Do you know this guy at Dominant Technologies?"

"Where are you calling from?"

Granger went to his main screen and clicked on the VPN icon. "It says Australia."

"And you dialed in on the blue line?"

"Of course. Can't you see that?"

"I like to double-check. So. Yes. Of course, I do. His name is Eric Figueroa."

"Who is he when he's at home?"

"Hahahahaha! You're a smash-up, Granger."

"Navid, get serious. They are onto him. This is for real. They've got a Fox News reporter trying to contact him."

"Good luck on that. Hahahahaha!"

"What do you mean?"

"Eric Figueroa, *c'est moi*, baby."

"You don't work at Dominant Technologies."

"Well, like duh."

"So how can you be Eric Figueroa?"

Navid put on a fey accent. "He's just one of my many online personalities, sweetie. You should get to know some of the others."

Granger was doodling on his legal pad. He had made a big circle, then drawn smaller concentric circles inside it, and now wrote "Navid" inside the innermost circle, the bull's-eye.

"I need to know what our exposure is," he said.

"We've got a backdoor man. He lets me in."

"So now there's two of you? Is there any way they can link you together?"

"Are you kidding? Hahahahaha! Dude, it's like I've been telling you. Navid is the man. Navid delivers. Navid disappears like he was never there."

That wasn't good enough for Granger. If Fox News got hold of the story, especially during the recount, other networks were going to smell a rat. It was only a matter of time before someone at the FBI or DHS started asking questions their guys couldn't shunt aside.

"I think you should start destroying any trace of this operation."

"You really do underestimate me, Granger."

"What if the FBI gets a search warrant and descends on your place?"

"I thought that was your job, keeping them away."

"Just sayin'. Be prepared."

"Even if they did, those Klondikes would never figure it out."

"Don't bet on it," Granger said. "And your backdoor man. It's time to make him disappear, too."

"That's harder."

"What do you mean?"

"He's right at the top."

"Oh, crap," Granger said.

If that was true, they had a real problem. A lower level official could be fired, or go on medical leave, or get transferred to another department, whatever. But someone at the top was visible. Worse, they most likely weren't an operative. Which meant, if squeezed, they'd get cold feet. They had too much at stake. They'd rat. And then it didn't matter that Eric Figueroa was Navid's fiction and couldn't be located. Eric Figueroa *was* Navid. And they'd find out because the backdoor man would tell them.

The time had come to pull the plug.

Granger took the SIM card out of his phone and, using an empty bottle of Maker's Mark, smashed the screen and the guts of the phone on the kitchen counter of his suite. *Sorry, Agent Jones. I left that phone on the roof of my car and it got run over.* He'd take the pieces later and dump them into the Intracoastal.

60

Governor Norton read a statement announcing the new rule issued by Secretary of State Shelley Hughes-Jackson at a 1:00 PM press conference at elections headquarters in Tallahassee that Friday.

"We already have results from the overwhelming majority of Florida counties in the presidential election and fully expect these results to be certified when the county boards meet tomorrow morning; however, in a half dozen of our largest counties—Orange, Hillsborough, Pinellas, Miami-Dade, Broward, and Palm Beach—the recount has been slowed by the relentless challenge of so-called out-stacked ballots. These are ballots which, for various reasons, cannot be read or counted by the automated tabulators. It is important that Floridians understand that these ballots constitute a very small percentage of the ballots that need to be counted—in most cases, less than one-fourth of one percent.

"In the interests of comity, and of ensuring that the votes of all Floridians get counted, the secretary of state this morning issued an interim rule setting aside all out-stacked ballots so they can be counted once the main recount is finished and the results known. As is their right, the Tomlinson campaign has sought an injunction of this rule, which we have now defended successfully before the Court of Appeals. So as of this moment, the recount will proceed without interruption."

The room exploded as reporters shouted out their questions. Norton stepped back from the microphone for an instant to whisper something in his secretary of state's ear and, looking somewhat amused, allowed the chaos to subside.

"That feels better now, doesn't it?" he said with a chuckle. "So first, let's hear from the *Miami Herald*."

"Governor," a female reporter began. "How can you continue to conduct a recount under the supervision of your secretary of state, whose husband we learned this morning has been taken into custody in Miami on charges of alleged rape? Do you still have confidence in Ms. Hughes-Jackson?"

Norton nodded. "She's standing right here next to me, as you can see. So, yes I do."

Next, he turned to Dean Estrada of the Tampa Bay Tribune.

"As you know, Governor, the entire Tampa-St. Petersburg metropolitan area falls within those counties that still have to report. What is your expectation for when they should be able to finish the recount and get to these disputed ballots?"

Norton deferred to his secretary of state.

"Well, Dean. The tabulators we have imported from Nebraska and other states, which as you know are identical to the ones certified for use here in Florida, can operate at very high speeds if they are allowed to run without the constant interruptions we've been seeing over the past twenty-four hours. So we expect all of the six counties—possibly with the exception of Miami-Dade—to complete their ballot run by 7:00 or 8:00 PM tonight. That leaves all day tomorrow for the lawyers to dispute the out-stacked ballots before the counties certify their results on Sunday morning."

The room again erupted into chaos as reporters shouted questions. Norton held up a hand and turned to his secretary of state to answer.

"No, I don't have a hard count as of yet of the out-stacked ballots. But as the governor said, our ballpark estimate as we look at the numbers from the counties that have reported so far is that they will be less than one-fourth of one percent, which does not meet the threshold for a manual recount, as you know."

"So you're just going to discard all those votes?" the reporter shouted.

"I didn't say that. Our counties will have a full twenty-four hours to look at them one by one, and I fully expect they will do that and meet early on Sunday morning, as required by law, to certify the results."

Norton returned to the podium and held up his hand for the reporters to quiet down.

"There is one more paragraph I have to read to you from my prepared statement, and I find it very curious that none of you were at all interested to ask the question. That relates to the results."

He could see the NBC national political correspondent already into her stand-up at the far end of the room, totally uninterested in the facts he was about to release.

"In the sixty-one counties that have completed their recount so far, forty-five are now reporting significantly different numbers than on election night. When combined, the clean retabulation of the paper ballots found that President Trump won significantly more votes than reported on election night. In some cases, this meant that Governor Tomlinson still came out ahead in that county, in other cases not. But when averaged out state-wide, it puts the president ahead by a three-percent margin so far. While we must await the results from the six remaining counties, if that tendency is confirmed, it means that the president will have won Florida by approximately 276,000 votes."

> *@realDonaldTrump: Bombshell press conference from Gov Kirk Norton. With all but 6 of Florida's 67 counties now reporting real results, Trump is winning by 3% statewide. Thank God for paper ballots! We need this in every state in America!*

Granger looked at the tweet and shook his head. *You fool,* he thought. *If you only knew.*

61

For Congressman Hugh McKenzie, the ten days since the election had gone by with agonizing slowness. At every moment, he had expected a knock on the door, an unexpected visitor, bringing bad news. He nearly lost it the day his opponent held that press conference calling for a recount in Montgomery County. He locked his door, turned on the TV, and replayed it again and again. His wife, Willie, was the only one who dared interrupt him. She peeked around the door and immediately saw what was going on. She let herself in then carefully closed the door behind her. He jumped.

"I thought you were the FBI!"

"Grow a pair," she told him. "You're playing with the big boys now. You should be happy."

"But what if they find out? They'll arrest me!"

Of course he had told her about Granger's "program." At least, he had told her the little that he knew, and she agreed, neither one of them needed to know anything more. That was how Washington worked.

"You don't know anything about the manipulation of voting machines," she'd told him. "Anyone in this office can testify that you can barely get the DVR to tape a show, let alone format a Word document."

"They'll know."

"No, they won't."

For days, McKenzie remained glued to the TV in his office, his door closed. But after the Norton press conference on Friday, he washed his face, straightened his tie, and had Willie crack open the outside door of his office suite to see if any reporters were outside. The corridor empty, they took the elevator down to the Rayburn basement, where they stepped into the Members-only subway car to the Capitol Building.

They were headed to the ornate office suite of Majority Leader Gus Antly, with its spectacular view of the National Mall. "I hope it's whip," Willie whispered as they waited in the anteroom. She would give anything for him to become majority whip—in effect, Antly's immediate deputy, the number three person in leadership.

"Don't hold your breath," he whispered back.

After aides brought them Diet Cokes and water, the South Carolinian whisked them into his private office.

"So, Hugh-boy. I see you got an over sixty-percent re-elect. So what was all that frettin' about?"

"Take nothing for granted, sir."

"No, that's right. I guess those Jews of yours came through."

"They did, Mr. Leader. I spent a lot of time with the rabbis."

Antly leaned back in his chair seeming to ponder this, his patrician blond curls and ruddy cheeks going to grey. McKenzie did his best to tamp down his rage. For some reason, Antly seemed to take pleasure in humiliating him. He wasn't going to fall for it.

"We've got ourselves a bit of a sit-iation down in Florida," the Majority Leader went on, gazing out toward the Washington Monument. "The way it's lookin', we could have four more years of Trump."

"We've got to impeach. Go to the mat this time. Tie him in knots. Draw it out."

"And we will. And that's why I called you in here, Hugh-boy. I've got an important task for you."

Antly explained that the party was concerned with the losses they had suffered in the 2018 pick-up districts, most of which Trump now had won back. The Ukraine impeachment ploy had backfired and now their majority was razor-thin. His job over the next two years was to rebuild their majority. He wanted to know if McKenzie was on board with that.

"Of course, I am. Everything depends on us keeping the House."

"So I want you to run the D-Triple-C in the upcoming cycle."

Inwardly, McKenzie groaned. Running the Democratic Congressional Campaign Committee, or DCCC, was the most thankless job on Capitol Hill. It meant spending every afternoon at DNC headquarters dialing for dollars—and not even for his own campaign, but for others! He wouldn't get stuck in a cubicle; that was for the plebs. But even in a corner office, it was a dreary task. And then, there was all the travel. He'd have to do events with backbenchers all across the country, smile and kiss the snot-nosed brats. It was two more years of campaigning.

"Do I have any options, sir?"

"Well, of course you do, Hugh-boy. Why, the last time you were in here you were whinin' about losin' your election. What's that I hear about some kid from the election office doing jail time for monkeyin' with the votin' machines?"

"I saw that."

"I'm sure you did. He wasn't one of yours, was he? Naughty!"

Antly didn't have to strong-arm his members; it wasn't his style. All he needed to get their cooperation was to dangle just the hint of unpleasantness and let their imagination do all the rest. With McKenzie, it worked like a charm.

"He wasn't one of mine. And you're right. The D-Triple-C is going to be tremendously important this cycle. I'd be honored to be named chair."

"So, we got a deal," Antly said.

"We've got a deal."

As they rode back on the subway to his office, McKenzie turned to Willie.

"Gus knows something. That's why I had to take the D-Triple-C."

"What do you mean?

"If we want to bury this, that's the deal."

62

NYPD Patrol Officer Ronald Caruso, who headed the security detail at Trump Tower that Saturday night, didn't see it coming. He'd been drinking hot soup with Tony Ferrara, his colleague from the 18th precinct, close to the main doors at the north side of the building, well out of the cold winds whipping down Fifth Avenue. Another pair of officers stood close to the Gucci display case on the south side. Jersey barriers formed a wall between them and the street, while the sidewalk south of the building was completely blocked off by metal barriers at East 56th street.

When the president visited Trump Tower, the iconic building he had called home until he moved to the White House in 2017, the Secret Service took charge and the NYPD blocked off the building's entryway with garbage trucks to prevent car bombs. But the president and his family were at Mar-a-Lago for the weekend, in expectation that the Florida recount would soon be called, so Caruso and his team were alone.

Caruso was blowing on his soup as he looked across the street and to the south, where a crowd of protestors had gathered demanding that Florida "Certify Now" and that Trump "Concede Now." They were noisy, as they usually were. Nothing out of the ordinary.

As it turned out, the real threat came from the north, to his right.

Shortly after 10:15 PM, Caruso heard a dull, thudding noise and knew immediately what it was: baseball bats against bullet-proof glass. He tossed his soup and ran out onto the main sidewalk and saw a gang of black-hoodied thugs swinging their bats and crowbars and pipe wrenches against the Gucci shop front and blew his whistle. No one backed off, and more of the thugs surged forward, so he retreated back to the main entrance of Trump Tower and keyed his walkie-talkie.

"Dispatch, this is Officer Caruso at Trump Tower. We've got a serious 407 and I mean like, serious and building. We need backup ASAP."

"Caruso, you've got a 407, copy, and you are requesting backup."

"Yeah. And fast. This is, like, Antifa thugs, not your garden variety leftie Trump-hating sign-holders."

"Stand-by, Caruso, I'm putting you through to the deputy commissioner."

"The deputy commissioner?" Caruso muttered. *Why do I need that piece of left-wing unsanitary refuse?*

The voice he had heard so many times on television came onto his walkie-talkie. "Caruso? This is the deputy commissioner. You are to stand down."

Caruso wanted to say unspeakable things.

"Not possible, sir," he said finally. "We are requesting backup."

"Stand down, Caruso. Do you hear me?"

"Not easy, Commissioner. Can you hear me?"

He keyed the walkie-talkie so this piece of political jerky could hear the utter chaos around him: screaming kids, cops with billy clubs, the crowd across the street, and everybody shouting.

"Stand down," the commissioner said again.

"Not possible, sir."

"Why the hell not?"

"There's no place to stand, sir. We're surrounded and they are swinging baseball bats and pipe wrenches. It looks like there are around two hundred of them, sir."

"Well, talk to them."

"Huh?"

"Talk to them. That's what the good cops are supposed to do."

Caruso heard it coming and held open his walkie-talkie so the deputy commissioner could hear it as well. After failing to smash the Gucci shop front with their baseball bats, a group of the hooded thugs grabbed a metal barricade, charged it into the glass and broke through with a crash.

"Hear that, Commissioner? How do you talk to that?"

"Do not use your weapons, Caruso. That's a direct order."

"10-1. 10-1. Can't hear you, Commissioner."

"Repeat: Do not use your weapons, Caruso. De-escalate. The Mayor has ordered no backup for Trump Tower. The President has changed his official residence to Florida? Let Florida protect him now."

"Oh, I get it. 10-4, Commissioner. No backup. And we are to disarm against baseball bats. Is that what you plan to say at our funerals? They obeyed orders and—"

Just then there was a louder crash as the hooded thugs swarmed around Caruso and broke through the bulletproof glass of another window. Caruso keyed off, pulled out his side-arm and fired two shots into the air.

"Form a cordon!" he shouted to his officers.

They fell back toward him in front of the main entry to Trump Tower, facing off with what appeared to be disciplined rows of Antifa thugs. The front rank held their baseball bats and pipe wrenches high, ready to swing. Those behind them held their weapons lower down, but Caruso could see them at the ready.

"Back off or we shoot!" he shouted.

An hour later, the president tweeted:

> *@realDonaldTrump: Shame @MayorNYC. No backup for brave NYPD officers vs Antifa thugs. 2 officers down, 200 thugs on the rampage. My condolences to the families of Officers Ronald Caruso and Tony Ferrara. This should never have happened.*

63

Judge Andres Delgado could think of many places he would rather be than in his courtroom on a Sunday morning at 8:00 AM. He could be preparing pancakes for his wife and their three children. He could be helping her to get them dressed for church. Or they could be wild and irresponsible and be packing lunch boxes for a fishing expedition on his boat in Panacea in the Gulf of Mexico. Instead, he was in Tallahassee at the appeals court building on Drayton Drive, playing the adult to a bunch of white shoe lawyers from Washington, DC.

"Remind me, Mr. Myers, why we are here on a Sunday morning?"

Myers, the chief attorney for the woman who, for the past ten days, had been treated by almost the entire nation as the president-elect, coughed.

"Your honor," he began. "We are here to request that you stop this unwarranted and out-of-control recount and certify the election night results."

Delgado knew that, of course. He also knew that Myers knew exactly how he would respond, and what the president's attorneys would say. This was just Kabuki Theater, made for the television cameras that now stained the walls of his courtroom.

"Your honor, if I may," said Josh Ridley. He was the chief litigator for the president. "We would like to join in the request of the plaintiffs and co-respondents. In part, at least."

Well that was novel, Delgado thought. *Maybe this wouldn't be a wasted hour after all.*

"You may proceed, counselor," he said.

Ridley argued that the president agreed it was time to certify the vote. There was no need to hold up the results, which were now clear from the recount, for the sake of 10,000 out-stacked ballots in a single county, Miami-Dade.

"You can't certify this so-called recount without counting all the votes," Myers objected. "If the state is to certify, they must certify the complete results, and the only complete results are from election night."

"Counselor, we've been through that six ways to Sunday. You lost that argument several days ago."

"The statutory deadline for counting the votes expires in less than one hour," Myers said. "If all the votes haven't been counted by that time, then the state must certify the election night results."

Delgado let his exasperation show. "This is like déjà vu all over again, counselor. I've already ruled to accept the recount on a county by county basis."

"You are talking about disenfranchising 10,000 voters," Myers objected.

"If we follow Mr. Myers's lead, we're actually talking about disenfranchising 370,000 voters whose votes weren't counted on election night," Ridley said.

"The Court agrees with Mr. Ridley," Delgado said. "In this case, the good of the many outweighs the good of the few."

"We are willing to make a concession, your honor," Ridley said.

"Really?"

"For the sake of comity, the president is willing to concede every one of the out-stacked votes to Governor Tomlinson, even though in all likelihood half of them or nearly half will be judged for him."

"Mr. Myers?" Delgado said.

"Isn't it ironic that the president is willing to disregard the will of thousands of voters if the end result comes out in his favor? So, Mr. Ridley, you are arguing that the ends justify the means?"

Ridley threw up his hands and turned in exasperation toward Ivo Silander, the president's personal attorney, who was observing the argument from the lawyer's box.

"Mr. Myers, I'll tell you what," Delgado said. "Under the Florida election law, I have the authority in exceptional circumstances to grant the boards of elections such time as they need to complete the vote count. I rule that your obstructive behavior and arguments constitute such exceptional circumstances, and grant the Miami-Dade board of elections such time as they need, without limit, for the unique and specific purpose of determining the status of these 10,000 out-stacked votes, at which time, Miami-Dade will certify their results. Mr. Ridley, any objection?"

"No, your honor."

"Now both of you, get back in your sand box and finish this up."

64

At noon the following Tuesday, the fourteenth day after the election, the Florida state canvassing board certified the election results, declaring that the state of Florida had gone for Donald Trump by 230,000 votes, or 2.5 percent. As it turned out, the Miami-Dade and Palm Beach County recount numbers differed less than other counties from the election night results, and that was what brought the overall percentage lower than Governor Norton had initially projected. Still, this meant Donald Trump was re-elected president of the United States with exactly 270 electoral votes to 268 for his Democrat opponent.

"She'll be back," the Crocodile said to Nelson Aguilar as they watched the final press conference in Aguilar's radio station office. "Like I said to ya. You keep your powder dry and live to fight another day."

Aguilar had vacated the campaign headquarters over the weekend and planned to find new tenants that week. But he was still perplexed by the apparent results of his election.

"What about Gordon and what he found? He says we actually won."

"Maybe. But nobody's going to believe ya. You're going to sound like one more sour grapes Roy Moore. What a self-righteous piece of work he turned out to be."

Something was nagging him. He couldn't quite put a finger on it. Something in the Crocodile's tone.

"Ken, did you know about this?" he asked finally.

"What do you mean?"

"That they were going to flip the results, just like they did in Florida?"

"Why would I know that?"

"You tell me. You seemed awfully chummy there at the end with McKenzie."

"I don't know what you're insinuating there, boss. Tell me I misheard."

"You didn't," Aguilar said, his tone hardening. "How come every time we seemed to have an opportunity to expose the vote switch, you always argued against it?"

"Whoa, boss. Now that's not fair!"

"How come when I wanted to pull out all the stops to get Gordon released from jail, you counseled me to back off, not to be seen actively supporting him in public?"

"That was for your own protection, boss."

The Crocodile started to sweat. *He never sweats,* Aguilar thought.

"Even Gail is saying I should file a complaint. How come you have pushed back on that relentlessly?"

"I'm just thinking about your image, boss. But if you want to file a complaint now that the results have been certified, be my guest. I'm going back to the Hill."

"Who are you going to work for, Ken? McKenzie?"

"That is over the line, boss. I think you are going to regret that."

Aguilar didn't answer. He watched the Crocodile gather up his leather portfolio, tuck it under his arm, and scurry out the door.

It was a shame to part on such terms. It was un-Christian, but in his heart he knew he was right.

65

The story by Fox News congressional correspondent, Jack Riley, went virtually unnoticed when it aired that evening. The nation's attention was on the official announcement of President Trump's re-election, with the talking heads dissecting it for hours on end. So when Riley interviewed Gail Copeland, a pro-bono elections attorney from Frederick, Maryland, about the landslide re-election of Democrat congressman Hugh McKenzie, it seemed like filler.

"Mr. Aguilar, the Republican challenger whom I represent, is still considering his options, Jack, but I am fairly convinced he will be filing an official complaint to the state board of elections."

She went on to explain that the campaign had learned that a state elections official had conducted a risk-limiting audit of one of the precincts in Montgomery County where her candidate had lost in a landslide—officially. "But when he brought in a ballot-counting computer from another county, the results turned out to be completely upside-down and my candidate won."

"You filed a recount petition at the time, but it was denied," Riley said.

"That's correct. Since that decision, we have discovered additional information that is extremely troubling and that could reveal what actually happened down in Florida, Jack. We learned that corrupt files sent by the manufacturer, Dominant Technologies, directly to the Montgomery County IT department infected their tabulators with an algorithm that switched votes from Mr. Aguilar to our opponent, Congressman McKenzie."

"Are you accusing the McKenzie campaign of fraud?"

"I'm not saying that, Jack. But what I can say is that our campaign has learned how those so-called patch files were sent and who sent them. And we have taken that information to the attorney general. Because we believe the same person or entities used the same type of scheme to infect the tabulators in Florida."

The next morning, the *Washington Times* reported on its local pages that an IT tech known to have worked for the Democratic National Committee, Navid Chaudhry, 31, had been struck and killed by an apparent hit-and-run shortly after leaving his office at 9th Street and Pennsylvania Avenue SE the night before. Witnesses said they saw a Cadillac Escalade with North Carolina plates stop after the collision and a tall, dark-skinned man get out from the passenger's side. Because he was wearing a broad-brimmed hat and a trench coat, it was impossible to identify him. Two passersby saw him stoop to the victim, put a gloved hand to his throat, apparently to check his pulse, and then get back in the car and drive off.

President Trump saw the Fox News piece with Gail Copeland and immediately dialed his attorney general, who confirmed the outlines of the story. He tweeted out:

@realDonaldTrump: MUST SEE: Fox News reporter Jack Riley blows the lid off of Maryland election machine manipulation. Similar to what happened to us in Florida! Coincidence???

Despite the apparent interest by the president, Gail Copeland remained frustrated. At the inaugural ball at the Washington, DC, Convention center on January 20, 2021, she ran into Austin Peters, the colleague from the Republican Lawyers Association who had taken her information to the attorney general two months earlier.

"It hasn't fallen through the cracks," he shouted into her ear over the deafening music. "The AG has appointed the U.S. Attorney for Central Florida to conduct an investigation into voter machine manipulation in the 2020 election. He will be calling you and your guy and the Maryland tech as witnesses."

It was another two months before she received the invitation to testify, and not until May 2021 that she and the U.S. Attorney, Cameron Davis, agreed to a date with the Grand Jury. She gave them everything Gordon had told her, including the name of Eric Figueroa from Dominant Technologies.

Davis sent a request to the NSA to run a trace on Figueroa. They were able to locate the emails he had sent to the chief IT manager for the Florida state bureau of elections, as well as those he exchanged with the IT manager for Montgomery County, Maryland. In their vast digital archive, which scooped up internet traffic from around the world for potential decrypt, Davis found a copy of the phony FTP site where Figueroa had uploaded patch files for the 51 Florida counties using Dominant Technologies voting machines, each of them using a different vote-shifting algorithm. But Figueroa himself had vanished as if he had never existed. Dominant Technologies could find no trace of him. No payroll. No office. No official email. No nothing. He was a ghost. And yet, he had total access to the Dominant Technologies computers and the network of VPNs they used to communicate with state and county elections directors. The NSA also found in the archive similar FTP sites for Pennsylvania, North Carolina, Virginia, Nevada, and Arizona, each containing a set of patches dated just days before the election. But when the NSA techs opened up the code, the files erased themselves.

In his initial confidential report to the attorney general, Davis noted that Figueroa's electronic footprint appeared to begin in Dayton, Ohio, the DT corporate headquarters. But when he turned over the data to the FBI elections division and their cyber team, they concluded that Figueroa had used IP spoofing software and that he really had been operating from somewhere on the outskirts of St. Petersburg, Russia.

Nobody questioned the FBI analysis, and nobody did a further trace of the IP address to discover that it pinged from Russia to Finland to Italy, then Australia, and finally to the basement of a townhouse at 9th and Pennsylvania Avenue, SE.

Davis was planning to interview Richard Foreman Hall, the controlling shareholder and a managing director of Dominant Technologies at the time of the election, even though he had resigned his director's seat and disposed of his stock in the third week of November 2020. By the time they got around to standing up a team to interview him in Silicon Valley, they learned that Mr. Hall had committed suicide by driving his red Lamborghini Centenario Roadster, one of just a handful imported into the United States, off the Pacific Coast Highway near Big Sur.

No one on Davis's team ever seriously suggested that they interview Governor Tomlinson or Senator Bellinger, who were serving out the remainder of their terms, or prominent DNC talking head T. Claudius Granger, the man with no first name.

The day after Navid's apparently accidental death, his colleagues in the cellar "war room" at 920 Pennsylvania Avenue, SE, smashed hard drives and USB sticks and left Washington, DC, for their former homes. The war room itself was rented out to a print shop.

In September 2021, President Trump invited Gordon Utz and his fiancée, Annie Bryant, to a private ceremony in the Oval Office and awarded him the Presidential Medal of Freedom. In the citation, he noted that Gordon "had made extraordinary contributions to the security of our nation's election systems." Later that afternoon, he tweeted:

> @realDonaldTrump: *Honored to have awarded the Presidential Medal of Freedom to a true unsung hero, Gordon Utz. After four years in this office, there are still agents of the Deep State out there...*
>
> *2/ whose sole purpose is to start wars, steal elections, enrich themselves, and smear anyone who tries to stop them. Thank you, Gordon, for your courage!*

Ken Adams, aka the Crocodile, went to Majority Leader Gus Antly shortly after the election and told him simply, "I know what happened in Maryland 8. And it's going to cost you." After a brief parley, they agreed on the price, and when the new Congress was sworn into office, Adams was appointed staff director of the powerful Ways and Means Committee under the Democrat chairman.

As for Nelson Aguilar, at the time this book went to print, his recount petition was still making its way through the courts.

ACKNOWLEDGMENTS

*T*he *Election Heist* is an entertainment, a term I have borrowed from British writer Graham Greene. He used it to distinguish between his "serious" novels, and those intended as, well, pure entertainment.

But to entertain does not mean dealing with trifles or the banal. My subject in this book is power, and the things people will do to acquire it and retain it. This is arguably the most serious subject any writer can approach.

A great deal of research is available on the flaws of our electronic voting machines. The interested reader can start by viewing this survey of seven ways our election systems can be hacked that was published just after the 2016 election: https://www.darkreading.com/attacks-breaches/7-ways-electronic-voting-systems-can-be-attacked/d/d-id/1327172. Another favorite of mine is Bev Harris's 2002 investigative classic, *Black Box Voting*, which can be downloaded here: http://blackboxvoting.org/black-box-voting-book/.

I consulted a number of cybersecurity experts as I was devising the scenario for this book, and want to single out for their input Tom Malatesta, Jarred Nicholls, Francis Kane, and Mike Hugenberg. Others who still work for alphabet soup agencies (and must therefore remain anonymous) discussed my scenario and reminded me that anything controlled by software can be hacked, a critical concept when considering the tabulators many districts use to count paper ballots.

A number of election officials in Maryland and Florida were generous with their time as I examined potential flaws in our voting systems. They, too, have requested anonymity. But you know who you are. Tim May and Frank Mitchell, co-hosts of the inimitable *Mid-Maryland Live* afternoon drive talk show on WFMD, deserve a shout-out for their cameo, as do Carol and Fred Wilson of Elk Run Vineyard.

Finally, the entire team at Post Hill Press has done a terrific job in producing, editing, and promoting this book. A special thanks to publisher Anthony Ziccardi, who has believed in me through thick and thin; to managing editor Madeline Sturgeon, for keeping the trains running during the Coronavirus mass hysteria; to publicist Meredith Didier, for getting the word out; and to remarkable copyeditors Monique Happy and Kiera Hufford, who not only smoothed out my rough edges but caught many errors and inconsistencies, all with good humor and grace.

ABOUT THE AUTHOR

Kenneth R. Timmerman is a nationally recognized investigative reporter, novelist, and war correspondent who was nominated for the Nobel Peace prize in 2006. He is the *New York Times* bestselling author of ten books on national security issues, as well as three novels and the critical biography, *Shakedown: Exposing the Real Jesse Jackson*. His work is regularly featured on FoxNews opinion, FrontPage Magazine, Breitbart, the *New York Post*, and elsewhere. In 2012, he was the Republican nominee for congress in Maryland's 8th district.

"Presenting the Nobel Peace Prize to Kenneth Timmerman and John Bolton will strengthen those in the world...who are today trying to find ways and means of putting a stop to the proliferation of nuclear weapons."—Nominating letter to the Nobel

Peace Prize Committee from former Swedish deputy prime minister Per Ahlmark

To schedule appearances, please email Ken directly: kentimmerman@comcast.net

Made in the USA
Columbia, SC
17 November 2020

24761286R00193